D0377452

HE RAISED HIS HANDS TO HER WRISTS, BUT THAT didn't stop her from sliding her arms around his neck, from pulling his head down for another kiss. He let her, let it go on too long, until he was too hot, too hard, until his skin had become slick with sweat and his hand unsteady, until, hell, he didn't want to stop her at all.

"Holly . . ." His voice was guttural, harsh. "I want—"

"I want, too," she murmured, leaving a trail of damp kisses along his jaw and down his throat, loosening his tie, unfastening a button or two.

His eyes closed, and he dragged in a deep breath for strength, then blurted out what he had to say. "Will you marry me?"

Holly had never known sexual ardor could be cooled so quickly, so effectively, with four small words. She stumbled back a step or two.

"I want to get married, Holly."

"To me," she said skeptically, and he nodded.

Then he added, "If you didn't think we were a good match, you wouldn't have been pursuing an affair with me for the past fourteen months."

"An affair—a few nights, no more! Not a lifetime commitment!"

"So I'm raising the stakes a bit."

"Look," she began, striving to keep her voice level. "Let's forget it ever happened, okay? Now . . . I believe I've had enough surprises for the evening. I'm going to bed."

"I don't want to forget that it ever happened, Holly. I want to get married. To you."

Bantam Books by Marilyn Pappano

SOME ENCHANTED SEASON

FATHER TO BE

FIRST KISS

FIRST KISS

Marilyn Pappano

BANTAM BOOKS

New York Toronto London Sydney Auckland

FIRST KISS

A Bantam Book / September 2000

All rights reserved.
Copyright © 2000 by Marilyn Pappano.

Cover art by William Schmidt.

No part of this book may be reproduced or transmitted in any form or by any means, electronic or mechanical, including photocopying, recording, or by any information storage and retrieval system, without permission in writing from the publisher. For information address: Bantam Books.

If you purchased this book without a cover you should be aware that this book is stolen property. It was reported as "unsold and destroyed" to the publisher and neither the author nor the publisher has received any payment for this "stripped book."

ISBN 0-553-58231-3

Published simultaneously in the United States and Canada

Bantam Books are published by Bantam Books, a division of Random House, Inc. Its trademark, consisting of the words "Bantam Books" and the portrayal of a rooster, is Registered in U.S. Patent and Trademark Office and in other countries. Marca Registrada. Bantam Books, 1540 Broadway, New York, New York 10036.

PRINTED IN THE UNITED STATES OF AMERICA

OPM 10 9 8 7 6 5 4 3 2 1

FIRST KISS

Chapter One

A FEW MINUTES BEFORE MIDNIGHT, Tom Flynn said good night to the last of his guests, left the caterer's staff to clean up from the party, and sought out his office. There he switched on the lights and opened the safe concealed in the mahogany credenza. The envelope he wanted bore a warning scrawled in careless writing: *Private. Keep out.* Ignoring it, he tore loose the tape that sealed the flap and withdrew the paper inside.

It had been written on his sixteenth birthday, with various additions and strikeouts added over the past twenty-four years. He'd been living then in a fifth-floor walk-up that was barely habitable. His mother had just died, he'd never known his father, and he'd come to the realization that if he was going to have any sort of life, he would have to make it for himself. And so he'd written out his goals.

The clock on the wall gave two soft bongs as midnight, and his birthday, arrived. Carefully he unfolded the paper.

His first set of goals had been simple. *Stay alive. Stay out of jail. Finish school. Find someplace warm.* And the last, written in capital letters and underscored: *GET SOME MONEY!!*

He'd added more goals over the years. *Go to college. Graduate from law school. Get a good job.* And later still: *Earn your first million. Buy a great house. Buy a Rolex. Buy a Porsche.*

Buy, buy, buy. That had been his primary activity for a lot of years. Buying whatever the hell it took to show people how rich and successful he'd become. Buying whatever it took to make him forget how poor he'd once been.

Every goal on the list had been marked off but two. *Earn your first 50 million.* Taking a pen from his desk drawer, he drew a line through it. As of yesterday, his net worth had rolled over 51 million, thanks to his CEO position at McKinney Industries.

That left only the last goal, written at the bottom of the page. *Get married.* It was the one thing virtually everyone he knew had already done, some two or three times over. He intended to do it only once, then finally he would be a satisfied man. With the acquisition of the perfect wife, he would have fulfilled more dreams than that cold, scared, hungry kid who'd started this list had been able to dream.

First he had to find the perfect wife. She had to be beautiful, sophisticated, and intelligent, able to discuss anything with anyone, plus be a consummate hostess. She would understand his reasons for marrying—would probably share them—and wouldn't burden him with messy emotional needs or demands.

She would be the envy of all the women she knew and would make him the envy of all the men he knew.

So where would he find her?

He didn't have a clue. But he *would* find her.

Grinning at the prospect, he started to slide the paper into the envelope when he noticed a line of writing—his handwriting—on the back side.

Fall in love.

Hell, he must have indulged in too much booze before he'd gone through this ritual last year, though he honestly couldn't imagine the amount it would have taken to make him think such an idea, much less add it to his list. The list was sacred. If he wrote a goal on it, he was honor-bound to do his best to achieve it. He *never* would have added that particular one.

But he had. The proof was there before his eyes.

Fall in love.

The idea was ridiculous. Impossible. Tom Flynn *wasn't* going to fall in love. He was a coldhearted bastard who felt nothing for anyone. Learn to love some woman? Wasn't gonna happen, not this year, not ever.

His first impulse was to scratch out the line. But if he'd ever allowed himself to tamper with the goals, he never would have gotten past the first ones. They'd seemed impossible, too.

Besides, *he* would know what it had said. He would know that in a weak moment, he'd wished for the one thing his money couldn't buy. The one thing his hard work and determination couldn't earn him.

Fall in love.

He had accomplished so much in the past twenty-four years, but he might have finally set for himself an unattainable goal. For the first time, he might face certain failure.

But he was honor-bound to try.

As soon as he figured out how.

THOUGH SHE KNEW THE STEADY TICK-tick of the grandfather clock in the foyer didn't carry more than halfway up the stairs, Holly McBride could swear she heard time counting down as she let herself into the second-floor suite reserved for Tom Flynn. Her invitation to his birthday dinner at the McKinney house was for seven o'clock, but she'd been delayed with a hundred and one problems around the inn. With each passing second, she was that much closer to being late, which she didn't really mind, and frazzled, which she did mind, but there were still a few small details to take care of before she could leave.

The two rooms were spacious and beautifully decorated with lots of warm color and texture. It was a perfect home away from home, not that Tom cared. He spent so much of his time here in Bethlehem working that she doubted he would notice if the rooms were stripped bare, as long as he had the ability to compute, fax, and E-mail. The same probably applied to his apartment in Buffalo. He was one of the few McKinney employees who chose not to relocate when Ross had moved the main headquarters from Buffalo to Bethlehem.

She straightened a vase of fresh flowers on the night table, then moved a dish of homemade chocolates from there to the sitting room. Next she laid the package she'd brought with her on the cocktail table, then moved it to the desk, the dresser, and finally the night table.

The wrapping and card were neither sentimental nor overly friendly, and the gift inside was impersonal enough to give to any acquaintance.

In fact, it was so small, she still debated giving it at all. She didn't know Tom that well, though not for lack of trying, and the fact that she'd like to know him better didn't count for a lot. Perhaps she should simply hand it to him without making a big deal of it. Maybe she should replace it with something fabulously expensive that would impress on price alone. Or maybe . . .

Hearing the relentless tick-tick in her head, she

drew back from the gift, spun around, and left the suite. The back stairs took her directly into the kitchen, where the pastry chef was putting the finishing touches on the cake Maggie McKinney had asked her to bring.

"Looks wonderful, Edward. Box it up, please, and I'll be back for it in five minutes. And the wine?"

"Over there," he said with a nod toward the counter.

So far, so good. Now if she could just get herself thrown together . . .

The closet in her private quarters at the back of the inn had been a guest room until her most recent remodel. But a woman who owned an inn had far less need of one more guest room than a woman who loved to shop had for closet space. Now she could see every outfit she owned. She just couldn't decide which one to wear.

Her latest purchase, a barely there little black dress, could get a girl arrested in some states. It had cost a fortune, looked fabulous on her, and all but shrieked, Look at me! Not that Tom would be paying attention.

So she went for a green woolen dress instead. Simple, elegant, and a good color for her, with her red hair and hazel eyes. She chose a pair of pumps and a handbag that matched, touched up her makeup and perfume, and switched earrings from diamond studs to dangling emeralds. On her way back to the kitchen, she fastened a bracelet around her wrist and shrugged into her black coat.

At the door she literally bumped into her newest employee. The young woman had recently moved to Bethlehem, had been at the inn only three days, was quite possibly the most inept person on the face of the earth, and went by the name of Bree. She'd been a disaster at every task she'd been given, but she tried, Holly kept reminding herself. She really did try. But even carrying a boxed cake appeared beyond her ability. Only Holly's quick grab saved it from a run-in with the floor.

Bree's fair skin turned pink. "Thought I'd save you a minute or two since you're running late."

Holly eased around the woman. "Do me a favor, Bree. Don't help me right now, okay? I just need to get the wine, and I'll be out of here."

"Okay." The girl stepped out of the way, hands behind her back, and gave Holly a clear path. She calmed herself on the drive and arrived at Maggie and Ross's place a mere five minutes late, looking as if she'd pampered herself all afternoon. The doorbell echoed through the old house, then a moment later the door was opened. By Tom.

The man looked incredible. His brown hair was mussed, and his blue eyes were penetrating. He leaned against the doorjamb, arms crossed, dressed in elegant clothes that couldn't disguise the strength of the body they covered. In her more vulnerable moments she wondered if he owned a pair of faded jeans and a snug T-shirt. Knowing that he did might be more than she could stand. She had a terrible weakness for him, and a terrible weakness for bad-boy types. Put them together, and she just might dissolve into a puddle at his feet.

He looked totally at ease, as if he were accustomed to answering other people's doors. She would have loved a chance to find out what other activities he was so totally at ease with. Billion-dollar takeovers. Meet-and-greets with the rich and powerful. Sex. Ah, yes, sex.

"So the mystery guest arrives," he remarked.

"You weren't expecting me?"

"Actually, I was. But no one acknowledged the fourth setting at the table, so I didn't ask."

She smiled coolly. "Maggie didn't have many options. I'm her only unmarried friend."

He took the wine from the crook of her arm and studied the label. "Nice vintage."

"I aim to please. If you approve of the dessert, do I get to come in and stay?" she said with a sarcasm-tinged smile.

He stepped back so she could enter, then closed the door behind her. "Let me help you with your coat."

His tone was dry, just a bit sardonic. She might have taken offense if she hadn't known that dry and sardonic, or arrogant and haughty, or disgustingly self-assured and commanding, were the faces Tom presented to the world. But, oh, boy, did she wish she'd actually worn the little black number. The snug-as-a-second-skin-and-backless-all-the-way-down-to-*there* black dress. Then she would carelessly stroll away and leave him with his eyes popped out and his tongue gathering dust on the floor.

Instead, as his long, warm fingers curled around the collar of her coat and brushed her skin, it was likely to be *her* tongue on the floor. Was he really taking his sweet time? Or was it merely wishful thinking on her part?

At last he pulled the coat free, and she gave a soft sigh of relief—or regret. "Where are Maggie and Ross?"

"In the kitchen."

"Maybe I should offer my help."

He took her arm—another touch, quite possibly setting a record for them—and steered her into the living room. "If what I've heard is true, maybe you shouldn't."

He set the wine on the coffee table. She laid the cake beside it, took a shrimp-and-rice hors d'oeuvre from the tray there, then sat in the nearest chair. "You should know better than to believe everything you hear. Why, if I believed everything I've ever heard about you, I'd be quaking in my Sophie Garel pumps." Crossing her legs, she displayed one pump to show how relaxed and steady she was.

"Are you implying that I can't make you quake?"

Her smile was slow, sensual. She'd smiled it at so many men so many times that it felt almost real. "I'm sure you could. And I'd be happy to return the favor."

"I'm sure you would." The acknowledgment

was all he offered. It wasn't followed by an invitation. It never was.

In a perfectly normal voice, she said, "Happy birthday."

"Yeah. Thanks."

"Not so happy?"

"I've had better."

"When?"

"Last year." He took a seat on the sofa and stretched out his legs. They were so long that his feet rested only inches from hers. If she moved just the slightest bit forward, they would touch. . . .

"What did you do last year?" she asked.

"I was in China. I didn't know a soul in the country, and I wasn't accepting calls that day from anyone outside the country."

"So you could pretend it was just another day."

"It *was* just another day."

She wagged one finger at him. "That's sad. You should always do something special for yourself on your birthday."

"I'm here," he said with a shrug. "And we had a party last night."

" 'We?' You and your latest blond bombshell? What's her name? Brandi? Tiffani? Cyndi?" Though she pretended ignorance, she knew. She'd heard a little about Deborah over Thanksgiving dinner, then a little less at Christmas.

"I've never dated a Brandi."

"But you plead guilty to Tiffani and Cyndi."

"Don't get too smug. Holly fits right in."

Her smile was cool and steady. "But you never dated me."

"I'd face an awfully long drive home when the evening was over."

"Not this evening." His suite was in the middle of the second floor. Her private quarters were at the back of the inn. A quick stroll through the kitchen, up the back stairs, and down the hall, and he'd be home. Better yet, he could give the housekeeper a break and just stay with her. She would make him feel right at home.

For a moment he looked as if he was considering the possibilities. Holly wondered what alway held him back. Loyalty, maybe, to the other woma temporarily in his life. Concern, perhaps, that h employer, Ross, might disapprove of a short-te affair with one of Maggie's close friends. More li an attraction that simply wasn't strong enoug overcome whatever misgivings he had.

Before he could respond, Maggie, looking in maternity clothes, came through the kitche "Sorry we weren't here to greet you," she sa hugged Holly. "I needed Ross in the kitche

"I volunteered to help, and Tom lo palled. What have you been saying b back?"

"Nothing that the whole town do your face," Maggie replied cheerful he's a fine one to talk. I bet he doesn where the kitchen is in his apartmen

"I know. It's the room where th

puts the cold beer." His tone was edged with caution, as if he expected Maggie to turn on him at any moment. Holly knew that things had never been smooth between them. She'd thought he brought out the worst in Ross's ambition. He'd believed she held him back. When the marriage had fallen apart, she'd wanted to put it back together. He'd wanted Ross to end it once and for all.

Maggie didn't hold a grudge, but then, it was easy to be gracious when you'd won. She'd gone from politeness to affection, something Tom couldn't quite accept as genuine because he did hold grudges. The same distance that cropped up between him and Holly was also present between him and Maggie. And between him and Ross. Between him and everyone Holly had ever seen him with.

Ross came in. "Hey, guys, dinner's ready. Holly."

She stood to greet him, presenting her cheek for his kiss. "I brought wine," she said, gesturing to the bottle Tom had picked up, "and cake, so far untouched by these incapable hands."

Ross grinned. "Your hands are quite capable. t's just that your talents lie elsewhere."

She gave both Tom and Maggie a smug smile, en went with them into the dining room. It s deep coral with white trim, with plenty of ht from a chandelier, welcoming warmth from fire sizzling and popping on the grate, and an ique table laden with an appetizing array of es.

Maggie and Ross sat on one side, Holly and Tom on the other. He held her chair for her, his fingers brushing across her shoulder as he drew back. That made three times for tonight. Ooh, maybe it was a sign. Put out the Do Not Disturb sign and warm up the bed sheets. This might be Holly's lucky night.

Rolling her eyes at her own sarcasm, she turned her attention to the wonderful meal. Before she realized it, dessert plates and ice cream were on the table.

Excusing herself for another trip into the kitchen, Maggie pitched her voice loud enough for them to hear: "What's the use of a birthday if you don't get a chance to wish for your heart's desire? So . . ."

Walking slowly, she came into the room carrying the cake on a platter. The flames of the candles she'd added wavered and sputtered with every step. "Happy birthday, Tom. Blow out the candles and make a wish."

He straightened in his seat and studied the cake, which Maggie set in front of him. Candlelight danced across his face, turning his skin golden. He looked uncomfortable, and Holly couldn't help but wonder why. Did he think he'd outgrown the tradition? Had it ever even been his tradition? He'd grown up poor, with no one but his mother. Maybe there had been no money to spend on luxuries like birthday cakes, and no hope to waste on futilities like wishes.

Or maybe he merely had nothing to wish for.

He was wealthy, powerful, admired, respected. Success naturally came his way. So did women. What more could he want?

After a moment, he leaned forward, drew a deep breath, and blew. How big a sin was it to make a wish on someone else's candles? Holly wondered as the flames flickered in a brief, wild dance. Probably a huge one, but she did it anyway. She closed her eyes and sent up her own silent wish: *Wish for me.*

For an instant, time stood still. Everything went silent—the conversation, the crackle of logs in the fireplace, the creaks and sounds of the old house. The lights overhead seemed to brighten, then dim. One instant in time drew out, lengthened, as the echo of her wish faded, and then, in a breath, everything was normal again.

Holly blinked once, twice. No one else seemed to have noticed that little burp in time. She must have imagined it. Earlier it had seemed that time was running out, and now it had stood still. It was just her frazzled brain playing tricks on her. Everyone knew time couldn't stop and wishes never came true.

Then Tom glanced at her and smiled, and she quickly revised that last thought. Wishes *rarely* came true. But hers just might.

TOM WATCHED THE LAST WISP OF smoke drift upward, then gave a shake of his head. For a moment, he'd experienced something akin to déjà vu. Not the sense that he'd done this routine before, but something . . . different. Weird.

But apparently no one else at the table thought anything odd had happened. Maggie was removing the candles from the cake, and Ross was pouring coffee. As for Holly, she was simply sitting there looking cool, composed, and beautiful, as always.

And attainable.

She'd made no secret of the fact that she was attracted to him. All she was waiting for was an invitation—a kiss, a touch, simple words. She would be more than willing, and he would be more than satisfied. But, although she was a gorgeous woman who preferred exactly the kind of no-strings relationship he liked, he'd never offered the invitation. He'd always had good reasons for it, but as he sat there beside her, he couldn't remember what they were.

He could even pinpoint the exact moment he'd forgotten—when he'd blown out the candles. When the weird feeling had come over him. Despite Maggie's command to make a wish, he hadn't. He'd been thinking about the fact that a year ago, he'd set one reasonable goal for himself—get married—and made one frivolous wish—fall in love. He'd been wondering exactly how a person went about falling in love, if it wasn't something he could research or find reliable how-to instructions for, and he'd blown out the candles and . . .

"What did you wish for?" Holly asked. Her

voice was a little on the husky side, full of promise, blatantly sexy, overwhelmingly feminine. It was a voice a man could dream about.

"Holly McBride!" Maggie admonished. "You know the rules. If he tells what he wished for, it won't come true."

Rules? For wishing? That seemed to miss the whole point. Not that it mattered. He couldn't tell a wish he hadn't made.

As they talked over cake and ice cream, he thought of all his birthdays past. The early ones had come and gone without parties, cakes, or gifts. The later ones had been marked by celebrations that hadn't meant anything to him. Like Deborah's party last night. It had been attended by a lot of people with money sucking up to others with more money.

That wasn't the case tonight. Ross was the single person he considered a friend, and he and Maggie didn't care about money. And all Holly wanted from him was the temporary use of his body.

Did she have any interest in getting to know him first? But why even wonder? When was the last time he'd let a woman see anything more than what was on the surface? When was the last time he'd trusted a woman, confided in her, cared about her? *Never.* And he liked it that way. He wasn't looking to change.

It was nearly ten o'clock when the evening ended. He shook hands with Ross, accepted

Maggie's kiss on the cheek, then walked out with Holly.

"So . . . happy birthday," she said for the second time.

"Thanks. And thanks for the cake. It's my favorite."

"I know. Maggie told me. It probably doesn't compare to being utterly alone in China, but as birthday dinners go, this one wasn't so bad, was it?"

"No, it wasn't," he admitted.

They stepped off the curb between their cars, and she turned left. On impulse, so did he. "Want to get a drink somewhere?"

She unlocked her door and tossed her bag inside before facing him, looking as surprised as he felt. They'd done a few things together—shared a meal or two, gone to a holiday party, even spent an afternoon at a carnival last summer—but always the invitations had come from Maggie and Ross. Tom had never suggested anything before tonight, and he honestly didn't know why he'd done it now.

"Bethlehem doesn't have a good place for just a drink. But the inn keeps a well-stocked liquor cabinet for our guests, and there's always a quiet place to sit in the lobby."

His suite was quiet, too, he thought about adding. He didn't, though. "I'll follow you."

Actually, he followed the distant sight of her taillights as she drove fast and braked hard through the quiet neighborhood. By the time he turned into the long drive that led to McBride Inn, she was out of sight. By the time he walked through the double doors, she was behind the registration desk, her coat already off.

"Either your insurance rates are sky-high, or you know all the cops around here."

She flashed him a smile. "*Know* 'em? I dated all of 'em."

She'd "dated" virtually every single man in the county, according to rumor, just as he'd "dated" every drop-dead gorgeous blonde in Buffalo. He wondered what she was looking for that she hadn't found with all those men, wondered if he'd kept his distance because he didn't want to be one more man who couldn't give her what she wanted.

But he'd disappointed dozens of women. What did one more matter?

He signed in for his suite, then accepted the key.

"Tell me your pleasure, take your bags upstairs, and meet me back here in five."

Tell me your pleasure. Simple words in that husky voice—all it took to warm his body. All he needed to form an image of him and Holly naked, her skin pale in contrast to his, her face flushed, her breathing ragged. He reached up to loosen his tie, but he wasn't wearing one. Letting his hand fall back to his side, he cleared his throat, then hoarsely repeated, "My . . . pleasure?"

"Your pleasure, your poison, your drink. Scotch,

brandy, cognac, wine, beer. If it's not on the list, ask. It may be in the cabinet."

The drink he'd asked her to have. It had completely slipped his mind. "How about coffee? Black."

With a smile, she headed for the kitchen in back. He picked up his bags and went upstairs.

The suite looked the same as it always did—perfectly done up, comfortable, but impersonal. Every little detail was perfectly matched to every other little detail. It was a space a thousand people would be happy in, like his apartment, designed to please all and to offend none.

But this time there was one unmatched little detail—the package on the night table. His name was on the outside of the card. The message inside: *Happy Birthday. Holly.*

At last night's party, there had been a table piled high with expensive gifts. Lots of crystal, silver, and gold, exotic leathers, gourmet chocolates, fine Havanas, and finer spirits. None of it suited him, because no one there knew him well enough to pick what he wanted. Not even Deborah.

How much closer would Holly come to the target? He was reluctant to find out.

He walked away from the package, then went back and picked it up. It was easy to tell through the paper that it was a book. If it had to do with business in any way, he could add it to the unwanted gifts at home. If it was something off-the-wall, something he might enjoy reading . . .

He tore the paper open to reveal the dust jacket of a hardcover by a mystery author he'd read for years. Inside it was autographed by the author to him.

How had she known he liked mysteries? Neither Maggie nor Ross did. His housekeeper was probably the only person in the world who knew, and that was because he paid her to dust his bookshelves.

But Holly had known, or made a lucky guess. Either way . . .

He read the inscription again, feeling . . . Hell, he didn't know. Vulnerable, when he'd worked too damn hard never to feel that way again. Turned on, because there was something erotic about receiving from a woman a gift that truly mattered. Threatened, because there was also something seriously dangerous about a woman who could choose a gift that truly mattered. Who the hell was Holly McBride to know him better than everyone else in his life?

He could go downstairs and find out. She was waiting for him. The thought made his chest grow tight, edged his temperature up a notch or two.

Or he could turn off the lights and crawl into bed. She would get the message when he didn't show. It was the coward's way out, and he'd taken it before when things threatened to get messy or emotional. It contributed to his reputation as a coldhearted bastard and led people to expect less of him.

But all Holly had done was give him a gift he could appreciate. She deserved better than to be stood up in her own lobby.

She deserved better. . . . Those were words he should keep in mind.

Chapter Two

McBride Inn had been in Holly's family for more generations than she could remember late on a Saturday night, though not always as an inn. Some ancestor had carved a farm out of the woodland to pass down through generations of McBrides. They had always been fortunate and prospered even when times were hard elsewhere.

Her grandfather had been the most prosperous of them all. He'd left a not-so-small fortune to his only child, Holly's father, Lewis, and Holly's mother had managed to run through much of it. Margery McBride had not been a happy woman. What good was a rich husband when he insisted on living in some drab little town where no one appreciated her? She'd required frequent trips to New York City, great sums of cash, and even greater reserves of alcohol to make her life bearable, while she'd made Holly's and her father's lives unbearable.

Holly gazed at the family portrait that hung in a lobby alcove. She was sixteen when the photograph had been taken, standing between parents who rarely spoke to each other and hadn't shared a bedroom in years. Margery had been tipsy, and Lewis had been his usual long-suffering self, and they had all pretended to be one happy family.

Rolling her eyes, she murmured with some scorn, "Can we say 'dysfunctional'?"

"Yes, and we can spell it, too."

She schooled herself not to startle at the realization that Tom had finally joined her. She'd first waited in one of two wing chairs in a dimly lit corner, then, too restless to sit any longer, she'd prowled the lobby, reflecting on family history to avoid thinking of what she feared was becoming obvious—that she'd been stood up.

But there was Tom at last. She'd thought he had regretted his impulsive invitation to have a drink, or maybe it had been the gift that changed his mind. Maybe she'd been right earlier, about it being too small. Or maybe he'd feared it meant more than it really did.

But whatever arguments he'd made in favor of standing her up, the arguments to show had won. She was glad.

He gestured toward the portrait. He had to have seen it before, but he'd never acknowledged it until now. "Mom and Dad, huh? And sweet, innocent Holly."

"No more than you at that age."

"You're still more innocent than I was at that age," he lazily disagreed. A moment later, he commented, "You look like your mother."

"You think so?" she asked dryly.

"Obviously you're not blond, but you've got her features and that sort of delicate look."

She studied Margery's face but couldn't find a hint of the resemblance he was talking about. But that didn't mean it wasn't there. She'd never wanted to see anything of her mother in her, and her mother had felt the same.

"Do they live around here?"

She wasn't surprised he didn't know. After all these months of coming to Bethlehem regularly, he still made no effort to get to know anyone, including her. She, on the other hand, had pumped Maggie for every last bit of information about him.

She gestured toward the wing chairs. The coffee she'd brought him, now lukewarm, sat on the mahogany table that separated them. "My father died a few weeks before I graduated from college, and my mother immediately returned from exile to New York City, where she was from."

"Do you see her?"

"No more than I can help." She sat down, crossed her legs, and watched nervously as he picked up his cup. Not that she had anything to be nervous about. Simple conversation—that was all he expected from her.

"So your father died and your mother moved

away, leaving you the family home. What made you turn it into an inn, or was it already one?"

"It was just an old farmhouse, less than half the size it is now." She gazed across the gleaming wood floors into the darkened dining room, one of the additions she'd made. "When my father died, he left the money to Margery and the property to me. He knew she hated it here. She would have sold it to the first person who came along. So she took the cash and split, and I got this great old house and a hundred acres of woods and farmland, but no means to take care of it."

"Why not sell it? You don't strike me as the sentimental type."

She'd spent a lot of years convincing people she wasn't the least bit sentimental about anything—not the family she both loved and hated, the teenage boys who'd broken her heart, the grown men who'd done it, too. Then one day she'd realized she was no longer persuading them to believe a lie. She really wasn't sentimental. She'd lost tender feelings somewhere along the way. She had become every bit as cynical as she'd pretended to be.

But sometime in the last few years, that trend had started to reverse. Despite her best efforts, she was developing a streak of sentimentality—but *not* about the men in her life.

"The place had potential," she replied with a shrug. "Bethlehem always draws tourists in the summer and crowds for the holidays, and it's not far from the best skiing the area has to offer. The only thing it was lacking was a place for all those people to stay. I was living by myself in a house with eight bedrooms. An inn seemed the only logical choice."

He looked as if he didn't quite appreciate her logic. Of course she'd had other options. She could have subdivided the house into apartments. Or she could have sold the timber, then put the land on the market. But neither would have left the property intact and still in the possession of a McBride. Back when she'd still been sentimental, an inn had been the only logical choice. Five years ago, she might have made a different choice. Five years from now, who knew?

"Obviously you're an only child."

"Obviously?" She stretched out a leg. "Need I mention that my Sophie Garels leave impressive bruises when applied to an unprotected shin?"

His chuckle was low, amused, warm. He rarely laughed and smiled only on occasion. He was a very serious man, but that was all right. She wasn't interested in his sense of humor.

"I imagine you leave all kinds of bruises on the unsuspecting men who come into contact with you."

"Just as you do with all those unsuspecting women."

He grimaced. "Not one of the women who deliberately seek out contact with me is unsuspecting. They know what they want, and they understand from the beginning what they'll get."

Like her. She wanted sex, pure and simple, and she believed that eventually she would get it. What happened after was anyone's guess. She had a tendency to remain friends with her former lovers, which was fortunate, since she saw many of them every time she went into town. Tom, on the other hand, tended to make enemies of his exes. If things between them ever degenerated to the point that he no longer was willing to be a guest at the inn, she had no doubt he would buy a house of his own, or build an inn of his own, or make her an offer she couldn't refuse. He wouldn't exile himself from Bethlehem. Exile would mean defeat, and Tom Flynn never admitted defeat.

But neither did Holly McBride.

Redirecting her thoughts, she also redirected the conversation. "Yes, I'm an only child. Does it show in my independent nature? My incredible maturity? My self-sufficiency?"

"Your belief that you have a God-given right to always get what you want?"

"If I'd always gotten what I wanted, I wouldn't be an only child. From the time I was little until I turned twelve, I wanted a brother or sister more than anything in the world."

"What happened when you turned twelve?"

God, what had made her bring *that* up? She hadn't even thought of it in years—the party she'd begged to not have, the elaborate tiered cake, the classmates she never would have brought into her home by choice, her mother too drunk to be on her feet, much less supervising a children's party. The embarrassment, the humiliation, the handprint on her cheek. And the tears.

What had happened when she'd turned twelve? "I grew up," she said shortly. Suddenly uneasy, she clasped her hands together, steadied her voice, and asked flat out, "Are you going to invite me to your room tonight? Because if you're not, then I'm going to bed."

He studied her for a moment, his features impassive, then gave a shake of his head. "Not tonight. Sorry."

She'd been rejected enough that at first it didn't bother her. But as she got to her feet, the smile that touched her mouth felt forced, and she had to dig deep to find the good-natured teasing she was looking for. "Sure you don't want to change your mind? It's going to be a long, cold night, and there are far better ways to stay warm than relying on blankets and furnaces. Trust me, you'll regret it."

"I probably will."

"But you're not changing your mind." Her sigh was soft, pouty, and totally put-on. "Why?"

"I have my reasons. Maybe I'll tell you once I remember them."

Sounding as natural as if this were one of their countless other friendly goodbyes, she said, "Then I'm heading off. I'll see you in the morning." She was already several feet away when he spoke.

"Holly? Thanks for the gift."

She turned back to see him looking awkward, almost shy, though surely that was impossible.

Suddenly her smile wasn't so forced. "You're welcome. He's one of my favorite authors. I'd seen you with a book a time or two, so when he was a guest here last month, I thought you might like him, too."

"I do. Thank you."

She walked a few more feet, then turned back to tell him good night. He was already halfway up the stairs. Going to bed alone. Like her.

But one of these nights he wouldn't turn her down, because she'd made a wish. One of these nights he would invite her to his room, and they would do incredibly wicked things the whole night through.

And then the game would be over.

Her smile faded as the ultimate result of her wish slipped into her mind. In effect, she'd wished for the game to end. For her fascination with Tom to disappear. For his presence in her life also to come to an end.

And sometimes wishes did come true.

YOU'LL REGRET IT, HOLLY HAD WARNED, and Tom had to admit she'd been right. Having her join him would have been a hell of a way to cap off his birthday—and a hell of a better way to stay warm than blankets and furnaces.

But no blanket ever expected anything from you the morning after.

Downstairs for breakfast, he tried to pay attention to the newspaper, but the front page headlines hardly registered. Ross and Maggie had invited him to join them at church this morning, but he had refused. Sixteen years of regular services at Holy Cross had been enough church for him.

Of all the changes Ross had made in recent years, the churchgoing would most astound everyone who had known him in Buffalo. There, his office had been his church, power and success his gods. McKinney Industries had been his top priority. But since Maggie's near-fatal car accident more than two years ago, Ross had turned his whole life upside down for her. Every decision he'd made had been based on her best interests, and it had apparently paid off. They were happier now than they'd ever been. They were going to have a baby. They were in love.

The idea of falling in love was foreign to Tom. It wasn't that he'd made a conscious decision not to fall in love. It had simply been incompatible with his decision to become rich and powerful. Achieving that had required single-mindedness, commitment, ruthlessness.

Maybe he could use the same principles to find a wife. If he applied himself as intently to it as he had to earning his first 50 million, wasn't he virtually guaranteed success? And if he concentrated on doing whatever it was women liked, on being the sort of man that appealed to them . . .

He smiled thinly. Only one kind of man appealed to the women he knew—a rich one. To make this venture successful, he would have to identify an entirely different segment and target his search accordingly.

As if by magic, a china pot appeared in front of him, pouring steaming coffee into his cup and distracting him from his thoughts. He waited until his cup was full before he raised his gaze in a slow journey from a black wool skirt to a blue silk blouse, open at the neck to reveal a sizable sapphire resting against pale skin. Up a long throat to a stubborn jaw, a sensual mouth, to the nose, high cheekbones, and deep-set eyes inherited from a mother she had little affection for.

She noticed his perusal and smiled smugly. "And good morning to you, too. Interesting news in the paper today. The stock market crashed. The IRS has raised taxes another ninety percent. Aliens landed in New York City and no one noticed."

Tom didn't have a clue as to what she was talking about.

Then she gestured to the newspaper he was holding. "Mind wandering a bit, huh? What were you thinking about?"

"Business." It was the one answer everyone would accept as gospel.

"It's too beautiful a day for that—and a Sunday, besides. It's still the weekend. You do understand the concept? Two days that come at the end of the week, when people normally relax and rest up for the next week? There are fifty-two of 'em every year. You should check 'em out sometime."

Folding the paper, he gestured toward the empty chair. "Want to join me for breakfast?"

"I'm afraid I can't. I'm working today, and the boss is a real slave driver."

"I don't doubt it," he agreed, earning him a warning glance from her hazel eyes. "Give yourself the morning off and order the others to double up."

"I can't do that. Sorry."

Her rejecting him. That was a change—and he wasn't sure he liked it. "What time do you get off?"

"Oh, you'll be long gone by then. Look me up before you go." With a bright smile, she left, making the rounds of all the tables, topping off coffee cups, chatting with diners, playing the gracious hostess. He wondered when she would find her way back to his table for a minute.

She didn't. If it were anyone else, he'd think she was upset about last night. But it *wasn't* anyone else. It was love-'em-and-leave-'em Holly, his female counterpart. No strings, no commitments, no expectations beyond great sex. It was the act that counted, not the partner. The physical satisfaction, not the emotional.

Not only did she not come back to chat, but he didn't see her again before he left. He did ask about her as he paid his bill and was told that she'd left on an errand and wouldn't be back for a while. Unfortunately, he didn't have a while to spare.

He was halfway back to Buffalo before he wondered about that "unfortunately." He'd never bothered to track her down to say goodbye before. After all, all there really was between them was business. She owned an inn; he was a frequent guest. He paid for certain services; she saw that they were provided. The fact that one—or both—of them might want something more was inconsequential.

In spite of those arguments, he still found it unfortunate that he'd had to leave without seeing her again.

Darkness had settled by the time he reached the building that housed his office and those of the few McKinney employees left in Buffalo. It was one of the tallest in the downtown area and offered dramatic views on all sides. Tom could look out his window and see his apartment, the neighborhood where Ross and Maggie had last lived—even, if he chose to find it, the neighborhood where he'd grown up.

He never made that choice.

He picked up paperwork, then headed for the apartment he called home. On the thirty-second floor of an exclusive building, the place had more space than he needed, was furnished to reflect the tastes of some anonymous decorator, and had cost a few million—double that for the antiques, the rugs, and the paintings. It was about as homey as any expensive hotel. If forced to leave that night and take only what was important to him, he could be out in thirty minutes or less. A few mementos, a few cartons of books, and he would have all that mattered.

Once he closed the door behind him, the silence was deafening. The building was so well designed for privacy that he lived in a vacuum. To assure himself that he wasn't alone in the world meant going out onto the balcony, where the street sounds filtered up. To know that it was storming meant pulling back a heavy drape and looking outside. To hear proof that he had neighbors in the building, he'd have to . . . Well, he didn't know what he would have to do. He'd never heard and had rarely seen his neighbors.

The damn place made him feel isolated.

He went to the office. The message light was flashing on the answering machine, and there was a stack of faxes. He hit the Play button on the answering machine, opened his briefcase, then flipped through contracts, bids, reports—nothing that required his immediate attention.

There were three messages from Deborah. The last one was decidedly blunt. "What's up, Tom? I've called and called. I even came by your apartment and rang the doorbell for ten minutes. Are you ignoring me? Did you have to go out of town unexpectedly? Are you seeing someone else?"

"Yes, I'm ignoring you," he muttered, stopping the tape in mid-rant. It was time to end things with Deborah. Time, maybe, to do something about this place where he lived. Time to formulate a plan for finding the woman he would marry.

But would it be wrong to have one last fling while he was looking? If he spent a few days, and most especially a few nights, with Holly? Why not indulge himself? Holly wouldn't expect anything more than he offered. There was no potential for wounded feelings or disappointments or betrayals.

But it felt wrong.

He gave a harsh laugh. He was too tired, too edgy, too *something*. What was wrong with him that he turned down an affair with a woman he'd wanted ever since he'd met her?

The phone rang and grated on his nerves. So did looking at the gifts piled high on a table in the living room. At least those he could do something about. He found several empty file boxes in the storeroom and filled them with every last gift. He didn't want the stuff, but Holy Cross was always in need of operating funds, and Father Shanahan would gladly accept them in the form of crystal, sterling, or gold.

He didn't load the boxes until he'd downed two scotches to ease the knotting of the muscles in his stomach. Going back to the old neighborhood was something he'd sworn he would never do, but he'd broken that vow little more than a year ago. Asked by Ross to dispose of a diamond and sapphire bracelet, he'd delivered it to Father Shanahan late one evening and renewed his promise to stay away. But here he was, heading back again.

It was late, and the streets were mostly deserted. These few blocks of Flaherty Street had always been poor, but they hadn't always been dangerous. These days they were both. Only the most desperate of Buffalo's residents called the area home. Abandoned buildings, condemned by the city, had been taken over by runaways, gangs, prostitutes, and drug dealers. Shops were closed down, their windows broken, their security grills little protection against the thugs who lived in the neighborhood. Weeds grew in cracks both in the sidewalks and the streets, and everything was marked with signs of graffiti, vandalism, or violence.

He drove slowly, his fingers clenching the wheel tightly. The little voice inside him, the one he surely should have silenced after all these years, was screaming, Get me out of here! God, he hated this place.

He was only a few hundred feet from the church when movement on the sidewalk caught his attention. It was a woman walking briskly, shoulders hunched, head ducked. She didn't glance up as she stepped from the curb into the street, not until the squeal of his brakes startled her. She stopped short, wide-eyed and frightened, as his car skidded at an angle toward her.

In spite of his best efforts, the right front fender clipped her, knocking her to the ground and out of sight. Muttering curses, Tom brought the car to a stop, then jumped out. She was already sitting up, dusting herself off, when he reached her. "My God, are you all right?"

She straightened the knitted cap on her head, then extended a gloved hand to him. "I think so. Help me up, will you?"

"Maybe you should wait— I'll call an ambulance—"

"You think an ambulance would come down here at this time of night? What world do you live in?" Without waiting for his assistance, she scrambled to her feet and dusted her backside.

Her clothing was shabby enough to suggest that she lived around there, too clean for her to be living on the streets. A fringe of curly blond hair showed underneath the black cap, and her fair skin looked even fairer against her red scarf. Her brown overcoat almost touched her tennis shoes and as she moved gave a glimpse of faded jeans underneath. It was impossible to guess how old she was, somewhere between twenty and forty. Probably closer to twenty, he thought, unless life had been kind. But life on Flaherty Street was never kind.

"Now where did my bag go?" Spying it against the curb, she walked over without so much as a limp and picked it up. After making sure nothing was missing, she slung the handle over one shoulder, then took another look at him. "You take a wrong turn somewhere?"

"I was on my way to see Father Shanahan."

"At this time of night?" She stepped closer and sniffed, then wrinkled her nose as if he offended her. "When you've been drinking?"

Abruptly he realized the potential danger in the situation. Anyone with a day's experience in poverty could take one look at him and see that he had money. He *had* been drinking, and he had run her down, even though it was her fault. When faced with a defendant with deep pockets, juries didn't care too much about fault. He could have hurt her badly. She deserved something for her trouble, and he deserved to stay out of court.

"I haven't been drinking," he said stiffly. "I had a few drinks. But if you hadn't walked right out in front of me . . ." Returning to his car, he got his checkbook and a pen, and braced the checkbook on the roof of the car as he began to write. "What's your name?"

"Sophy. Sophy Jones."

"How much do you want?"

"How much do I want for what?"

"To forget this. To let it end here."

"I don't—" Suddenly, understanding dawned, and her eyes widened. "I don't want your money. I'm not hurt, and it was my fault, and even if I were hurt, I would never try to profit from an accident I caused!"

"You wouldn't, huh?" He'd learned over the years not to believe any woman who protested too loudly that she wasn't interested in his money. That was usually just before he found her up to her elbows in his bank account. "What is it? You want to talk to your lawyer first? Find out who I am and how much I can pay? Are you afraid of settling for a hundred grand tonight if there's a chance of getting a million or so in court?"

She gave him a look that was equal parts disbelief and amusement. "Oh, yes, of course my lawyer is just sitting around waiting for my important calls. In the meantime, he keeps my accountant and my stockbroker in line, and worries along with my personal physician about my late-night walks through this neighborhood." She came closer, raising her hand as if she were going to check for a fever, and he automatically stepped back to avoid her touch. "Maybe you should call that ambulance, mister. Maybe you bumped your head when you stopped."

He watched her suspiciously. "You expect me to believe that you don't want anything."

"I don't care *what* you believe. I'm just grateful your reflexes are as fast as they are, and I'm sorry I walked out in front of you without looking."

She eyed him up and down again. "You're a very wealthy man, Mr. Flynn. It's easy for a wealthy man to give away large sums, isn't it? A hundred thousand dollars? Small change to a man like you. A million? Petty cash."

A chill shivered down his spine. He prided himself on being able to anticipate his opponents' moves, on identifying and undermining their strategies. But he didn't have a clue as to what Sophy Jones was up to.

"All that money, all that success, and what do you have to show for it? Probably a beautiful office. A showplace home. A Porsche." She gingerly rubbed her hip. "Expensive clothes, incredible luxury, never a moment's worry about money. But that's all."

"All?" Tom echoed. "What more could I want?"

"Oh, I don't know. A family. Friends. Someone whose life is better because you're in it."

His mouth thinned to a flat line. He had no desire for a family, merely a wife. Friends were overrated. And as for making that kind of difference in someone's life . . . That sounded like a sappy definition of love. His ridiculous, impossible goal. "And where do you propose that I acquire these things? At the family-and-friends store at the mall?"

"Your money won't help you with that. Money can't buy a wife or friends—at least not the good ones. To get that, you have to rely on the warmth of your personality, your trustworthiness, your character, your generosity, and your sense of humor." She appeared to consider what she'd just said, then gave a shake of her head. "Or maybe not."

"Thanks for the vote of confidence," he said dryly. Time to steer the conversation back on course. "Now are you sure you're all right? If you become persuaded differently and choose to see a doctor, let me know. I can get the top specialists in their fields—"

"I won't be persuaded differently," she said firmly.

He wished he could believe her, wished he didn't think that Sophy Jones of Flaherty Street saw him as her ticket to a brighter future.

She sighed, then said, "Boy, are you a case," as if she'd read his mind. She started walking back the way she'd come.

"Hey! You were going the other way."

She turned and walked backward while smiling sweetly. "I know a shortcut—one that gets me away from you. Enjoy your visit with Father Pat. And don't be surprised if you see me around sometime." With a wave, she spun around and disappeared into an alley.

Slowly Tom closed his checkbook and slid it

into the breast pocket of his overcoat. He wasn't the least bit relieved by her insistence that she didn't want his money. She'd known who he was; her last comment no doubt meant he would soon be hearing from some two-bit lawyer claiming that nothing less than millions would ease her pain and suffering.

Damn, he'd tried to do a priest a favor, and look what it got him.

Swearing as he climbed back into the car, he finished the drive to Holy Cross. The iron fence surrounding the church was rusted, the gate propped open on broken hinges. It was a wonder the diocese hadn't shut the place down years ago and left the souls of the residents of Flaherty Street up for grabs.

Though the doors should have been locked and barred, they weren't. Tom carried the boxes inside, set them in a corner, and left as quietly as he'd come. He didn't want to see Father Shanahan, didn't want to hear the voice that had dogged him enough in the first sixteen years, he would never forget it. *You're a good boy, Tom. Why do you give your mother such grief? In trouble again, Tom? Why don't you direct all this energy into something worthwhile instead of causing such misery for yourself? Let her go, Tom. It's time. Tell her you love her and let her die in peace.*

She had wanted a better life for her son—had worked herself to death trying to give it to him—but what he'd achieved wasn't what she'd had in mind. Their definitions of "a better life" had varied greatly. To Lara Flynn, it had meant a safer neighborhood, enough food, a decent job, a family, a home, and services at Holy Cross at least once a week. To him it had meant succeeding beyond his wildest dreams. She might have been impressed by all that he'd done, but she would have deeply regretted all that he'd sacrificed to do it.

She wouldn't be proud of the man he'd become.

It took a long time for the knots in his stomach to unravel, and the tension that constricted the muscles in his neck to ease. The more distance he put between himself and Flaherty Street, the better he felt. By the time he got home, he was ready to return to his agenda.

How best to end things with Deborah?

How to find the perfect wife?

And the most important question of all: What to do about Holly?

Chapter Three

MONDAYS WERE GENERALLY SLOW at the inn, but this Monday also happened to be the end of the month. Holly had about a million entries on her things-to-do list, and not a single one of them said, Take a walk in the woods. So, of course, what was she doing? Taking a walk in the woods.

If it weren't the end of the month, she would have gone shopping, had dinner in a restaurant not her own, stayed in someone else's hotel, where all the worries and crises fell on someone else's shoulders. She might even have asked some handsome man to stay there with her.

Or not, she admitted as she scuffed through fallen leaves and pine needles. It had been a while since her last date. It wasn't that she hadn't had any invitations. She simply lacked the desire. What did it mean when she preferred the company of friends over an evening out, and a night in, with a handsome man? Or, worse, when she preferred a quiet evening alone?

"It means," she said aloud, "that you're getting old." She was thirty-seven. Too young to be a crotchety old spinster—her goal in life—and too young to consider giving up men completely, but too old for a good number of the available men in town.

Once upon a time, she'd had dreams of growing up, falling in love, and living happily ever after. The dreams had never included marriage, though—not with the example her parents had set for her. Marriage had made them both desperately unhappy. Her father had wanted out of the union, and her mother had wanted out of Bethlehem. They'd both gotten their wishes with his death.

Be careful what you wish for. You may get it.

Holly smiled thinly. Wherever her father was, she had no doubt he was happier than he'd been with Margery. At least he had peace. She'd never given him one day of it the entire twenty-some years they'd lived together in Bethlehem.

The trail she was following abruptly lost its gentle meandering curve and ran in a straight shot to the top of a not-very-steep hill. On the other side was her lake, both in ownership and in name. Years ago, before life and Margery had defeated her father, he'd brought her out here to fish and skip stones, and he'd christened it Holly's Lake in her honor.

It had seemed the biggest and best of all lakes

back then, though it was really just a pond. Some summers she'd swum in its waters, but most of her time there had been spent sitting on the dock her grandfather had built, hiding from her mother, mooning over the latest boy in her life, dreaming of a different life. All that was left of the dock was the pilings that had supported it, and all that was left of her dreams was . . .

Oh, who cared about stupid long-ago dreams? she thought crossly as she sat cross-legged on a flat rock at the water's edge.

It was a chilly day, but the sun was shining and felt good on her face. Tilting her head back, she closed her eyes and concentrated on breathing deeply. The air smelled cool, crisp, and clean, and it filled her lungs, forcing out tension, old memories, old disappointments.

Something plopped in the water, and she opened her eyes. Her first thought was that a fish had broken the surface, but the second and third plops proved her wrong.

"I realize I'm trespassing," said a woman's voice from behind her. "I hope you don't mind. I wanted to take a walk, and this seemed the best way to come."

"I don't mind." Holly lied, then asked, "A walk from where?" The only property for a good long way in any direction was hers. Wherever the woman had come from, she wasn't just taking a walk. She was doing a cross-country march.

"That way." She gestured to the northeast. "I'm visiting friends on Hillis Road."

Holly pointed to the southeast. "Hillis Road is a few miles that way."

The woman laughed, tossed the rest of her stones into the water, then dusted her hands before coming close to offer a handshake. "I'm Gloria, and I have a lousy sense of direction, but thankfully I never get lost."

"I'm Holly McBride," she said, studying the woman. They were about the same height—five-five, five-six—but Gloria was probably twenty pounds heavier. Her short brown hair was touched with gray and cut in a simple style. She was probably in her forties and not particularly pretty, but there was something compelling about her. Her eyes, or maybe that wonderful laugh, or the sense of comfortableness that surrounded her. She looked like someone's mother. Like someone you could trust with your deepest secrets.

"Holly McBride," Gloria repeated. "I've heard about you." She started to join her on the rock, then stopped and asked, "Do you mind?"

Holly shook her head. "Good or bad?"

Gloria sat down, then sighed. "It's a lovely place you have here."

For a moment, Holly allowed herself to be distracted. It *was* a lovely place—surrounded by trees, yet open to the sky, with no noise but bird calls and the occasional rustle of wind in the trees. As a kid, she'd planned to build a house right there, with a deck that extended over the water. Occasionally, as her business had grown, she'd thought about it again. Maybe she would. Or maybe she would save it as her place to go when she needed to be alone.

Or not alone, she thought as she glanced at Gloria. The woman appeared to be ignoring her question, but just as Holly had decided to repeat it, she spoke.

"I suppose it depends on what you consider good and bad. Things that insult some people amuse others."

"Hmm. What have you heard that I might consider an insult?" She could well imagine. In a small town like Bethlehem, with small-town values, her too-active sex life raised more than a few eyebrows and spurred its share of gossip.

"Well," Gloria began, "they say you're softhearted."

Holly stared at her for a moment before bursting into laughter. "You must have me confused with somebody else. I'm not softhearted. I'm a cynic. A first-class skeptic. I don't have a soft spot anywhere in my body."

Gloria ignored her disagreement. "They say you'll give a job to anyone who needs it, whether they can do it or not."

Holly thought of Bree, who'd managed that morning to break an antique teapot, wash a load of white sheets with a red tablecloth, and clog the vacuum so thoroughly that they'd had to send it out for repair. "That's not being softhearted," she defended herself. "Ask anyone in the hotel industry. Help is hard to find. I pay my employees a fair salary, but I expect them to earn it."

"See what I mean?" Gloria's smile was bright and pleased. "Most people wouldn't be offended by the suggestion that they were kindhearted." She stretched her legs out in front of her and sighed. She wore navy slacks and a navy parka, and her lace-up shoes were navy, too. It was a no-nonsense outfit, except for the wildly patterned socks. "So tell me, Holly McBride, why aren't you married?"

Holly thought about pointing out what a personal question that was, but passed on that. Instead, she offered the truth. "I have no desire to be."

"Ever?" Gloria looked scandalized. "But what if you fall in love?"

There wasn't much chance of that happening. It seemed to Holly that, with all the men in her past, if she were destined to fall in love it would have happened by now. Since it hadn't . . . "Falling in love has nothing to do with marriage. If I fell in love, I would have a long and satisfying relationship. No marriage. No misery."

"Ahh. You've had a bad experience."

"Or two."

"But marriage can be a beautiful thing. Why, look at Emilie and Nathaniel Bishop."

"Nathan Bishop," Holly corrected. Emilie was her assistant manager and one of her best friends. She and Nathan had been married two years, had a son, and were providing a home for Emilie's two nieces and nephew. Even the most cynical soul couldn't deny that they were incredibly in love.

"And what about the McKennas?" Gloria continued.

"McKinneys."

"Them, too. And Alec and Melissa Thomas, and the chief of police and his lovely wife, Kelly."

"It's Alex, not Alec. And Shelley, not Kelly."

"Right, Shelby." Gloria's half-smile, half-grimace was all charm. "I have a terrible time with names. Until I've known someone a decade or two, there's no telling what I might call them. Anyway, Holly—it *is* Holly, right?—my point is that you shouldn't write off marriage for yourself just because your parents' marriage was unhappy. They were the exception, not the rule. Your friends are proof of that."

Holly tried to ease the frown caused by the mention of her parents, but it refused to be eased. She knew people gossiped about her affairs. Some of them even debated which was stronger—her desire to seduce Tom or his desire to remain unseduced. She wouldn't have been surprised if some enterprising soul was giving odds on the outcome.

But she'd never guessed that anyone gossiped about her parents' marriage. She would have bet most people in town didn't even know the truth of it.

"For someone who's just visiting, you've certainly learned a lot," she said stiffly.

"Oh, I'm not visiting. I'm in Bethlehem to stay.

And you're right. I have learned a lot. I guess I just have one of those faces that make people want to talk."

Standing up, Holly dusted the seat of her pants, then slid her hands in her jacket pockets. "Well, Gloria, right now I'd rather not talk. And for the record, I'm not foolish enough to think that all marriages are destined to fail because my parents' failed. And I really don't appreciate having a total stranger take me to task for choices I've made that you know nothing about. Now if you'll excuse me, I need to get back to work."

"Oh, please . . . I'm sorry . . ." Gloria scrambled up the hill after her, then stopped at the top. "Don't leave on my account. Stay here and enjoy the peace. Don't go away mad. . . . Oh, fiddlesticks!"

Holly was halfway to the inn before she slowed her steps. It was stupid of her to get annoyed. All she had needed to do was change the subject, and Gloria would have taken the hint.

It was particularly foolish of her to be annoyed when Gloria was right. She didn't look kindly on the institution of marriage in large part because of her parents' spectacular failure. She'd never wanted to find herself in the same situation.

Not that it mattered. The truth was, no man had ever proposed to her. There was only one thing they wanted from her. The same thing the high-school boys had wanted when she was a starved-for-affection teenager, the same thing all those college boys had wanted. It wasn't marriage, and it sure as hell wasn't love.

And it was all she wanted, too. Remember?

HARRY'S DINER WAS AN INSTITUTION in downtown Bethlehem. It occupied the best location on Main Street, directly across from the town square, and had for the last thirty-nine years. Every morning Harry Winslow arrived at five o'clock, entering through the back door. Within a minute or two, his head waitress, Maeve Carter, who'd been with him every one of those thirty-nine years, walked in the front door.

Right on time Wednesday morning, Harry let himself in. The first thing he did was turn on the heat. It was a cold dawn and wasn't likely to get much warmer. The weatherman was predicting snow, and the ache in Harry's bum knee agreed. Didn't matter much to him. Snow or not, he'd be there until closing at eight that night, and he would be right back again in the morning. He was open seven days a week, fifty-two weeks a year.

Since his kids had moved away and his wife had died, God rest her soul, the diner was his life.

A sound came from the dining room. As he measured out the ingredients for his famous sticky buns, he called, "Mornin', Maeve."

Six days a week, fifty-two weeks a year, she answered back, "Mornin', Harry." But not this morning. And the dining room lights were still off, except for the ones over the counter that burned all the time.

Dusting the flour from his hands, he went to investigate. He was standing there in the dining room, doing just that, when Maeve let herself in with her key. She set her handbag down, removed her coat and the scarf that covered her hair, and said, "Mornin', Harry."

"Mornin', Maeve."

She glanced at him, then gave him a second, more curious look. "What're you looking at?"

He gestured toward the corner booth, the one with the bench that curved practically all the way around. She came to stand by his side and looked, too. "Why, who on earth is that?"

Harry shrugged. "The more important question is, what is she doing spending the night in my diner?" Anticipating Maeve's elbow to the ribs, he sidestepped, getting only a gentle poke instead of the jab she'd intended.

"Harry Winslow, why do you think she spent the night here? Because she had no place else to go, that's why!" Leaning across the table to better see the sleeping girl, she went on. "I remember her. She's had dinner in here every night this week. Just before closing time. Nice girl. Quiet. Kinda sad. I wonder who she is."

"Wake her up and ask her."

Maeve shot him an annoyed look. "I will not! The poor child looks exhausted. You get back to baking your sticky buns, you old grouch, and I'll take care of her."

As he returned to the kitchen, Harry shook his head. Maeve had a tender heart. She should have had a houseful of kids to mother, but she'd only had the one, and only one grandchild. Her husband had been gone almost as long as his Mary Sue, but Maeve had adjusted better. She worked, baby-sat her granddaughter, helped out at the church, and tried to make him feel not so alone. She was a good friend. A good woman. It was a wonder some old rascal hadn't snapped her up. She sure could brighten a man's life.

Of course, if someone did marry her up, Harry would be sorry. It wasn't likely that a man of an age to interest Maeve would want his brand-new wife working all the time. He'd want her home with him, and available for traveling to visit family and friends, maybe, or to go see the Grand Canyon and the giant redwoods and maybe even Disneyland. Harry sure would hate to lose her, but of course he wouldn't stand in her way.

Hearing voices in the dining room, he moved to the pass-through. The lights were on, and the girl was awake. The first of a few dozen pots of coffee was brewing, and Maeve was sitting in the booth, watching the kid eat a slice of pie left over from yesterday.

"What's your name, honey?" she asked when the girl was finished.

The question was met with suspicion and a grudging answer. "Bree."

"What a pretty name. Is it short for Sabrina? Brianne? Gabrielle?"

"Just Bree."

"You new in town?"

Just-Bree nodded.

"Having kind of a tough time, huh?"

Still looking suspicious, Bree huddled in her jacket. It was old, inadequate for an upstate New York winter, and needed cleaning, repairing, and . . . Oh, heck, it needed throwing away and replacing with something warmer. With her straight brown hair and big hazel eyes, the kid looked about ten years old, though Harry would wager she was probably twice that. She looked scared, too. And lost.

Harry gave himself a mental shake. He was starting to feel as softhearted as Maeve, and he wasn't that at all. He was cantankerous, and no one could prove any different.

"I'm doing all right," the girl said defiantly. "I don't need help from anyone."

Maeve's laugh brought a smile to Harry's face. "Well, honey, you're doing a lot better than me. I'm fifty-ni—well, a lot older than you, and I've needed help from someone every single day of my life. Where'd you come from?"

"Rochester."

"Do you have any family or friends here? Besides Harry and me, of course."

"Who's Harry?"

Without looking over her shoulder, Maeve said, "He's the nosy old man back there peeking through the window. He owns this establishment, but I run it."

Bree's gaze shifted to Harry, and she nodded once in greeting. There was something vaguely familiar about her. Maybe he'd met her before, or her mama. Or maybe she just had one of those faces.

After returning her nod, he said gruffly, "What you run around here is your mouth, Maeve. Can't you talk and work at the same time?"

He didn't mean anything by the words, and Maeve knew it. She just winked at the girl, flashed a grin at Harry, and went on talking. "He's an old grouch, but we put up with him around here because he's a fairly decent cook . . . for a man."

He harrumphed because she expected him to, and then she repeated her question. "You got any family around here, hon? Any place to stay?"

Bree wiped her nose with the back of her hand, then went on the defensive. "I didn't take anything from you. I didn't eat or drink anything. I just slept on the bench and used the bathroom. That's all."

Harry gave up any pretense of working and came out to the dining room, pulling up a chair from the nearest table. The sharp look Bree gave him, edged with fear, made him realize that he blocked her exit from the booth. Without a word, he scooted closer to Maeve, so the kid could get out if she wanted. "How did you manage that?"

"I—I came in for dinner about seven-thirty. Just before you closed, I paid the bill, then went to the bathroom. I stayed there until you were gone."

He made a mental note to start checking the bathrooms at night.

"Hon, you can't keep sleeping in here," Maeve said. "If we can get you a job—"

"I have a job. I'm not looking for charity or anything. I got a job my first day in town."

"Where at?" Harry asked.

An odd look came across her face—part guilt, part distrust, part bitterness. "The McBride Inn. I'm a maid there."

So she could make the beds there, but she couldn't sleep in one of them. Then Harry immediately regretted the thought. If Holly had known the girl had no place to live, she would have helped her out. Anyone in Bethlehem would have. Holly liked to pretend she was a coolheaded businesswoman, with all the compassion that implied, but no one was fooled. Like Maeve, Holly had a tender spot for people in need.

"Have you told Holly—"

Wide-eyed, Bree burst out, "No! She doesn't need to know! It's none of her business!"

"But you must have given her an address, a phone number."

It was Harry's turn to nudge Maeve. The girl had to have lied to Holly.

That girl now slid to her feet and grabbed the battered backpack she'd used as a pillow. Harry suspected it contained everything she owned. "Look, I'm sorry I borrowed your place without asking, and I promise I won't do it again, but you've got to promise you won't say anything to Holly." She looked anxiously from Harry to Maeve, then added, *"Please!"*

With a sigh, Maeve said, "All right, hon. We promise."

Relief spread across Bree's face as she turned toward the door.

"Don't you want some breakfast, hon?" Maeve called. "It's on the house. The best breakfast in town."

The only answer was the closing of the door.

Harry watched the girl go, then looked back at Maeve, one brow raised. "You want to tell Holly, or should I?"

Chapter Four

LIKE MOST SMALL TOWNS, BETHLEHEM loved its celebrations, and Valentine's Day was no exception. Every year, the place to be on the Saturday before the fourteenth was the Sweethearts Dance, held in the grand ballroom at the Elks Lodge. It was a rite of passage, since no one under eighteen was allowed. Holly remembered her first Sweethearts Dance, her last, and every one in between. They were a tradition in her life, one that she loved. This year she was donating her time and services, as she always did, as part of the planning committee, meeting that afternoon in her dining room, but it looked as if she wasn't going to have a date for the dance.

Oh, Jim Watters had asked, but she made it a rule not to date the newly divorced. There was nothing quite as boring as spending an entire evening listening to a man lament the one who got away. She'd also had an invitation from Kenny Gallagher, a sweet young man who swore the difference in their ages didn't matter, but it mattered to her. Especially since she'd dated his father first.

Though she hadn't dared admit it to anyone yet, she thought she might skip the dance this year. She could have Edward make his hazelnut dacquoise for her, put on her comfiest jammies, watch some terribly maudlin movie on cable, and have a great pity party for one.

Corinna Winchester, co-chair of the committee with her sister Agatha, consulted her notes, then recapped. "All right, ladies. Melissa is donating the centerpieces, as usual. Emilie and Kelsey are in charge of the decorations, with help from all of you under the age of fifty." She offered that last with a charming, seventy-some-year-old smile. "Shelley is taking care of the music, and Agatha will be in charge of the child care. Maggie, along with the inn's staff, will provide the food, and Holly . . ."

"I'm advertising and reservations."

Miss Corinna made a note. "Yes, and you're supplying the pink tablecloths. It was quite a happy accident, wasn't it?"

Holly glanced at a distant table that held the linens her disaster-prone employee had turned from white sheets into pink tablecloths and smiled dryly. "Quite."

Miss Agatha leaned close to Holly. "Maybe she'll turn the new ones green in time for St. Patrick's

Day. And we could use some pastels for the big Easter egg hunt at City Park."

"I'll keep that in mind." Holly sat back in her chair and let her attention wander while the elderly sisters continued to tie up loose ends. They were community leaders in every way, volunteering at church, the hospital, and the library. They gave generously of their money and more so of their time. They were classy broads, she thought with a grin, and someday, when she was too old to be wicked, she might be just like them.

"If there aren't any questions, this meeting is adjourned," Miss Corinna said.

After Miss Corinna and Miss Agatha left, the remaining women huddled around the table, as if they were having their traditional Friday get-together lunch. Shelley looked at Kelsey and said, "Okay, tell us about Bud."

Bud Grayson was Kelsey's father-in-law. He'd come to Bethlehem for a few weeks last summer to help while J.D. had temporary custody of the four Brown kids. Bud's few weeks had turned into a permanent move, and J.D.'s temporary custody had become a formal adoption. He'd also regained custody of his own son from his first marriage. Kelsey had married a man with no one in his life on a permanent basis, and had wound up in very short order with five kids and a father-in-law. She was a braver, stronger woman than Holly, who surely would have run screaming in the other direction.

"I was telling Bud about the Sweethearts Dance,"

Kelsey said, her eyes bright, "and I asked him if he would like to go with J.D. and me. He said no, he'd stay home with the kids. So I mentioned that they were providing child care and that Miss Agatha was in charge of it, and you should have seen him perk up! He decided that maybe he would go, after all, and if he got tired of dancing, then maybe he'd offer his help taking care of the kids."

"So Bud is sweet on Miss Agatha," Emilie said. "Ooh, this should be fun. We can play matchmaker for the matchmaker."

The Winchester sisters did consider themselves matchmakers of a sort. They'd given J.D. more than a few nudges toward Kelsey, had taken a great interest in keeping Maggie's marriage to Ross intact, and helped Emilie and Nathan get together, too. If Shelley could remember that long ago, she and Mitch had probably had their share of Winchester help. Melissa and Alex, though, hadn't needed it. For them, it had been love at first sight. And as for Holly . . . even matchmakers had their limits. They couldn't force a match between two people wishing to stay unmatched.

But that hadn't been her wish, an annoying little voice pointed out. *Wish for me.* That was all she'd thought. She hadn't put any stipulations—for a night, a week, or a lifetime, for an affair, a relationship, or marriage—on the wish. Just *Wish for me.*

"I always wondered why Miss Agatha never married," Melissa remarked. "She's got so much love to give. I can't imagine no one offering."

"I prefer to think she chose spinsterhood," Holly said airily. "Some of us do, you know."

Shelley looked knowingly at her, then turned to Maggie. "Is Tom coming to town this weekend?"

Emilie and Maggie both shook their heads, leaving Holly to wonder if Tom had any idea that his boss's wife and a woman he'd barely met tracked his movements.

"So why don't you go to Buffalo?"

Holly looked at Shelley as if she'd spoken in a foreign language. "And what would I do in Buffalo?"

"What you do everywhere you go—shop. Try a new restaurant." Shelley grinned. "Maybe seduce a handsome lawyer."

"Do it for us," Melissa teased. "You're the only one whose life allows any spontaneity. You don't have kids to farm out or a husband to convince. Just turn the inn over to your most capable assistant manager—"

"Who's scheduled to work this weekend anyway," Emilie added.

"—and go off and have fun. Give us something to drool over next Friday."

Holly tried but couldn't change the subject. Until Janice, working the desk while Holly and Emilie attended the meeting, stepped into the double doorway. "Phone call, Holly."

Excusing herself, she rose from her chair with relief, turned . . . and walked smack into Bree. Unfortunately the girl was delivering a dessert, the inn's latest Valentine's creation—a concoction of cream cheese, raspberry sauce, Dutch cocoa, and rich chocolate.

For an instant, the table went silent, then Holly heard two simultaneous gasps—hers and Bree's. She stared down at the mass of cream cheese plastered right in the middle of her chest, staining her white silk blouse raspberry red.

"I—I—" Bree's hands were trembling so badly, she dropped the plate that had held the dessert. It was only Melissa's quick grab that saved the delicate china. A cry escaping her, Bree ran from the room.

"You take your call," Emilie said, handing Holly a napkin to wipe her blouse. "I'll check on Bree."

Holly scraped away as much of the dessert as she could, then went to her office to answer the phone. She sat down and began writing Bree's final paycheck at the same time as she said hello.

Ten minutes later, she said goodbye to Maeve and tore up the check.

Oh, hell. It wasn't her fault that the girl was homeless, or that she was apparently all alone in the world. She was a walking disaster, for heaven's sake. If she stayed around much longer, she would break, ruin, and burn Holly out of business.

True, it wasn't her fault . . . but wasn't she somehow responsible? Didn't she have an obligation to consider the best interests of the people she employed? Didn't everyone have some obligation to look out for everyone else?

She wasn't great with questions of conscience.

Right now she would change clothes, then return to the dining room. Later she would discuss the problem with Emilie. Her assistant manager was the softhearted one. She would know what to do.

Holly was in her closet, putting on a deep purple blouse, when the hall door opened, and Emilie called her name. "I'm in here," she replied.

"I believe the tears have stopped for a while," Emilie said with a sigh. "She doesn't seem like an overly emotional person most of the time, but then something goes wrong and she just falls apart. I don't have a clue what's wrong with her."

"I do." She told Emilie about Maeve's phone call.

"She's been living in Harry's Diner?" Emilie gave a bemused shake of her head. "When we were homeless, I recall wishing Harry's was open twenty-four hours so I could just sit there awhile, but it never occurred to me to try moving in."

"No, you just went out and stole a whole house." Though her words were true, Holly softened her tone. Emilie had been desperate when she'd gotten stranded in Bethlehem two Thanksgivings ago. Broke, on the run with her sister's three kids, stuck with a car that had died in a blizzard, she'd made the best of her very limited options. The house she'd moved into had stood empty for years, and if the neighbors had assumed she was the owner, well, she couldn't be responsible for what people thought. Eventually she'd been found out, of course, but by then she'd made friends who were only too happy to help her, and she'd had Nathan, who'd fallen head over heels in love with her.

Bree didn't appear to have any friends, and there was no sign of a white knight waiting to come charging to her rescue.

"What are you going to do?" Emilie asked.

"I don't suppose I can rent an apartment for her, give her some cash, and fire her, can I?" Holly asked hopefully.

Emilie shook her head.

"But I don't have a guest room."

"You have a whole floor of them."

"But most of those are rented every weekend. I can't very well ask her to move out every Friday and stay gone until Monday, can I?"

"No, but you can turn that junk room into a guest room. You've been saying for months that you're going to clean it out and do something with it. Here's your chance."

The junk room had been a screened-in porch before Holly's last remodel had turned it into a room with real walls, a window, and a door that opened just a few feet from the door into her own quarters. It stayed locked now, and was home to everything Margery had left behind. That was the real reason Holly had never cleaned it out—cleaning it would mean dealing with her mother, and she tried very hard to avoid dealing with her mother.

But Margery had been gone fifteen years. Holly had provided her free storage long enough.

"All right. But you owe me," she said as she

checked her appearance in the full-length mirror mounted on the door. She wasn't sure whether she was talking to Emilie, herself, Bree, or God, but just to make sure the message got across, she repeated it. "You owe me big-time."

Maybe she owed herself big-time, she thought as they returned to work. She did need a break. For years she'd indulged herself often with weekend trips and enjoyed them tremendously. At the moment, though, she couldn't remember the last such trip.

Which meant it had been too long. She didn't have to go to Buffalo, but even if she did, she didn't have to call Tom. If she set her mind to it, she could have a great time without thinking about him even once.

First thing on Saturday morning, she would pack a bag, drive to the airport, and buy a ticket on the next available flight, no matter where it was going. She might wind up in Toronto, St. Louis, or sunny San Diego.

But just in case it was Buffalo, it couldn't hurt to take along that little black dress, now could it?

Chapter Five

AFTER PUTTING IN A FULL DAY'S work at the office on Saturday, Tom rode the elevator down to the garage, where his car was the only one occupying the entire level. For a moment, he stood half on the elevator, half off, then abruptly stepped back on. He didn't want to go home, not just yet. If there were someone he could call to meet him for drinks and dinner, he would, but Deborah had finally gotten the hint and he hadn't yet found a replacement.

Hell, he didn't mind eating or drinking alone. And if he did, well, there was always someone on the make in the place where he was headed.

The restaurant was on the twenty-fifth floor of the building across the street from his office. The view was nice, the food good, the prices outrageous. He didn't mind, since it helped cut down on the Saturday-night crowds. Even so, there would be a thirty-minute wait for a table, even for a regular customer like him. He went into the bar and claimed a stool.

"What can I— Well, imagine meeting you here."

He jerked around from his perusal of the place to stare at Sophy Jones. When he'd awakened the morning after the accident, he'd half hoped it had all been a bad dream—the trip to Flaherty Street, the run-in with Ms. Jones. After all, he would never, in his right mind, choose to make another trip to Holy Cross. There were no marks on the Porsche to indicate an accident, and that night had a sort of surreal feel to it.

But he'd known it was real. And only two days later, he'd run into Sophy again. She and Father Shanahan were eating in a restaurant he'd been forced to step in to make a phone call on the walk over to a business lunch. His cell phone, which never left his side, had gone on the blink even though it had been working properly that morning. Father Shanahan had thanked him for the gifts, and Sophy had told him to take an aspirin. The pained expression on his face must have let her know he had one hell of a headache. Had she also known she was partly responsible for it?

Now here she was again.

"What are you doing here?"

"Working." She made a showy gesture with both hands to indicate her white shirt, black trousers, and red bow tie that matched the other bartender's outfit. With her broad grin and the blond curls falling across her forehead, she looked even younger than usual.

"You work in a bar? Does Father Shanahan know?"

"It's not a regular job. I just fill in sometimes. Tip well. I'll deserve it."

"Are you even old enough to be in a bar?"

"I'm much older than I look. What will you have?"

"Scotch."

She picked up a glass and a bottle, then asked, "Are you driving tonight?"

"Not for a while."

"Good, because, you know, drinking and driving don't mix."

He glared at her smug look and reached for the drink, then waited for her to go away before taking the first sip.

She didn't go, though. Instead, she leaned her arms on the bar that separated them. "Did you work today?"

"Yeah."

"Is that all you do?"

He opened his mouth to deny it, but it was hard to deny the truth. "Yeah, pretty much."

"All work and no play makes Tom—"

"A very rich man."

"In some ways. Very poor in others. You don't even have someone to share dinner with you on a Saturday night."

Rather than argue the point with her, he asked,

"How do you know I didn't come here for the purpose of meeting somebody?"

"Say you did. I bet I know exactly the type you go for." She stretched onto her toes to gaze around the bar, mumbling to herself as she passed from one woman to the next. Tom turned to look, too, wondering what kind of woman she would pick for him. Probably some female version of himself, someone who'd spent an entire Saturday in her office, who hadn't heard another voice besides her own all day and had nothing to go home to but an empty apartment she didn't even like.

He saw several candidates, but Sophy passed over them. She also dismissed a couple of Deborah clones, an attractive redhead he'd pegged for a very expensive hooker, and a drop-dead gorgeous woman in green who looked exactly like—

"There she is," Sophy said triumphantly. "The blonde holding court in the middle of all those men. That's your type."

"Uh-huh." Without looking at the blonde, he picked up his drink and started across the room to drop-dead gorgeous. The man she was talking to looked vaguely familiar, but Tom paid him no mind. Instead, he fixed his gaze on her. "Holly."

She broke off in midsentence, looked at him, and smiled coolly. She looked . . . incredible. Like every erotic dream, fantasy, and experience he'd ever had all rolled into one. "Tom."

He had to swallow before he could speak again, and the sarcasm he was aiming for was barely recognizable. "What a coincidence running into you here."

"My being in Buffalo is a coincidence," she admitted. "My being here right now is the result of information from Maggie."

The man seated across from her cleared his throat, and she started as if she'd forgotten him. Good. "Oh, Tom, I'd like you to meet—" She gave the guy a brilliant smile. "I'm sorry. I didn't get your name."

He answered too low for Tom to hear, but she caught it. "Greg Everett, Tom Flynn."

Greg half-rose to shake hands, then stiffened. "Tom Flynn . . . the lawyer? Um, yeah, nice to—to meet you. Holly, take care." Forgetting his drink, he disappeared into the crowd.

"Well, there goes my evening's entertainment." She didn't sound too disappointed. "You two have a history, or do all intelligent lawyers run the other way when you appear?"

"Maybe I'm suing him or putting him out of a job." He slid onto the tall stool Everett had vacated as she made a *tsk*-ing sound. "If I'm suing him or someone he represents, he deserves it. If I'm putting him out of a job, he'll find another. Lawyers always do."

Leaning back, he sipped his drink while giving her a thorough look. Last Saturday night she'd been wearing a green dress, too, but that was where the similarities between the garments ended. Last week's dress had been simple, dark, perfectly suitable for church. This dress was emerald green, flashy, and revealed a lot of shoulder, arm, and leg. It fit as if made for her body.

To entice his body.

Or, more properly, Greg Everett's body.

"What are you doing, picking up someone whose name you didn't even ask?"

"Ooh, something you've certainly never done." She gave him another of those cool smiles. It made his fingers tighten around his glass and his jaw hurt. It was the sort of smile she might give someone she didn't know, or someone she didn't like. It sure as hell wasn't the way she should be smiling at him.

She didn't give his question any more of an answer. It wasn't necessary. He could guess her plan. Come in here, wait to see if he showed up alone, try her luck with him if he did, find someone else to—how had she put it?—entertain her if he didn't. Take him out of the plan, and it became one of her old routines.

It was one of his old routines, too, but it was different for him. He wasn't sure how. He just knew it was. "If you don't change your ways, one of these days some hotel housekeeper is going to find you with your lovely throat slit ear to ear."

"I'm available, not reckless."

"Yeah? Tell me what you know about Greg Everett."

She leaned toward him, the deep V neckline giving him a view that made his throat go dry. It was nothing he hadn't seen a dozen times before. Just the beginning swell of her breasts, the shadowy valley between them, the soft creamy skin. And it made him hot. Made his hand unsteady and his heart beat faster.

"I know he's a lawyer," she said in a husky, seductive voice. "He works in your building across the street. He's divorced, has no kids, makes six figures a year, drives a Lexus, and thinks he's the best thing to ever happen to a lonely woman on a Saturday night. I also know that I had no intention of going anywhere but the dining room with him." Sitting back, she raised her voice to normal. "You, on the other hand . . ."

She didn't need to finish. His imagination was way ahead of her, in an anonymous hotel room, clothes scattered everywhere, the two of them naked in bed. Aw, hell, why had he been telling her no for months? He couldn't remember.

Truth was, he didn't *want* to remember that she was Maggie's friend. He didn't want to remember that she wasn't his type. Wasn't tall enough, blond enough, thin enough, greedy enough. He didn't want to remember that she had plenty of money of her own and wasn't interested in his. Money was what drew women to him, what made them stay, and, in the end, it was money that made them leave.

He damn sure didn't want to remember that she was the only woman who attracted him, tempted him—hell, just flat-out tormented him—and whom he hadn't used and discarded. She was the only one of all those women for whom he felt some measure of . . . respect.

Tom Flynn feeling respect for a woman he wanted in the worst way. *That* was an event to remember.

"Where's Deborah?"

He shrugged.

"So another affair bites the dust." She traced the rim of her glass with one fingertip. "How long did this one last? Eight weeks? Nine?"

"About that." For some reason, he wasn't comfortable discussing Deborah with her. He wasn't sure why. They'd talked about his women and her men before, but now it felt . . .

Felt. There was that damned word again.

Holly slipped off the tall stool and picked up her handbag. "I'm going to the ladies' room. Listen for my name, and I'll let you share my table."

Along with half the men and women in the place, he watched her walk away, then he downed the rest of his drink in one swallow. With one hand, he tugged his tie, loosening the knot that was strangling him. Unfortunately, the extra inch of breathing space didn't ease the constriction in his throat, or his chest.

"She's lovely, but I wouldn't have thought she was your type."

He glanced idly at Sophy as she placed his empty glass and Everett's mostly full one on a tray, then wiped a water ring from the table. "She's not."

"I don't believe in types myself. If you limit yourself to a certain type, think of all the wonderful people you miss out on. You might never meet the woman you were meant to spend the rest of your life with just because she doesn't match your preconceived notion of your type. Wouldn't that be a pity?"

He turned his narrowed gaze on her. "What makes you think I'm looking for someone to spend the rest of my life with?"

"A man can spend every waking hour working for only so long. He needs someone there when the work's finally finished. Someone to grow old with. Someone to make all that money, power, and success worthwhile. Do you deny that you've given it a thought?"

He neither denied nor confirmed it.

"Is she the woman you've chosen?"

Marry Holly? He choked back a laugh. She'd made it clear she had no desire for a husband, wanted no children of her own, and was perfectly capable of taking care of herself with no help from anyone. Even if he could change her mind, she would have no patience for his moods or his selfishness, none at all for his long hours at work. She was too independent, too capable, and too intelligent ever to consider spending the rest of her life with him. Plus, she would never give up Bethlehem for the city.

But she also met or exceeded every requirement on his short list for the perfect wife. She was beautiful and sophisticated. She was the perfect hostess—people didn't keep coming back to her inn for the chocolate mints on the pillows—and she was intelligent and well educated. She had opinions on every subject under the sun and didn't mind sharing them, and would probably understand his reason for marrying as well as, if not better than, he did.

The only question was her emotional needs. How much of a burden would they be?

"Not answering me, huh?" Sophy grinned. "That must mean the answer's yes. You've made a wise choice. She'll make the right man a wonderful wife."

"You can tell that by seeing her for ten seconds."

"I'm a great judge of character. I was right about you, wasn't I?"

"I have no character. I'm a lawyer, remember?"

"Here she comes. Her table's ready in the dining room, so why don't you deny these juvenile males the pleasure of seeing her climb up on that stool in that dress?"

"What if I want to see it, too?"

"You'll get plenty of chances in the next sixty years." Picking up the tray, she disappeared into the crowd before he thought to ask how she knew Holly's table was ready when she didn't know Holly's name.

Then Holly was standing in front of him, and he didn't care how Sophy knew anything. She was easing the short, tight skirt of her dress a little higher to climb onto the stool. He stood up and caught her arm. "Our table's ready."

"Oh, well, drag me away then."

He grimaced, eased his grip. "Sorry." As he followed her toward the door, he saw the admiring looks she drew from damn near every man they passed. Messy emotional needs aside, marrying Holly just might be an interesting experience. At least he would never get bored—or too comfortable, he thought, noticing the dazzling smile she turned on a few of those men.

And being neither bored nor complacent wouldn't be a bad way to live.

DINNER WAS INCREDIBLE, AND THE food hadn't been half bad, either—at least, what Holly remembered of it. That part of the evening was something of a blur, though she'd bet she could recall every word Tom had spoken, every expression that had crossed his face, every movement he'd made. To say he was dynamic was a major understatement. He could very easily fascinate her, if he wanted to. If she wanted him to.

Their dinner dishes had been cleared away two hours ago, their dessert plates an hour later. They'd talked their way through a bottle of wine and two cups of black coffee and had ignored the waiter's eagerness for them to leave. The young man had discovered great reserves of patience once Tom had slipped him a folded bill.

With a sigh, she gazed out the window at the millions of lights below. It was the same view from her hotel window, similar to what she saw in every other city she visited. It was impressive and breathtaking, but it was nothing compared to home.

"Thinking about Bethlehem?"

"How did you guess?"

"You have this look Ross gets after he's been here a few days. Maggie comes here wearing it." He shook his head. "I can't believe they're happy living in a—"

"Watch it. That's my hometown you're about to malign."

He thought better of what he'd been about to say. "It's not a bad town. I guess, as small towns go, it's fine. It's just so small. And intimate."

"We like it that way."

"You know what struck me most about it when Ross and Maggie first moved there? The trees. Where I grew up, the only place to see trees was in a park, and there for damn sure weren't any parks in our part of town. Even now, the only trees where I live are in containers on balconies and in the lobby. All those millions of trees around Bethlehem impressed me."

That was sad, though of course she didn't comment on it. "Where did you grow up?"

His mouth thinned, and his jaw tightened. "Here in Buffalo."

"Where?" She looked out the window again. "Can we see your neighborhood from here? Point it out."

He didn't bother looking or pointing. "It was a place called Flaherty Street, and it's not worth talking about."

She wanted to know more, but something in his eyes stopped her. She couldn't identify it exactly.

Bleakness. Bitterness. Wariness. He wasn't proud of where he'd come from—only of where he'd come to. But one didn't have much meaning without the other. Surely growing up poor on Flaherty Street was a large part of what made his success so sweet. But he obviously didn't want to discuss it, so she changed the subject. "Do you think we've tied up their best table long enough?"

In answer, he stood up. After a stop to pick up their coats and his briefcase, they got in the elevator together.

"Can I get a cab downstairs?" she asked.

"I'll give you a ride."

"A cab's no trouble."

"Neither is a ride."

She suppressed a smile as she watched the numbers flash on and off. When they reached the lobby, he steered her out the east door and across the street.

"What would you have done if I'd decided not to eat at that restaurant tonight?" he asked as they were buzzed into the lobby by a security guard.

"I told you. Greg Everett was my entertainment for tonight. I would have had dinner with him, then caught a cab to the hotel, ordered ice cream and chocolate from room service, and seen if *The X-Files* was on any of the two hundred channels available."

"And that would have been. . . ?"

Was he fishing for compliments? Wanting to hear that an evening with him far surpassed the best possible evening with any other man? She suppressed another smile. "Not bad. Not the best time I've ever had, but not the worst, either. But I'm glad you did decide to eat there."

They took an elevator to the top level of the parking garage. It was a vast, empty, shadowy place, and it gave her the creeps. "I know you think Bethlehem is a tiny little burg without much to offer, but at least there's not one of these things for miles around. I'm happy parking my car in my own driveway."

"You don't have a driveway. You park in a lot."

"Yes, but it's *my* lot, and it's only a few feet from my door, and it's open to the sunlight—"

"And the wind, rain, and snow." He unlocked the doors, then started to circle around to the driver's side. Abruptly he came back, scowling, and opened the door for her.

She wasn't sure what to think of his behavior tonight. When he'd first joined her in the bar, if she hadn't known better, she might have thought he was jealous. But a man had to care about a woman before he could get jealous over her. It wasn't as if Tom wanted her for himself. He'd certainly turned down plenty of opportunities to have her. No doubt, when they got to the hotel, if she invited him to her room, he would turn her down yet again.

But that would be all right. She'd had a lovely evening. It had been almost like a real date, and a woman with her reputation didn't get many of those. There was always the expectation of "payment" before the evening was over. Tom, she was sure, didn't expect anything more than a thank-you.

He stopped at the garage exit. "Where are we going?"

"I honestly don't know," she answered absently. Then, realizing what she'd said, she forced a laugh and gave him the name of her hotel.

When he pulled into the hotel driveway, she expected him to drop her off at the door. Maybe, if he was feeling chivalrous, he would see her to the elevator. She *didn't* expect him to hand the keys to a valet, walk inside with her, and turn toward the bar at the rear of the lobby.

"Need another drink?" she asked dryly.

"No." He gestured at the dance floor. "Want to dance?"

"Dance."

"You know, music, rhythm, moving together. I know you know how."

"Of course I do. I just never imagined you getting away from your desk long enough to learn."

"My job requires that I attend a lot of boring parties. If you don't dance, you have to actually talk to people."

"And so you'd rather not talk to me anymore?" she teased.

"If that were the case, I would have dropped you off at the door." He made an impatient gesture. "Do you want to dance or not?"

She glanced from him to the couples on the floor. The music was familiar, old jazz standards, and the dances were intimate. "Yes, I do."

They checked their coats, then moved onto the floor. Dancing, she believed, told her a lot about a man—at least, about her and that man. When they stumbled, unable to match each other's rhythm, the sex between them was usually awkward, too. Some of her partners were technically accomplished on the dance floor but lacked passion for the music, the movements. Sex with them lacked passion, too.

But Tom . . . When he took her in his arms, it was as if she'd been there a million times. Her body knew his, recognized his steps, anticipated his moves. Having his arms around her was the sweetest, most natural thing in the world. Even her fingers knew the feel of him.

Sex with him would be so fantastic, it might not be mere sex. It would be so incredible, so intense it might demand to be called by another name. Like making—

Harshly she shoved that thought out of her mind. Sex was sex was sex. Sometimes it was mediocre, usually passable, and on occasion it was toe-curling fabulous. But it was still sex. Nothing more.

She was working on convincing herself of that when Tom brought his mouth close to her ear, and murmured, "Did I mention I like your dress?"

His breath was hot and made her shiver. It was all she could do to shake her head.

"I do." He rubbed his hand slowly up and down her spine, generating more heat than the simple gesture could account for. "You're a beautiful woman, Holly."

She'd heard the words before, more times than was fair. So why did they sound more sincere, more significant, coming from him?

Wishing the temperature in the room were about twenty degrees cooler, she cleared the hoarseness from her throat. "If you like this dress, I have another one that you'll love. It's quite amazing."

"A dress is just fabric and thread. It's the woman wearing it who makes it amazing."

"Such flattery," she said with a nervous chuckle. "I never would have guessed you were capable of it."

He gave her a long, steady look. "I don't flatter. I just tell the truth."

And the truth was he'd never paid her so much attention, never made her feel so . . . special.

They danced silently through three more songs. When she caught him covering a yawn, she laughed. "I believe it's time to call it a night before your carriage turns back into a pumpkin." And the charming, attentive date turned back into the keep-his-distance man she knew better.

"A pumpkin?"

"You know, Cinderella and the pumpkin? Or wasn't your mom big on fairy tales?" she teased.

"No," he agreed as they left the bar. "She worked one job full-time and another part-time. There wasn't much time for fairy tales."

Not for living them, Holly thought somberly.

He might view Bethlehem through a critical big-city eye, but it was too bad his mother hadn't lived there. She could have found help, could have made her own life and her son's life easier. She might have lived long enough to actually enjoy life.

She thought he might say goodbye in the lobby. He didn't. Not at the elevator, either. And not once they reached her floor. He walked her to her door and waited while she unlocked it. When she turned back to him, he simply stood there, studying her intently. Then, as if he'd reached a decision, he cupped her face in his hands and bent forward, bringing his mouth within a whisper of hers . . . and then stopped. So close she could feel his breath against her lips, so close she could imagine the taste of him, and he *stopped*. "Good night, Holly," he murmured. "Sweet dreams."

Then he walked away.

THE WEARINESS THAT HAD STRUCK HIM on the dance floor was gone by the time Tom got home. Despite the fact that it was late and cold outside, he went onto the balcony, rested his forearms on the railing, and leaned comfortably to think.

He wouldn't credit Sophy with too many good ideas. After all, she thought walking on Flaherty late at night made perfect sense, and she hadn't given a second thought to stepping out into the street without checking for traffic first.

But his marrying Holly . . . That just might be the best idea Sophy Jones had ever had.

So, what now? He'd never considered what he would do when he found the right woman.

If Holly was the right woman. There were still minor problems to consider. She didn't want to get married. She wouldn't show him much tolerance. She wouldn't leave Bethlehem.

The last was easy. He could live in Bethlehem at least part of the time. It wasn't much more than an hour away by plane, less than two if he took one of the company helicopters. As for her insistence on staying single . . . The secret to successful salesmanship was to convince your target that she wanted or needed what you were offering. So he would convince Holly that she not only wanted to marry but wanted to marry him. And as for tolerance . . . If she couldn't tolerate certain behaviors of his, there were only two courses of action—increase her tolerance, or change the behaviors. Simple in theory, likely to be a little tougher in practice. Still, he'd always liked a challenge.

The question at the moment was what to do next. He suspected Holly would respond to a proposal of mutually beneficial marriage with anything from hysterical laughter to smashing something over his head. Though he preferred blunt honesty, this situation might require more finesse, maybe even a little trickery. Fortunately, he'd been known to excel at both when necessary.

So . . . He would pop the question, have the wedding. And then what? Hell, if he succeeded with this plan, he might turn his attention to the other goal on his list.

He might learn how to fall in love.

Chapter Six

IT WAS THE MIDDLE OF SUNDAY NIGHT, and the inn was as quiet as it ever got. Bree Aiken wore her usual nightclothes, a T-shirt and cotton shorts, with a pair of thick gym socks, as she wandered around the first floor.

The night clerk, a redhead named Peggy, had gone home at midnight. Holly had gotten back from her trip around seven that evening, looking as if she'd had a very good time.

What would it be like, Bree wondered wistfully, to be able to just jump on a plane and go wherever it went? Born and raised in Rochester, she'd never been anywhere except for an occasional trip within the state. A few times they'd visited her mother Allison's relatives in Albany, and she'd gone to Buffalo a time or two. Once, when she was seven, her father had taken them to New York City in December to see the holiday decorations and bought them both fabulous gifts there. It had been the best Christmas she'd ever had.

A few months later he'd died, and nothing in life had ever been the same. Everything good and bright in her mother had simply faded away. There'd been no more laughter, no more singing, no playing, no fun. Though he'd left them a sizable insurance policy, by the time Bree had started high school, the money had run out. They'd survived those four years by moving into a cheap apartment, selling the house, and living off the proceeds.

The older Bree got, the more her mother clung to her, wanting her close all the time. Allison had barely given her enough freedom to finish school, and she'd hated the job that had taken Bree away for nine hours every day. Living with her had gone from sheer happiness, fifteen years ago, to cloying suffocation.

She hadn't told Allison where she was going when she left Rochester—hadn't even told her that she *was* going. She'd sneaked out of the apartment early one morning with only what she could carry in her backpack. She'd left a note on the dining table that said, "I'm safe, don't worry about me, I'll call you," and she'd walked out without one look back. But not without worries and fears.

She walked through the dimly lit lobby, rubbing her hand over the back of the leather sofa, straightening the shade on a lamp, gazing at the hangings on the wall. There was an old sampler, signed by a McBride and dated 1854. Next to it was a painting of some McBrides, looking stern and prosperous and quite elegant for farmers. More portraits were scattered all over the inn, an impressive display of family and history.

She didn't have a single photograph of her father, and all she knew of her mother's family history was one-sided. After high school, Allison had left Albany for New York City, then had settled in Rochester. Her relationship with her family was shaky, so they'd never had much contact with them. Besides a few visits, Bree could recall a few cards, a few phone calls. Even when her father had died, the strain had overshadowed the sympathy.

She paused, as had become her habit, to study the photograph of Holly and her parents. They didn't look happy, and she wondered why. They'd lived in a great town, in this great house, and had plenty of money to spare. They'd been an old and respected family in Bethlehem for generations, and everyone in town had looked up to them.

Bree didn't know yet if she liked her boss. Honestly, Holly intimidated the hell out of her. It wasn't that she was tough to work for. On the contrary, she'd been more than patient with all of Bree's screw-ups. What got to her most about Holly was that she seemed so perfect. She had everything Bree had wanted at some time for herself—a solid background. A nice home. Money. Beauty. Confidence. A sense of belonging. A sure sense of who she was. There was nothing, it seemed, that Holly couldn't handle. She had no doubts, no fears, no insecurities.

Sometimes Bree felt that was *all* she had.

"What are you doing up?"

Bree spun around so quickly that she bumped the table beside her, making the vase it held wobble dangerously. She grabbed it with both hands and steadied it, then gave a sigh of relief before turning to Holly, standing in the hall that led to the kitchen. "I—I couldn't sleep."

"Me neither. Want some cocoa?"

Bree hesitated. The idea of sharing anything with Holly made her hands shake. But the idea of having Holly's attention all to herself, especially when there were no lectures to be delivered, overcame her nervousness. "Sure."

Sliding her hands into the pockets of her robe, Holly returned to the kitchen. Bree followed. "Can I help?"

"Just have a seat and keep your hands where I can see them." Holly poured more milk into the saucepan on the stove, took another cup from the cupboard, then set a plate of oatmeal-raisin cookies on the table. "How was your weekend?"

Bree had spent the last two days working and still marveling over the fact that she was living at McBride Inn. Granted, her room was an old storeroom, and her bathroom was the employee bathroom, with its cramped shower stall, but it was still the inn. It was a huge step up from the apartment she had shared with her mother. But, of course, her boss didn't want to know any of that. When she'd asked about the weekend, she'd meant work. "Fine." Then she blurted out, "I didn't damage a thing."

"I'm glad to hear that," Holly said dryly.

"How—how was your weekend?"

"Surprising."

"Is that good?"

"I think so. Also rather confusing." She carried the mugs to the table, then sat down. "Bree's a nice name. Is it short for something?"

"Sabrina." She smiled self-consciously. "My mother loved the movie—you know, the one with Audrey Hepburn. It—it reminded her of falling in love with my father. She used to watch it all the time until . . ." Her nervous smile faltered. "Until he died."

"I'm sorry," Holly said, sounding as if she meant it.

"Me, too. I miss him."

"Where is your mother?"

"In Rochester." Bree swallowed hard. "What about your parents?"

"My father's dead, too. My mother's in the city. May God keep her there for years to come."

"What's she like?"

Holly was silent for so long that Bree thought she'd decided the question was too personal and wasn't going to answer. But, after a time, she spoke. "She's . . . difficult to describe. We were never particularly close. She moved away the day after my father's funeral, and I wasn't sorry to see her go."

"What about your father? Were you close to him?"

"For the most part. He traveled a lot on business, so I didn't see as much of him as I would have liked. He told great stories, and he loved to fish. In the fall, he'd go hunting with his friends, and I always pleaded with him not to shoot any Bambis or Thumpers, and he never did—or, if he did, he gave them to his buddies rather than bring them home. In the winter, one evening every week, he'd take me to the ice rink over at City Park, just the two of us, and we'd skate and have cocoa and hot-dogs."

She picked up her mug and gazed at the cocoa as if remembering. Then, with a shake of her head, the wistful look disappeared. "I take it you're not close to your mother."

"Why do you say that?" Bree asked cautiously. She loved her mother, even if Allison did suffocate her, but she figured the less said about her, the better. She didn't want anyone getting the idea that her mother was worrying about her. She didn't want anyone calling her mother. That wouldn't be good at all.

"Considering your financial state when you arrived here . . ."

Instead of explaining that her mother had had no money to help her, she ducked her head, shrugged, and murmured, "I'd rather not talk about it."

"Relationships are tough, aren't they? And confusing."

Bree nodded. She was often ambivalent about the people in her life. She loved her mother dearly, but was glad to be away from her. She liked her co-workers at the inn, but would probably never get close to them. She wanted to like Holly, but was afraid of her, and more than a little envious.

"I'll see you in the morning. Good night."

Bree murmured a response, then reached for a cookie. In the morning, things would be better. She wouldn't have any accidents while working. She wouldn't get so nervous whenever Holly came around. She would get a better grip on her feelings, especially the envy.

In the morning she could do anything, everything. But tonight she needed sleep.

THE BALLROOM AT THE ELKS LODGE was one of the grandest places in all of Bethlehem. Located on the second floor of the hundred-year-old building, its ceiling was twenty-five feet high, and huge arched windows filled all four sides. The wood floor was polished to a high sheen, and the mural painted on the ceiling glowed above the light of a dozen chandeliers.

It seemed a vast space as Holly walked from the grand entrance to the opposite side, but come Saturday night, it would be filled with all the people it could accommodate. She hadn't yet decided whether she would be one of them.

As she reached the table where Emilie, Melissa, and another woman were working, Emilie not so subtly moved the spools of wired ribbon closer, where she could guard them. Holly gave her a sarcastic smile and said, "I saw that, Emilie. You don't have to worry. I'm not here to help you make your bows. Not even Martha Stewart could help these hands form a bow that looks like a bow."

"I know. I remember the last time you tried."

Holly perched on the edge of the table, then extended one hand to the third woman. "I doubt you remember me, but I'm—"

"Holly McBride, the innkeeper," the woman said, laying a tangle of ribbons aside to shake hands. "Of course I remember you. And I'm Noelle." After a moment, she added with a blush, "Noelle Rawlins. I keep forgetting . . ."

"How's your husband?" Gabe Rawlins, everyone agreed, was one lucky man. He'd been passing through Bethlehem on New Year's Eve, stopped for a break, and walked into the middle of an argument gone sour. Only the paramedics' quick response had saved his life, though no doubt the surgeons at Bethlehem Memorial who'd repaired the damage from the gunshot wound would appreciate some of the credit. It was a good thing for Gabe that all the dire predictions of Y2K computer crashes had never come to pass. If the 911 system had gone down, as doomsayers had expected, Noelle would have buried Gabe in the new millennium, not married him.

"He's fine," Noelle replied, her smile brilliant with gratitude. "The doctors released him to go back to work, and not a day too soon. He says working for Mr. McKinney is a lot less stressful than stripping paint, sanding woodwork, and hanging wallpaper for me."

"Sounds like a man," Emilie said. "Nathan will entertain the kids for hours, he'll take care of dinner, do the laundry, and even change Michael's dirty diapers, but I ask him to do something simple like plane the bottom of the closet door so it doesn't drag on the carpet, and suddenly there's someplace else he *has* to be."

"Alex, too," Melissa agreed. "He never misses the chance to tell me that he went to law school so he could pay people to do those little handyman chores for him."

As the conversation about husbands went on, Holly felt just the tiniest bit left out. It was the weirdest thing. All her friends were married, and they all talked about their husbands whenever said husbands were absent, and it had never bothered her before. She'd just listened and never wished for half a second that she had anything to contribute.

The last thing in the world she wanted was a husband. What use did she have for one? She was self supporting, she already had a handyman on the inn staff, and lovers were easy enough to find. What else could a husband possibly provide that she couldn't get without one? Love? A long-term commitment? Companionship, someone to belong to, someone to grow old with? She could get all those with the right man without having to slip a noose over her head and tighten the knot.

She just hadn't found the right man yet.

The husband talk was interrupted by Maggie and Shelley's arrival, because their husbands, as well as Emilie's, were with them. Miss Agatha and Miss Corinna arrived right on their heels. While Miss Corinna supervised the men in setting up the tables and chairs stored in the back corner closet, Miss Agatha and Holly began folding a huge stack of white linen napkins.

"If you don't want to miss the dance, Miss Agatha," Holly said, "I could probably get a couple of my younger employees to watch the kids."

The white-haired lady laughed. "Oh, I've been to a hundred of these dances, Holly, and frankly, they don't hold the same appeal they did when I was twenty. I'd just as soon spend the evening with the children."

"When you were twenty, you were probably the belle of the ball, with all the young men in the county lined up for a chance to dance with you."

"Not all of them. Just one in particular." Miss Agatha's smile was sweet and fifty-some years distant. "His name was Samuel. Samuel Thomas."

"Any relation to Alex Thomas?"

"He was a cousin to Alex's father and his uncle Herbert. He had black hair, brown eyes, and a smile that made you feel as if the sun had just come out in the middle of the night."

"You were in love with him," Holly said softly.

"Oh, yes. From the time I was seventeen. We were going to be married as soon as I graduated from high school, but the war was going on, and Sam joined the army. He was shipping out to

Europe that February I was twenty, and he was able to spend a few days here on the way. The Sweethearts Dance wasn't so fancy in those days, what with the war and rationing going on, but we did our best. He looked so handsome in his uniform, and I was so proud of him, and so much in love with him."

Miss Agatha's smile slowly faded, and the light in her eyes dimmed as her hands stilled their work. Then she blinked a time or two, straightened her shoulders, and with rapid, sure movements began folding napkins again. "It was the last time I saw him. He was killed later that year. At Omaha Beach."

Holly locked her gaze on the napkin in her hands. All her life she'd assumed that Miss Agatha had never married because she'd never had the opportunity. She hadn't guessed the old lady was still mourning the love she'd lost so many years ago.

"And you never met anyone who could take his place," she murmured.

"Oh, honey, you don't replace people like that. Sam's a part of me and always will be. But, no, I never loved anyone else. But you know . . ." Her gaze took on that distant look again, and her sweet smile returned. "It's never too late. As long as there's breath in my body, you never know what might happen."

Was she thinking about Bud Grayson? Did she know he was sweet on her, as Emilie had put it? Did she have feelings for him, too? Keeping her voice level and natural, Holly remarked, "You might have help with the kids Saturday night. Kelsey said her father-in-law is coming with her and J.D. and he mentioned that he might help out with the child care when he got tired of dancing." She sneaked a look at Miss Agatha and was rewarded with the beginnings of a blush.

"Oh . . . well . . . Isn't that sweet of him? He's a dear man, and J.D. and—and—"

"Kelsey."

"Yes, of course, Kelsey. They're lucky to have him."

"He's a handsome man. Seems any woman of a certain age would be happy to have him," Holly said slyly. "If I were older, I'd certainly grab him up before someone else did."

The blush in Miss Agatha's pale cheeks deepened, and she changed the subject rather pointedly. "And what about you, Holly? Which young man have you chosen to favor with your company Saturday night?"

It was on the tip of her tongue to blurt out that she didn't think she was coming, but she caught herself. "I haven't decided yet."

"Still waiting for an invitation from Mr. Right?"

Instantly Holly thought of Tom. A few days ago she would have said the odds of his ever asking her anywhere were somewhere between zero and none. But after last weekend . . . Maybe she should have mentioned the dance to him. Maybe he would have asked her to go, and she would have had the best Sweethearts Dance ever. But she hadn't thought to mention it, and there was no way she could do so now without being pathetically obvious.

"Now, Miss Agatha, you know me better than that. I'm not wasting my time waiting around for Mr. Right. I'll happily settle for Mr. Right Now."

Miss Agatha gave a shake of her head. "One of these days, Holly, you're going to fall in love with one man so hard and so fast that it'll take your breath away. You'll be amazed at what you've been missing."

"Not me," she disagreed brightly. "I'm never giving up my good times." But even to herself, her denial sounded less than convincing.

They worked in the ballroom for several more hours. By the time Holly left to return to the inn, the tables and chairs were set up all around the perimeter of the room, the tablecloths were spread, and dozens of huge bows ranging in color from palest pink to deep crimson were swagged over the windows. Melissa would bring the centerpieces from her nursery early Saturday morning, and the food would start arriving that afternoon. It would all be lovely and romantic, and Holly was just almost certain that she would rather miss it than go alone or with just one more of her Mr. Right Nows.

At the inn, she parked around back and was halfway between the kitchen and the lobby when the voices reached her. One belonged to Janice, who'd filled in while she and Emilie were at the lodge. The other . . . Aware of a sudden ache in her stomach, Holly walked a little faster, and breathed a little faster, too. Surely that strident, demanding voice couldn't possibly belong to . . .

Coming around the corner, she came to a sudden stop. Her first thought was too profane to speak aloud. So was her second. She waited until the woman opposite Janice paused in her tirade to take a breath, then quietly said, "Hello, Mother."

She felt it the instant Margery McBride's gaze reached her—felt the chill, the dislike, the resentment. "It's about time you got back. I've been waiting here for hours."

Typical Margery. No hello, how are you, it's been ten freaking years since I've seen you. Start with a complaint and a criticism and go downhill from there. "Impossible, Mother. I've only been gone three hours."

"You really must do something about the caliber of employees you hire. This—this person"—she stabbed the air with one deadly red-tipped finger in Janice's direction—"refused to give me a key to a room or to let me into your quarters. She's made me sit out here for *hours,* waiting for you to return. I want her fired."

"Not in this lifetime. What are you doing here?"

"Why, I got your message."

"What message?" Her only message to Margery in ten years had been short and direct: *I'm shipping your belongings to you.*

"I came to sort through my things, to decide what I want and what you can keep."

Holly took a breath for patience. "Your things aren't here. I shipped them to you. Remember? *That* was the message."

"Oh." With the wave of one hand, Margery dismissed her mistake. "Well, I needed a break from the city anyway. I'll stay a few days—"

"Only a few days. All of our rooms are booked for the weekend. You'll have to leave Friday around noon." It was only a small lie. One suite—Tom's—wasn't yet taken.

"Unbook one of them."

"I can't do that."

"Of course you can. You call the person, tell him a pipe burst or there was a fire or a damn meteor crashed through the roof and landed in the bed." On the last words Margery's voice turned brittle and hard. It was the voice Holly remembered most from her childhood, the voice that had screamed at her, cursed at her, and made her cry a thousand times. It was that voice, more than anything, that meant *mother* to her. "You can tell him whatever it damn well takes to get your mother a room to sleep in."

Holly moved behind the counter and picked up the key to the suite. When Margery imperiously extended her hand, Holly laid the key on the counter. "Until noon Friday. Then you'll have to leave."

Margery smiled sweetly, perfectly capable of being nice now that she'd gotten her way. "Thank you, sweetie. See that someone parks my car and brings up my luggage. Oh, and I'll need a little late-afternoon cocktail delivered immediately. You know what I like."

Holly and Janice watched her sweep up the stairs, looking for all the world like some Hollywood star of the forties making a perfectly scripted grand exit. Once she was out of sight, Janice let out the breath she'd been holding. "I'm sorry, Holly. She said she was your mother, but . . . I couldn't let a stranger into your apartment on nothing but her say-so. I offered to rent her a room, but she refused to pay. She said— Well, never mind what she said."

Holly could well imagine. For a lady of breeding, as Margery liked to refer to herself, she could match curses and insults with the best. "I apologize for her, Janice. She's . . ." Self-centered. Demanding. Difficult. Amazingly vulgar. ". . . Not easy."

"Want me to get her bags?"

As Bree came out of the dining room with an armload of soiled linens, Holly shook her head. "Bree? Can you meet me outside after you drop those off?" Maybe she would break everything in them.

The rental car was parked under the porte cochere, blocking the drive, which, of course, was inconsequential to Margery. The trunk was filled with luggage—three large suitcases and two smaller ones. Which ones held the breakables? she wondered as Bree came out the door.

"I need you to take this luggage upstairs," she said as she began unloading bags.

"Wow. How long is this guest staying?"

"A couple of days. And she's not a guest. She's my mother."

The bag she'd just handed Bree slipped to the ground, landing on its fabric side in the muddy drive. Hastily, the girl bent to pick it up. "I—I—"

"It's okay. Just get the bags upstairs and leave them in the hall. I'll take them in."

"I don't mind."

Holly looked at her, so young and innocent, and smiled. "Honey, if she saw you drop one of her bags, she'd eat you alive. You'll have plenty of opportunities in the next two days to face the dragon. For now, just get these upstairs for me."

She closed the trunk, then slid behind the wheel. The interior of the car smelled of Margery's perfume and, more faintly, of liquor. She supposed it was too much to hope that her mother had gained control of her drinking in the ten years since they'd last seen each other. She *knew* it was too much to hope that Margery would remain on her best genial-drunk behavior while she was there.

What was that popular prayer? "God, grant me the serenity ?" After parking the car, then starting back to the inn in the cold, Holly offered her own version:

God, grant me the strength to not kill her tonight. . . .

Chapter Seven

When Tom left the office Wednesday evening, a cold rain was falling. The car wipers swept back and forth as he waited at a red light—and was immediately distracted by the figure on the curb waiting to cross the street. There must be thousands of blondes in Buffalo, but he had little doubt who this particular blonde, with hair curling underneath a black knitted cap, was.

He tapped the horn to get her attention, then rolled down the window. "You want a ride?"

Sophy gave him a bright smile. "Yes, thank you." When she climbed into the car, she brought with her the cold fresh scent of rain, and immediately shivered. "This is kind of you, Mr. Flynn."

"No, it's not," he disagreed. There was nothing

kind about giving her a ride. It was just . . . decent. "Where are you going?"

"To the grocery store up ahead."

"You walk all the way over here from Flaherty to buy groceries?"

"It's the closest store. The one your mother used to shop at closed years ago."

Even that store had been a good walk from Flaherty, though not this far. He and his mother had made the trip every Saturday, sometimes carrying home enough food to last a week, sometimes not.

When he pulled in front of the supermarket to let her out, she gave him a chiding look. "Be sociable. Come in with me." Before he could turn her down, she coaxed, "Oh, come on. I'll bet you can't even remember the last time you set foot in a grocery store."

She was right. He couldn't. So he found a parking space and went inside with her.

Ten feet inside the door was a garish display of red cardboard hearts filled with candy, heart-shaped balloons, and scraggly red silk roses in cheap vases. Sophy looked from it to him and smiled. "What are you doing for Valentine's Day? Spending it with the future Mrs. Flynn?"

"What makes you think there's going to be a future Mrs. Flynn?" But he couldn't deny that her question immediately brought to mind an image of sleek auburn hair, hazel eyes, and a wickedly sexy smile.

"You didn't deny it when I asked you Saturday

night," she said as she pulled a shopping cart from the line.

"I didn't confirm it, either."

She waved one hand, as if that were of no consequence. "Seriously, what are you doing for her for Valentine's Day?"

In truth, he didn't know. Holly was intelligent, reasonable, and, he was certain, above that hearts-and-flowers crap. But then sappy holidays had a way of turning even intelligent and reasonable women a bit goofy.

"The least she deserves is a nice dinner. If you can drag yourself out of the office at a reasonable time, you could pick her up after work and take her to—"

"She doesn't live here."

"Oh. Where does she live?"

"In Bethlehem. The one in the mountains, not the one south of Albany."

"I know where Bethlehem is. Lovely little town." Her eyes brightened. "I bet they have a really special Valentine's Day celebration. Why don't you call her and ask?"

The idea held more appeal than he wanted to admit. Since Sunday, he'd found himself wondering what excuse he could use to call Holly. After all, he couldn't put his marriage plans in motion without seeing her, talking to her, spending time with her. Besides, she wasn't a sure bet. If he couldn't convince her that she wanted him, then he would have to start all over again. That would throw him way behind schedule.

"What's the matter? Are you afraid?"

He scowled at her as they rounded the corner from produce to canned goods. "You know, Sophy, you are probably the nosiest and the pushiest woman I've ever met."

"Thank you," she said with a smile. "I'm glad you noticed. Are you going to call her?"

"None of your business."

"Aha! That means you are. Be sweet to her. Don't sound all grumpy like this. No woman wants to spend an entire evening at a Valentine's Day dance with a grumpy man."

She let the subject drop while she finished her shopping. He couldn't let it go as easily. He kept remembering the Saturday-night dance with Holly in that incredible little green dress, kept thinking that a chance to dance with her again, to hold her like that again, just might be worth celebrating even a schmaltzy holiday like Valentine's Day.

Sophy paid for her four bags of groceries with a handful of wadded bills, and he picked up two of them. "How would you have walked all the way back to Flaherty with all this?"

She smiled confidently as he unlocked the car doors in the rain. "I would have managed. Things always work out, you know."

"No, they don't. Things *never* just work out. You have to *make* them work. You live on Flaherty Street, and you haven't figured that out yet?"

"If you have faith—"

"In what?"

She smiled cheerfully. "God. Your friends. Your neighbors. The kindness of strangers."

He shook his head. "You can only count on yourself. Everyone else will let you down."

"Your mother would be sorry to hear you say that."

Rain dripped from his hair and ran down his neck, sending a chill through him. "What do you know about my mother?"

"Father Pat talks about her from time to time. He says she was a good woman, a good mother, and a good Catholic. He says she very well might have been the only person you ever loved."

He didn't speak again until he reached the intersection where he'd first made her acquaintance. "Where to?"

"Straight ahead three blocks."

He didn't have to ask which building. There was only one that was even close to habitable. The one across from it had been condemned when he was a kid, and the one across the side street hadn't been fit for living in while he'd still lived in it.

She offered to carry the bags herself, but for reasons he didn't understand, he insisted on taking two, on walking her inside and up two flights of dark stairs.

It was all depressingly familiar. The wood floors, worn bare of varnish. The graffiti-covered walls. The broken bulbs in every light fixture along the hall. The smells of food, of poverty, of hopelessness, and despair.

His breathing was shallow, forced into a quick,

steady rhythm to keep in check the discomfort building inside him. When she stopped in front of a door, he was more than happy to hand over the bags, say good night, and head back to the stairs.

Halfway there, he turned back. "This isn't a safe place to live."

She pulled off her cap, combed her fingers through her hair. "It's not bad."

"Pick an apartment in a better part of town. I'll pay for it."

"I'd rather stay here." Then she smiled. "But I appreciate the generous offer."

Again with the *generous* bit. He scowled at her. "If you change your mind, let me know. I'm sure I'll be seeing you around."

"I'm sure you will."

Her good humor made him scowl harder. He took the steps three at a time, burst out the door into the cold night, and breathed deeply to cleanse the smells from his nose.

When he got home, he went to his office to work, but his attention kept wandering to that gaudy Valentine's Day display and the idea Sophy had planted of doing something with Holly. No doubt, Bethlehem did have some sort of Valentine's Day celebration. They celebrated everything, and sometimes nothing. But if they did, it was a sure bet that Holly had been asked weeks ago. She'd never suffered from a shortage of male attention, and she wasn't the sort to break off a date with one man because someone better had come along.

Someone better? His snort echoed in the room. Who the hell did he think he was better than?

He turned back to the computer, which was waiting patiently for a command, but he didn't give it. Instead, he looked up the number for the McBride Inn and sat there tapping his finger. What if she didn't have a date? What if, by some strange luck, she was available and willing to go out with him? A nice Valentine's celebration could go a long way toward achieving his goal of finding a wife.

And if she was already spoken for? Hell, he'd been rejected before. It wouldn't kill him. Reaching for the phone, he dialed the number.

"McBride Inn." The voice was familiar, husky, sexy as hell—a voice to dream about, whether asleep or awake.

He settled back in his chair as the tension seeped from the taut muscles in his neck. "Holly, it's Tom. Tell me something. What does Bethlehem do about Valentine's Day?"

THERE'D BEEN A TIME WHEN THE sweethearts Dance was a formal event, with the women in gowns and the men in tuxes. As Holly got dressed Saturday evening, she half wished that was still the case. She hadn't worn a gown since the senior prom and thought it might be fun to do so again, but the real reason for the wish was Tom. She'd seen him in suits—standard attire for the men at the dance—dozens of times, and she thought he would do incredible justice to a tux.

After his unexpected call Wednesday evening, she'd taken off Thursday to go shopping for the perfect dress, and she'd found it. The dress was a green so dark it was almost black, and was perfectly modest. It covered her from shoulders to knees, and the neckline bordered on chaste. It fit as if it had been sewn together on her body, but thanks to the miracle of modern fibers, she could still breathe. Paired with matching three-inch heels, a simple diamond teardrop on a platinum chain, and diamonds in her ears, she looked . . . elegant. Sexy. Perfectly nice, but more than a little naughty.

From down the hall, she heard heels clicking in her direction. As she looked in the mirror, she saw the tension spreading, starting in her jaw and working its way into wrinkles across her forehead and a pulse that throbbed at the base of her throat.

She'd known that Margery wouldn't leave until she was ready. She had come to make Holly's life miserable for a certain number of days, and by God she wasn't going home until she'd succeeded. Twenty-four hours more just might be more than Holly could bear, now that Tom had checked into the suite and Margery had been moved into Holly's quarters. She'd claimed them as if they were her own, offering criticism and insults every step of the way.

Margery stopped in the doorway of the closet/dressing room and leaned against the frame. "Oh, little girl, you look lovely," she murmured in her liquor-roughened voice.

Six small words, with the power to sweep Holly more than twenty years into the past. It had been a Saturday night then, too, and she'd been standing in front of this same mirror in her old room upstairs, primping for her very first honest-to-God date. She'd been nervous and excited, and her mother had stood in the doorway and said those same words.

The date, Holly remembered, had been a success. She'd learned an important lesson—that teenage boys would gladly give her, for a time at least, the affection she was missing at home, and all they wanted in return was sex. A fair enough trade, she'd thought at the time.

These days she wasn't looking for affection. She liked sex for its own sake.

Shaking off old memories, Holly gave Margery a long look. "You don't look so bad yourself."

Her hair, once perfectly blond, was now perfectly champagne. Her skin was smooth and firm, cosmetic surgery having won the battle against unwanted lines. She'd always looked best in classic styles and subdued colors, and that was even truer now. She was a lovely woman.

A lovely, sharp-tongued, bitter, alcoholic woman.

"So you're off to the Sweethearts Dance. When are you going to find yourself a sweetheart?"

"If I ever start looking for one, I'll let you know." Holly selected a handbag from the shelf, a small silver-mesh bag, and switched the essentials from her purse.

"You're not getting any younger, you know. Another few years, and no man wanting a family is going to want you."

"Good. Because I have no intention of having a family." She'd decided against having kids long ago, when she'd watched Margery tear through the house on her ten thousandth drunken rage, lamenting the terrible betrayal she'd suffered and the wonderful life she'd lost, thanks to Holly and her father. She'd taunted Holly that someday she would get what she deserved. *She* would get stuck with a whiny, snot-nosed kid who would ruin her life, and then she would pay for the torment she'd put her own mother through.

"And do you have no intention of getting married?"

"Why should I? So I can be miserable the rest of my life like you were?"

"I loved your father."

"Could have fooled me." Margery *had* fooled everyone in town. Holly didn't think a soul in Bethlehem had a clue of how miserable Margery had made both her and her father. If people did know, they'd had the courtesy to keep it to themselves.

"I loved him," Margery repeated with a distant smile. "He was the handsomest, most charming man in the city. People vied for his attention. Women vied for his affection. But he chose me.

We made a beautiful couple, and we were happy. Until . . ."

Holly had heard the story a dozen times before. Until her grandfather had his first heart attack and Lewis had been called home to Bethlehem. His bride had thought they would live the rest of their lives in the city, partying, going to the theater, playing at working. She'd never dreamed she would wind up in a little burg like Bethlehem, with a husband who actually held a job, without much of a social life, with none of the glitter and glamour she thrived on. She'd certainly never dreamed she would be stuck raising a kid.

"I never would have married him if I'd known. . . ."

Then maybe Lewis could have been happy, Holly thought. And maybe she, if she had ever come to be, would have some idea what a normal daughter was supposed to feel for her mother. Because all she felt was anger. Resentment. Bitterness.

Holly picked up her bag, checked her reflection one last time, then eased past Margery.

"Have a good time," Margery called after her.

"As soon as you get out of my life," Holly whispered beneath her breath.

She got her coat and made her way to the lobby. She'd arranged with Tom to meet there instead of her quarters, wanting no chance of Margery asking for an introduction. By the time she came through the kitchen, she'd pasted a smile on her face. The fake smile gave way to a real one, though, the instant she saw him.

The first time she'd ever met him, she'd been unimpressed . . . for about two minutes. She'd thought he was rude, arrogant, and hardly worth her time except for the minor pleasure she'd found in annoying him. She'd been convinced that he wasn't her type, and vice versa, but she'd left their brief meeting with the awareness that she was willing to disregard types for him.

Now she thought he was amazingly handsome. His dark hair always looked as if he'd combed it with his fingers, his features were rugged, and his eyes were hard. Everything about him was hard—evidence of his difficult upbringing. Not that she was complaining. She found him far more interesting to look at than conventionally handsome men.

Far more interesting to fantasize about.

"Didn't your mother ever teach you that a lady always keeps her date waiting?" he asked dryly.

She shot a look at him. Had he heard something about Margery from one of the staff? Or was he asking an innocent question? Hoping for the latter, she shrugged. "You're making two major assumptions—that my mother taught me anything at all, and that I'm a lady."

His dark gaze raked her head to toe, then he slowly smiled. She waited for a smug comment, but none came. Instead, he gestured toward the door. "Shall we go?"

They drove in his car to the lodge. The massive stone building was ablaze with light and music echoed around them, along with the sounds of children at play, as they entered the lobby.

Their first stop was the coat check. The woman behind the counter said, "Well, if it isn't Holly McBride, looking lovelier than any woman should. You'll be the envy of all the men at the ball, Mr. Flynt."

It took Holly a moment to place the motherly woman—the pond, a Monday walk, and a nosy intruder with a bad memory for names. "Gloria."

The woman smiled broadly as if pleased to be remembered. "Make a wish for a fine time tonight, because it's sure to come true. The music is lively, the ladies are lovely, and the gentlemen are handsome. 'Love is in the air,' " she sang off-key as she handed a ticket to Tom. "Enjoy yourselves."

"Friend of yours?" he asked as they started toward the stairs.

"Not exactly. We met a few weeks ago when she was trespassing in my woods."

"And, of course, it never occurred to you to report her to the sheriff."

"Of course not. She wasn't doing any harm. She'd just gone for a walk and wound up at my pond." She gave him a sidelong glance. "Here in Bethlehem, we try not to sic the authorities on someone unless they've actually done something wrong. It's a little quirk of ours."

He returned her gaze, then took hold of her

arm. "Well, Gloria was right about one thing. You do look lovely."

Holly wasn't sure whether the sudden warmth flooding through her came from his compliment or his touch. Maybe, logic suggested, it was just because they'd reached the crowded second floor. Whatever the reason, she felt as if she were starting a slow burn from the inside out. She thought that once they started to dance—once he took her in his arms and held her so close she could smell his cologne, feel his breath against her hair, and feel his heart beat beneath her cheek—she would be lucky if she didn't burst into flames.

They found their seats at a large table in the corner. Her closest friends—the Friday lunch bunch and their husbands—were all at the same table, or would be if they ever stopped dancing at the same time. She greeted the ones who were there, refreshed Tom's memory of their names, then gestured to the floor. "Want to dance?"

She wanted to be held close, to risk going up in flames.

Innocently he agreed, following her onto the floor, taking her into his arms.

The band was from Howland, and their repertoire for the evening was heavy on romance. Lots of slow songs, lots of close dances. The ballroom's lights were bright around the perimeter, dimmer above the dance floor. It was as romantic a setting as Holly could have wished for.

"Why were you available for this dance at such a late date?" Tom asked well into the second song.

"Maybe you were the first to ask me."

"I don't think so."

She tilted back her head far enough to see him. "You're right. I'd been asked, but not by anyone I wanted to go with. I actually intended to stay home tonight and watch a movie."

"And miss out on all the admiring looks you're getting in that dress?"

She didn't glance around to see if anyone else was looking. The only admiring looks she cared about were his, and he was giving them often. His dark gaze was smoldering, and it made her feel . . . Excited. Filled with anticipation for what was to come.

"If you had plans to stay home tonight, why did you accept my invitation?"

"You know the answer to that."

"Tell me anyway." He pulled her nearer, his hands big and firm where they held her, his body sheltering hers. She'd never been one to look to a man for protection, but she suddenly understood why some women did. There was something undeniably comforting about being in the arms of a man big enough, tough enough, strong enough to protect her—a sense of security, of safety. A promise that nothing could hurt her.

A promise she wasn't foolish enough to believe, of course, but still . . . It was tempting. Enticing.

She drew a breath that smelled only of him, then murmured, "Because I wanted to be with you."

His smile was lazy and smug, but his response

was neither. "Good," he said quietly, as if her answer satisfied some need in him she knew nothing about. "Very good."

THE DANCE HAD STARTED AT SEVEN o'clock. By eight, the last of the guests had arrived, and the final tally in the temporary child-care center was higher than Agatha Winchester cared to count, though, of course, she did. She could have handled twice the number of children alone—a lifetime of teaching had taught her that—but that evening she had help.

Mandy Lewis, whose grandfather pastored one of Bethlehem's churches, and a half-dozen of her teenage friends had volunteered their services. They were all a year or two younger than the minimum age of eighteen required for attendance at the dance, but this way they didn't feel totally left out. In a few years, they would come to dance the night away with their young beaus, and girls like Alanna Dalton, Emilie's older niece, would do the volunteering and dreaming about their own first Sweethearts Dance.

And Agatha would be there, too. Down below with the children. Not upstairs with a sweetheart.

"That sigh sounded positively forlorn."

Agatha looked up from the baby she was rocking to find Gloria in the doorway. She knew little about the woman, but her instincts told her she could trust Gloria with her life, and Agatha Winchester's instincts were never wrong. "Oh, no,

I'm not forlorn," she said hastily. "I was just thinking about the dances and how quickly time flies."

Gloria came to sit on a folding chair nearby. "Why are you stuck down here with the kids instead of upstairs having a good time?"

"I'm not stuck. I love being with the children. I was never blessed with any of my own, but I've been fortunate enough to care for others' babies. They keep me young."

"I'm sure they do, but wouldn't you rather be upstairs, where all the action is? Where a certain gray-haired gentleman is?" Gloria's smile was teasing. "I have it on good authority that Mr. Grayson is hoping for a dance or two with a certain lady, if she ever sets foot in the ballroom."

Color bloomed in Agatha's cheeks. She had thought she'd kept her interest in Bud Grayson a secret, but Holly had guessed, and now so had Gloria. How had a virtual stranger seen what everyone else remained blind to? It was somewhat disconcerting.

"I've danced my share of dances," she said as if it were the honest truth. "Leave it to the young folks. They're the ones who enjoy it most."

"I beg to differ, Miss Agatha. Every heart can find joy in a dance, particularly in the arms of a special someone. Love knows no age limits, and neither does romance." Gloria leaned closer and whispered conspiratorially, "Go on. Have one dance."

"But I have responsibilities—"

"And they're all well in hand. You've got seven

competent helpers, and I'll be right next door at the cloakroom. I can keep an eye on things until you get back."

"Well . . ." Agatha thought of a dozen reasons why she should refuse, and only one why she should accept—because she wanted that one dance. After more than fifty years of living with her memories, she wanted to find joy in a special someone's arms. Foolish or not, too old for it or not, she wanted those few moments with Bud.

"If you're sure you don't mind . . ."

"I'm sure. Go upstairs and show those youngsters how it's done."

Agatha rose from the rocker and handed the baby into Gloria's waiting arms. When she hesitated outside the door, Gloria made a shooing motion with her free hand, sending her on her way. Halfway up the stairs, she stopped, touching a hand to her hair, wondering if any of her lipstick remained or if she'd kissed it all off greeting the children earlier. Maybe she should go to the ladies' room and make repairs, or forget it entirely. She hadn't come prepared to dance or even to celebrate at all. She'd dressed for her duties with the children, who loved her no matter how she looked.

But something—Gloria whispering, "Go on, have one dance"—pushed her to the top of the stairs, where she paused in the broad doorway to the ballroom. It was made for grand entrances, and she'd made plenty of them in her younger days, but at that moment, no one was expecting an entrance of any kind. The band was playing a Cole Porter tune, and half the guests were on the dance floor. She saw Maggie and Ross McKinney glide past, so lost in each other that the rest of the world had ceased to exist. Harry Winslow, looking dapper in his Sunday best, waltzed past with a glowing Maeve Carter in his arms. Holly and her beau, a fine-looking couple, were leaving the dance floor, and Alex and Melissa Thomas were taking it.

But there was no sign of Bud. Perhaps he'd decided against coming, after all. Perhaps Gloria had mistaken someone else for him. Or perhaps he was dancing with someone else, or in a private corner romancing someone—

"Ah, the belle of the ball has finally arrived." Bud moved around the tall palms that had blocked him from her view and stood two steps below her, gazing at her as if . . . well, as if he liked what he saw.

Agatha felt her cheeks grow warm again and hoped, with the profusion of pinks and reds everywhere, he wouldn't notice. Perhaps he didn't. More likely, he was too much the gentleman to comment. "I imagine every man here would argue with your bestowing such a title on me."

"They're entitled to their opinions, but mine is fact." He moved one step higher and took her hand. "May I have this dance?"

"It would be my pleasure."

"Oh, no, Agatha," he said quietly as he slid his arm around her waist. "The pleasure is all mine."

If her dance skills were somewhat rusty after years of disuse, he pretended not to notice. He was an excellent dancer himself, and he more than made up for her occasional stumble. By the end of the second dance, she had rediscovered the grace she'd once had, and had proved Gloria right. There *was* joy to be found in a dance with the right person.

"One more?" Bud asked as the band started up again.

"I'd love to," she said, automatically following his lead, "but I really should get back to the nursery. I don't want to impose on Gloria for too long. She volunteered to check coats, not wipe runny noses and change diapers."

"Could you use some help? I've become quite adept in the last six months at taking care of kids."

"And it's made life worth living, hasn't it?" she asked softly. "You know, there was a time a few years ago when Corinna and I filled our days baking, crocheting, and volunteering at the hospital—typical old-lady activities. Then Emilie moved in next door, practically penniless, with three children and in dire need of child care while she worked. We began taking care of little Brendan during the day, and the two girls after school, intending it to be a short-term arrangement, to help only until Emilie was back on her feet financially."

"But here you are, over two years later, still keeping the Dalton kids, as well as the baby, and helping J.D. last summer with his four." Bud gave an admiring shake of his head. "Anyone ever tell you that baby-sitting young children is too much work for people our age?"

"Yes, but they're wrong. The children keep us young. They're one of the most important—"

"And most satisfying."

"—parts of our lives." Agatha smiled, pleased that he shared her opinion, then returned to his earlier question. "I don't actually need help—I have plenty of that—but I would certainly enjoy your company, unless you'd rather stay here."

"No," he said firmly. "I wouldn't."

They stopped dancing before the song ended and started toward the steps. They hadn't gone more than a few feet, though, before Agatha became aware of tension seeping through the room. She craned her neck to see the reason and located it at the entrance. "Oh, dear," she murmured.

Margery McBride was making the grandest of entrances, moving regally if unsteadily into the room, dragging her fur behind her like a train. Her head was held high, her bearing imperious, but her dress looked as if it had suffered a roll or two in the gutter, and her makeup looked worse. She smiled at familiar faces, nodded to strangers, but spoke to no one.

When Agatha stepped in front of her, Margery had no choice but to stop her staggering journey. She lifted the bottle she carried like a scepter, tilted back her head, and took a long drink.

"Margery," Agatha said, trying to hide the

disapproval that tightened her smile. "How nice to see you. I didn't know you were in town."

"My daughter didn't want you to know. She's kept me hidden at that god-awful farm since I got here. Ungrateful little wretch." She raised the bottle again, realized it was empty, then flung it away. The crash when it hit the floor was deafening and drew the attention of everyone who hadn't yet noticed her arrival.

Agatha looked anxiously toward the corner where Holly sat and saw her head slowly turn toward them. The color drained from her face, and, even from a distance, Agatha recognized the shame that crept into her shocked expression.

"Margery, it's been such a long time since we've had a chance to talk," she said, moving forward to take the woman's arm. "Let's find a quiet table and catch up on everything that's happened."

Margery jerked free of Agatha's grip with such force that Agatha stumbled backward into Bud's arms. Without sparing her even a glance, Margery staggered away. "Didn't come to talk to you, old woman. I came to see my ungrateful wretch of a daughter. I came to cel'brate with her. Where is she?"

Agatha watched as Margery wove her way to the bandstand, where she stopped and swayed drunkenly out of time with the music before suddenly spying Holly, now standing woodenly at her corner table. She marched toward her daughter, pausing only long enough to grab two glasses of champagne from a waiter. She drained one, then raised the other in salute.

"There you are, little girl, looking so pretty. And which one of them"—she indicated the men at the table with a wave—"did you do all this for? Which one's going to get lucky tonight? Course, knowing you, prob'ly every man in here's been lucky at least once. Never could keep your clothes on, could you? From the time you were fifteen . . . I warned you. I told you what boys thought of girls like you, and you did it anyway, just to spite me. You were always so good at that. So good . . ."

Nathan Bishop left his wife's side, and Mitch Walker came off the dance floor. Both men reached Margery at the same time, each claiming one arm. When Nathan removed the still-full champagne glass from her hand, she cursed, turned to Mitch to complain, then smiled flirtatiously instead. "I don't believe we've met. I'm Margery."

"I'm Mitch. And I'm taking you outside for some fresh air."

Everyone stepped back, clearing a path to the door. Somehow, in the crush, Holly escaped first. Agatha caught only a flash of auburn hair and dark green dress disappearing down the stairs. When she looked back at the table, she saw that Tom Flynn was gone, too, no doubt to catch Holly. On occasion, Mr. Flynn proved himself to be a better man than he wanted most people to think—though why any man would want people to think badly of him was a mystery to her.

"Are you all right, Agatha?" Bud asked.

She gave him an unsteady smile and patted his hand where it rested on her arm. "I'm fine, thanks to you. Poor Holly. She didn't deserve this."

"No, she didn't. And poor Margery . . ."

His expression was so pensive, so lost, that Agatha wanted to wrap her arms around him and assure him everything was all right. Margery's display must have brought back painful memories of J.D.'s own battle with alcohol. It had cost him dearly—his psychiatric career in Chicago, his wife, his son. It was no less than a miracle that he had not only survived but recovered. He'd made a new career for himself here in Bethlehem, dealt with his guilt and grief over his first wife's death, fallen in love all over again with Kelsey, and gotten his son back, as well as four more children to love and treasure and a stronger, deeper relationship with his father. No less than a miracle.

"Well . . . shall we go downstairs and see what those grandkids of mine have been up to?" Bud asked, forcing a lighter tone into his voice.

"Yes," Agatha agreed. The children would cheer her up, would make her forget these past few minutes. The children were nothing less than miracles themselves. God love them, because she certainly did.

Chapter  Eight

BY THE TIME TOM REACHED THE lobby, there was no sign of Holly, but her trespassing friend Gloria was standing near the bottom of the stairs, holding both their coats. "I called to her, but she didn't stop," she said worriedly. "She was heading toward the town square."

The night air was cold enough to make his breath catch. Carrying Holly's coat, he pulled on his own as he took the steps to the sidewalk two at a time, then turned toward downtown. His car was parked on the far side of the square, and the inn was in that direction, too. Maybe she'd just gone for a walk, or would be waiting for him at the car. Maybe she'd decided to walk home.

So that was Holly's mother. Even though the only time he'd seen her was in the photograph at the inn, he would have recognized her. She'd changed very little since the picture, thanks, no doubt, to the best cosmetic surgery money could buy. She was still beautiful, and she still bore some resemblance to her daughter. Mostly what she reminded him of were the drunks who'd been abundant on Flaherty Street when he lived there. The only difference was that he'd pitied those drunks. He didn't feel anything but anger for Margery McBride.

As he turned at the next corner, a breeze from the west made him shiver. It was a hell of a night for a walk.

Halfway up the block, the square came into sight. It was located in the exact center of downtown, with benches and a bandstand. He'd attended two Christmas Eve services there with the McKinneys and Holly, had sat through a concert with a local bluegrass band last summer with them and their friends. At the time he'd felt out of place, an intruder who didn't belong. Looking back, though, he realized that he'd had a good time.

Gloria had guessed right. Holly had gone to the square. She was standing in the shadows in the bandstand, her arms folded across her chest, her head bowed. Tom entered the park and quietly climbed the closest set of steps. Walking up behind Holly, he wrapped her coat around her shoulders, then left his hands there for a moment. There was something he should say, but he wasn't quite sure what it was. Offering comfort and sympathy wasn't among his usual skills.

She curled her fingers around the edges of her coat and pulled it tighter, then gave a heavy sigh, followed by a sound that was mostly choked laughter. "Remember on your birthday, when we were talking, you asked what had happened when I turned twelve?"

Though she didn't look at him to see, he nodded.

"My mother was in one of her rare gotta-prove-I'm-a-good-mother phases. She insisted that I have a party—the biggest, best, most fabulous birthday party anyone in Bethlehem had ever seen. I begged her not to do it, but she insisted. Dad was out of town—he traveled a lot on business—so he couldn't help me. She invited my entire class, including the kids whose favorite pastime was making me miserable." She did look at him then, offering a wan smile. "It might surprise you, but I wasn't always this popular or self-confident. When I was twelve, I was a homely, clumsy, insecure mess."

He couldn't imagine that. She gave the impression of having been born beautiful, gregarious, well liked, and self-assured. But people changed. Look at him. There wasn't so much as a hint of the Flaherty Street punk he'd once been left in him now.

"Planning the party consumed Margery's life. She was so excited that she even forgot to keep a drink in hand at all times. I actually dared believe that everything might turn out all right, after all. Then the party came. She was so drunk she could barely stand up. She was loud, vulgar, and her temper was explosive. I won't bore you with all the details," she remarked, rubbing one hand lightly over her cheek. "Suffice it to say that it came as an incredible relief when she passed out face-first in my birthday cake. And that I wished she would suffocate in the frosting."

He still didn't know what to say, but he took a stab at it anyway. "So that's when you learned that wishes don't come true."

She gave him a long, steady look before turning to lean beside him. "Some wishes, maybe. Others . . ."

"What is she doing here?"

"I swear, she came for the sole purpose of ruining tonight. She's got some sort of instinct about special times, and she never misses doing whatever she can to turn them into disasters."

"The evening's not ruined."

This time her look was chastising. "If you think I'm walking back into that ballroom after the display she put on . . ."

"No, I wasn't going to suggest that. I just meant that we could go back to the inn, have a dance or two, a glass of wine, and . . . talk." That last part made him wince inwardly. He suspected that the last thing most women wanted to do as part of their Valentine's Day dates was talk. It was a sure bet none of her friends at the dance would be wasting time on words when they got home.

She stood motionless for a moment, then suddenly shivered, as if she'd just realized how cold she was. She slipped her arms into her coat sleeves and tightly belted it, then walked to the top of the steps. "That sounds nice."

They got into his car and drove the short distance to the inn. At her request, they went in the front door, where the night clerk and another of the inn's employees, a young girl who he thought was about Sophy's age, were chatting over a game of solitaire. The clerk glanced at them, then at the grandfather clock, and said, "Gosh, you're home early. We weren't expecting you until the clean-up crew danced you out the door. What hap—" Her gaze shifted toward the back of the inn, and her features took on a worried look. "Mrs. McBride has been so quiet back there that we figured she'd gone to bed early. She didn't . . . ?"

Holly's smile was still wan. "Yes, she did. Do you know if anyone is in the library?"

"No, it's all yours. Could I bring you a glass of wine or maybe some dessert?"

Holly looked from her to the young woman, who stood in silence. "Why don't you let Bree do it? Do you mind?"

Abruptly twisting around, Bree knocked half the cards to the floor. "S-sure," she said, her face red. "I—I'd be happy to, if—if you're sure *you* don't mind."

She was still standing there, blushing and bewildered, when Holly led Tom through the lobby, past the family portrait, and into the library. The built-in bookcases that filled most of the space were cherry, and the thin strips of wall surrounding them were painted deep red. There were two windows on the west wall, with sills wide enough for seating, and a stone fireplace on the north. The wingback chairs were leather, the tables cherry, the lamps brass. It was what he'd had in mind for the office in his apartment, but the designer hadn't captured it.

Holly shut off all but two lamps, then switched on the stereo that filled one bookcase shelf. The music was quiet, unobtrusive, and perfect for dancing.

Before he could do more than remove his overcoat, there was a knock at the door. Bree came in. She carried the tray so unsteadily that he heard the silver clinking and actually saw one wineglass sway before she set it on a cherry table with a sigh of relief. "Would you like me to pour for you?"

"No, thank you. We'll take care of it."

She rushed out, closing the door behind her.

"A relative of yours?"

"No. Why do you ask?"

"I can't think of any other reason for a level-headed businesswoman to keep such a klutz around."

Holly shrugged as she filled two glasses with wine. "Maybe I'm soft at heart." She said it as if expecting him to laugh, but she'd get no argument from him. She'd expended some effort at creating an illusion of herself as hard-hearted, but not many people were fooled by it.

Drawing her into his arms, he rested his cheek against her hair and easily found the rhythm of the music. As they moved together, he rubbed his right hand slowly up and down her spine, occasionally pressing her closer, mostly just savoring the feel of her. So soft, so feminine, and yet strong. Oh, the things he could do to her, with her, and the things she could do to him . . .

"This is nice," she murmured, her voice little more than a whisper, a breath of sound that disappeared almost before it formed.

"Nice" wasn't a word he used very often, but, he realized with a start, she was right. Holding her like this, with no one to disturb them, nothing to come between them, was very nice.

Holding her even closer, with nothing at all between them, would feel even better, he admitted as his body reacted to hers. For a perfectly nice conclusion to the evening, they could dance their way upstairs, remove each other's clothing, and spend the rest of the night—hell, the rest of the weekend—sharing the most incredible sex either of them had ever known. She wanted it. He wanted it. Why shouldn't they have it?

Because he respected her, remember? Because she was the only woman he'd ever wanted from whom he hadn't simply taken what he wanted and walked away. Because he wanted more from her than mere sex—even the most incredible sex he'd ever known.

Because he didn't want to treat her like every other woman in his life. He didn't want other people to think of her the way they thought of the women who'd come before her.

He wanted to marry her.

She rubbed enticingly against him, a movement that had little to do with the music and everything to do with what he was thinking, what he was feeling. It would be so easy to peel off her dress, to strip off his own clothes and lay her down, slide inside her, find the pleasure and the satisfaction she promised with every look, every move. So easy to tilt her head back, like so. To lower his head until his lips brushed hers. To accept her silent invitation, to slide his tongue inside her mouth, to lift her so her hips pressed hard and welcoming against his erection.

She clung to him, sucking his tongue, wringing a strangled groan from him with no more than the easy thrust of her hips. Her fingers rubbed up his neck over taut muscles, then slid into his hair, pulling him nearer while she greedily demanded more from their kiss.

So damn easy . . . and almost more than he could manage to stop.

He forced her back a few inches, dragged in a searing breath, then gasped as she boldly caressed him. "Holly." Her name was little more than a groan, his efforts to keep her hands off his body halfhearted at best. "Listen—there's something I want— Wait—"

Her smile was sensual, her hazel eyes hazy. "We can talk later. Right now I want—we both want—" She freed her hands and touched him again, not in an overtly sexual way this time, just rested her hands possessively on his upper arms.

The effect on him, though, was overtly sexual, and painful, and pleasurable.

He raised his hands to her wrists, but that didn't stop her from sliding her arms around his neck, from pulling his head down for another kiss. This time she was the one doing the teasing, her tongue mimicking his own earlier thrusts, and he let her, let it go on too long, until he was too hot, too hard, until his skin had become slick with sweat and his hands unsteady, until, sweet hell, he didn't want to stop her at all.

"Holly . . ." His voice was guttural, harsh. "I want—"

"I want, too," she murmured, leaving a trail of damp kisses along his jaw and down his throat, loosening his tie, unfastening a button or two.

His eyes closed, and he dragged in a deep breath for strength, then blurted out what he had to say. "Will you marry me?"

HOLLY HAD NEVER KNOWN SEXUAL ardor could be cooled so quickly, so effectively, with four small words. She stumbled back a step or two, felt the table with their wine behind her, and spun around to drain one glass, then the other, in quick succession. She wanted to pretend she hadn't heard him, or that she couldn't possibly have heard right. She wanted to go on as if he'd never asked the question, wanted to ask if he'd had too much to drink when she wasn't looking, or if he'd just decided to go freaking crazy!

She took a deep breath, clasped her trembling hands tightly together, and said in her best faked-calm voice, "Should we do the polite thing and ignore words you surely did not intend to say to me, or laugh about it and then forget it?"

"I did intend to say them, and only to you." Looking as unruffled and in control as if he were in one of McKinney Industries' boardrooms, closing a multibillion-dollar merger, he circled her to reach the empty glasses, refilled them, and offered her one. She wanted the drink desperately but shook her head rather than let him see how badly his question had unsettled her. With a shrug, he placed it on the table beside her, then took up a position leaning against the mantel a few yards away. "I want to get married, Holly."

"To me," she said skeptically, and he nodded. "When did you reach that decision?"

"Last weekend."

Funny. She'd thought they were playing a drawn-out game of seduction. The dinner, the dances, the almost-a-kiss good night . . . She'd thought they were leading up to sex, to one hell of a fling. She'd never dreamed he would offer a marriage proposal!

"You have to admit we're a good match."

Oh, no, she didn't. "I'm not your type. You're not my type. You like society blondes. I like men who go away when told. The only thing either of us knows about relationships is how to stay out of them. This is ridiculous!"

"If you didn't think we were a good match, you

wouldn't have been pursuing an affair with me for the past fourteen months."

"An affair—a few nights, no more! Not a lifetime commitment!" She was tempted to pound her fist against his chest to drive home her point, but feared getting so close to him. A few more touches, a few more kisses, and the devil only knew what she might agree to.

"So I'm raising the stakes a bit. If you'll think about it rationally, it makes sense. We each find the other interesting. We each want to have sex with the other. We're both in business, so we each have an understanding of the demands on the other's time. Neither of us wants children, so that's not a problem. You've got money of your own, so that's not a problem, either. It seems perfectly reasonable to me."

"Reasonable," she echoed, then shifted into a syrupy-sweet voice. "My, oh my, what more could a woman possibly want?"

"Tell me, and I'll give it to you," he said seriously.

She turned away, going to the window to stare out into the night. It truly was the most outrageous suggestion anyone had ever made to her. Get married? Not in this lifetime. To Tom Flynn? Not in a million lifetimes. She just wanted to ravish his body, to have fabulous, wicked sex with him, then walk away. She wanted eight or sixteen hours of his time, twenty-four tops. Not the rest of his life!

"Look," she began, striving to keep her voice

level. "Let's write this off as too much wine, too much dancing, too little sleep, whatever, and forget it ever happened, okay? Now . . . I believe I've had enough surprises for the evening. I'm going to bed. Thank you for taking me to the dance. I had a—" Unable to utter the word that would be an absolute lie, she simply left it out and went on. "A time."

He let her get as far as the lobby before he spoke again. His voice was clear enough to carry to the registration desk and beyond. "I don't want to forget that it ever happened, Holly. I want to get married. To you."

Behind the counter, Peggy gasped. Bree, seated on a tall stool, stared openmouthed. Holly felt like slapping both women—hell, and the man, too. Instead, she all but ran down the hall to the kitchen and into her apartment, where she slammed and locked the door, then leaned against it for good measure.

A marriage proposal! That was the last thing she'd ever expected to hear from Tom. Acceptance of her offer to make his wildest dreams come true, yes. Polite rejection, maybe. A marriage proposal, never.

And such a romantic one at that. No hearts and flowers for this man, no, sir. Instead, he'd used words like "rationally." "Interesting." "Understanding." "Reasonable." If she were ever inclined to accept *any* man's proposal, it sure as hell wouldn't contain words like that.

Not that she would ever be so inclined.

A light tap on the door made her jump. She

jerked away as if the door could somehow transmit some measure of Tom's craziness to her, then guardedly asked, "Who is it?"

"It's Bree. I forgot to tell you that you had a message from Miss Winchester. She said that she and her sister were taking your mother home with them to spend the night and that you shouldn't worry about her."

"Damn. I'd hoped Mitch would lock her up in jail."

"Your own mother?" Bree sounded scandalized, apparently realized it, and quickly apologized. "I'm sorry. It's none of my business. One other thing."

"Yes?"

"Congratulations."

Holly unlocked the door and opened it a few inches. "I'm not getting married."

"Oh. But . . . he said you were."

"He's misinformed." And arrogant. Egotistical. And a liar, too.

"Oh. Well. Proposing after the Sweethearts Dance . . . it's just so romantic. And he seemed so certain. . . ."

Overconfident. Smug. Presumptuous.

"He's awfully handsome. And rich. And he seems like a—a good catch."

Conceited, overbearing, and—hell, where was a thesaurus when she needed one? "He is handsome," she agreed cattily. "And rich. And I'd rather catch a cold."

"But—"

"End of discussion. Thank you for delivering the message. Good night." She closed the door in Bree's face, then immediately jerked it open again. "Not a word of this to anyone. Do you understand? What happened here tonight is between you, Peggy, Tom, and me."

A guilty look crept into Bree's eyes. "But Peggy—I, uh, all right. I won't say anything to anyone."

Not wanting to know what Peggy had already done, Holly closed and locked the door again. The man had incredible nerve. He'd made her forget the unpleasantness at the dance. Hell, he'd damn near made her forget her name. And then he'd gone and spoiled it all with that stupid suggestion. She should be undressing in his suite instead of her dressing room, should be facing a long, steamy night instead of throwing things across the room.

This was undoubtedly the worst Sweethearts Dance ever, and it was all Tom's fault.

Of course she had trouble sleeping. And what little sleep she got was disturbed by dreams that were sad, silly, and ridiculous. They starred handsome, sexy, perfect Tom, and Holly. In a wedding dress. Holly with her hair bleached blond. Holly in virginal white lace running through a throng of well-wishers, seeking escape like a panicked rat in a maze.

Rolling onto her side, she stared out at the early morning sky, bright with stars. "Someone up there has a sense of humor," she whispered sourly. "This wasn't exactly what I had in mind when I made that wish. I just wanted his attention, his body, sex. I *never* wanted this."

No response. The stars just seemed to twinkle even brighter, as if amused by her predicament.

Holly wasn't amused then, or three hours later when she finally gave up the pretense of resting, got dressed, and wandered from her apartment in search of caffeine. The kitchen staff was already at work on breakfast and the Sunday dinner desserts, but that didn't stop Edward from swinging her around in an embrace.

"I have the perfect cake in mind. A sponge cake delicately flavored with amaretto and wrapped in white fondant, each layer draped with an ivory fondant lace handkerchief and—" Abruptly he broke off, and his animation turned downward into a pout. "Unless, of course, he has his own pastry chef and you would prefer that *he* make the cake."

"What cake?"

"Your wedding cake, of course."

Holly pulled away from him. "I'm not getting married. Everyone hear that? Regardless of what you've heard, I am *not* getting married."

Everyone looked at her. Some of them even nodded. But no one appeared to believe her.

Forget the coffee. She had enough adrenaline in her system to make caffeine unnecessary. Bypassing the pot, she went straight to the registration counter, where Janice was filling in. "I'm going to get a head start on the cleaning. Has anyone checked out yet?"

"Only Mr. Flynn."

Holly almost gaped. "He what?"

"He got a call right after I arrived this morning and left soon after, mumbling something about a factory and a fire."

"Did he—" She swallowed hard, hating the need to ask, hating the faint, hopeful plea in her voice. "Did he leave a message for me?"

Janice shook her head. "But don't worry, boss. I'm sure he'll call you just as soon as he gets a chance. After all, it's not every day that a man gets engaged. Congratula—"

Her assistant's words barely registering, Holly walked away into the dining room, where Kate was setting tables for breakfast. Without speaking, Holly picked up an armload of tablecloths and started at the other end.

The night before, he'd asked her to marry him. This morning, he'd left without so much as a goodbye. What did that mean? That the proposal had been a spur-of-the-moment mistake? Bad judgment? Worse, some sort of bad joke? Or did it mean anything at all? He'd often left for Buffalo without seeking her out to say good-bye . . . but not after proposing to her.

It was just as well that he was gone, she decided when Emilie walked in. Her friend's expression was so stunned that Holly knew she wasn't there to discuss Margery's behavior at the dance. Emilie picked up a tablecloth, gave it a shake, then spread it over the table where Holly stood. After they'd evened the edges, then placed the centerpiece, salt and pepper, dishes and napkins, Emilie finally spoke. "I don't know whether to offer my congratulations or ask if you've gone insane."

"My, gossip travels fast."

"Tom Flynn, coldhearted snake, proposing marriage to Holly McBride, confirmed marriage-hater? At the speed of light, honey. What happened after you two left the dance?"

Holly moved to the closest wait station, poured two cups of coffee, then joined Emilie at the table they'd just set. "He'd had too much to drink."

"I don't think so."

"He was so overcome with lust he didn't know what he was saying."

"If anyone could make him that hot, it would be you. But I hear he was as calm and cool as can be. Next excuse?"

"Temporary insanity?" That was the likeliest explanation. She'd suffered from it herself on occasion, in those moments when she opened her mouth and all the wrong words came out. Thank God she hadn't had a bout of it last night. She might have actually said yes!

"What are you going to say?"

"He wasn't serious. I don't have to say anything."

"But what if he *was* serious? What will you tell him?"

"I already told him no. Hell, no. Not in this lifetime." She stared broodingly into her coffee. "This is what I get for stealing his birthday wish."

"You what?"

Her face felt as warm as the fire blazing across

the room. "I—I stole his wish. At Maggie's. On his birthday. We had a great cake, his favorite kind, and Maggie had candles, and she told him to blow them out and make a wish, and . . . Hell, you know him. What does he have to wish for? He's got everything he could possibly want. So, since I knew he wouldn't make a wish when he blew out the candles, I did. I wished for him to wish for me."

Concern had crept into Emilie's expression. "And you think that's why he proposed to you? Because you wished for it?"

"Of course not. And I didn't wish for it. I wished for an affair. Aw, hell, don't pay any attention to me. I'm sleep deprived and mortified by last night. I know I've got to face my mother when she comes back here, and I don't know how to do it without smacking her senseless, and I'm surrounded by people who insist on congratulating me on an engagement that doesn't exist to a man who left without even saying goodbye. I'm doing what any respectable woman would do. I'm taking leave of my senses. I'm going to steal a half-gallon of chocolate ice cream from the kitchen, grab a can of chocolate syrup from the pantry, and I'm going to curl up on my bed and not come out until they're both all gone."

Emilie's lips twitched with a smile. "I'd be happy to donate the kids' Valentine's candy to the cause. I bought them some of those wonderful chocolate-covered marshmallow things that you put in the freezer and the marshmallow gets hard and chewy."

"I love those." She paused. "I understand the Winchesters took Margery home with them last night."

"Mitch didn't want to lock her up, but he didn't want to bring her back here, either."

"I'm throwing her out today. I swear I am." When Emilie didn't say anything, Holly glared at her. "Go ahead and say it."

"Say what?"

" 'You can't throw her out. She's your mother. Family's important.' "

"Family is important, but that doesn't mean you have to accept and forgive everything they do. Being your mother shouldn't give Margery any more latitude in her behavior than anyone else would get."

In her head, Holly knew what Emilie was saying was right. In her heart . . . She didn't want to be as bad a daughter as Margery was a mother. "Relationships suck," she muttered. "I don't know what you people see in them."

Emilie merely laughed. "You're not nearly as tough as you think, Holly."

That, Holly admitted silently, was part of the problem.

THE MORNING LIGHT STREAMING THROUGH the windows was the first thing Margery noticed when she awakened. She lay on her back, feeling the warmth on her face, and wondered exactly where she was. It wasn't the first time she'd awakened in a strange room. On occasion, there was a strange man beside her, but more often she was alone. She hated being so damn alone.

Once she fully opened her eyes, it took her weary mind a moment to realize that the field of white she was staring at overhead was a canopy. The ruffled and tucked fabric was dotted with barely noticeable white flowers, was very pretty, very feminine, and not something she could place. Seeing the rest of the room offered no help—not the lace curtains at the windows, the fine antiques, or the cabbage-rose wallpaper.

With a groan, she slowly pushed herself into a sitting position. Her clothes were gone, and in their place she wore a voluminous flannel nightgown, gathered at the sleeves and the high neck, something an old granny would wear, but never, ever, Margery McBride. Where was she? How had she gotten there? Whose nightclothes was she wearing? And how had she shamed herself this time?

A tap sounded at the door, then it immediately opened. A tray appeared first, with a cup of coffee, a glass of juice, and a china saucer holding some sort of cake. Carrying the tray was an older woman, white haired, serene, moving assuredly. When she saw that Margery was awake, she smiled politely enough, but there was an undertone of disapproval. "I thought you might be waking up soon. It's almost lunchtime." She balanced the breakfast tray over Margery's outstretched legs, then withdrew to the end of the bed.

"Breakfast in bed." Margery's voice was hoarse, raspier than usual. "That's a luxury I haven't had in ages." She sipped the orange juice to soothe her parched throat, then sniffed the cake cautiously. It was a rich, moist coffee cake, and thankfully it didn't threaten her already-upset stomach. "Do I know . . ."

"I'm Corinna Winchester."

The name brought back more memories than Margery wanted. Last night, the dance, the too-many drinks she'd imbibed. Making her grand stumbling appearance, shoving Agatha, humiliating her daughter. Again. The queasiness that hadn't appeared earlier rushed through her now, bringing a sheen of perspiration to her forehead, making her hands unsteady. "I—I don't remember much about last night."

"You look as if you remember enough."

"Holly—"

"Probably isn't eager to see you today." Corinna folded her hands together. "You need help, Margery."

"I'm not—" Her defensiveness left as quickly as it had come. She couldn't repeat the lie that had seen her through the past thirty years. *I'm not an alcoholic,* she'd insisted every time her husband had suggested she seek treatment. *I just like a drink now and then,* she'd sworn whenever one of her friends got bold enough to mention it. *I don't have a problem,* she'd persuaded herself whenever she'd awakened in a strange place with no recollection of how she'd gotten there.

Pitiful lies. Pointless denials. She wasn't kidding anyone but herself, and she was too damn old to be kidded.

"Was it horrible?" she asked hesitantly.

"Yes."

"I'm so sorry—"

"It's not me you should be apologizing to. It's not me you insulted in front of her friends. You know, Margery, your daughter is a smart, capable, admirable young woman. Most people in this town care a great deal about her. It's a shame the same can't be said about her mother."

There was nothing she could offer in her own defense. She'd loved, hated, and resented the hell out of Holly since the day she was born. Part of it was the alcohol that made her mean and shrewish. Part of it was her own unhappiness. Part of it was . . . Hell, she didn't claim to understand herself. Sometimes she'd tried, but it was always easier, and a lot less painful, to open another bottle of whiskey.

"It's been years since Lewis died," Corinna said. "Sometimes I think you were alone even when he was here. But you don't have to die alone. You've got a daughter to make any mother proud. It's not too late to be her mother."

"Sure it is," Margery said miserably. "It's been too late since she was twelve years old." The details were fuzzy, as with so many events in her life, but she remembered enough. Lewis out of town again, the credit card receipt she'd found in his pocket for a piece of jewelry he hadn't given her, the middle-of-the-night phone calls to his motel room to find he wasn't there, and the whiskey. Too much whiskey.

The next thing she remembered clearly was waking up the following morning on the dining-room floor, with a pillow under her head and a blanket tucked over her. She'd found bits of dried cake frosting in her hair, on her blouse, her face, and the remains of a party gone bad, and Holly, sitting at the table where she'd spent the night, looking decades older than her years.

Margery had had a hell of a hangover, but she'd tried to apologize. Holly had walked away from her, and things had never been the same again.

"It's never too late," Corinna said with the assurance of someone who'd never ruined a relationship or even treated someone unfairly in her life. Then she conceded, "Well, it may be too late for the usual mother-daughter relationship, but perhaps you can still be friends."

Friends with her daughter. Margery considered the possibility with more than a little longing, but she refused to be hopeful. Nothing had turned out right in her life, and, no matter what Corinna said, she didn't expect that to change.

The day she'd married Lewis had been the happiest of her life. She'd thought their lives were perfect and would stay that way forever. How long had it taken for things to fall apart? Two years, when they'd moved to Bethlehem? The following year, when Holly was born? Or the year after that, when Lewis began spending more and more time on the road, or so he'd claimed?

She had suspected almost immediately that work was only an excuse to cover his infidelities, and before long she'd had proof. She'd hated him for cheating on her, but loved him too much to leave. And Holly had gotten caught in that love and hate. If not for her, Margery had thought, she could have taken better care of herself, traveled with Lewis, kept him from straying.

In the end, they'd all been miserable. She'd failed her husband, her daughter, and herself, and she'd spent the rest of her life paying for it.

She didn't deserve to be friends with her daughter.

Chapter Nine

IT WAS LATE SUNDAY NIGHT WHEN TOM finally settled in his motel room in Laurel, Alabama. It wasn't much more than a wide spot in the road in the northeast corner of the state and had been home to McKinney Industries' newest acquisition. Until four o'clock that morning. Witnesses had reported hearing three explosions, which had been followed by a tremendous fire. Not much of the factory had been left standing.

Stretching out on the bed, he called Ross in Bethlehem. "The plant's a total loss," he said without preamble. "One worker was killed, and a half-dozen others suffered minor injuries, as well as three firemen. The cause of the explosions hasn't been determined yet. The investigators say it will take some time."

"I picked a hell of a time to buy a new factory, didn't I?" Ross said dryly.

"Look at it this way. You just got a ten-million-dollar loss for this year's taxes."

"I'd rather have the factory and its profits. Of course we'll take care of the injured workers and their families."

Of course. "What about the uninjured workers? They'll want to know whether they're out of a job temporarily or for good."

"I don't know. Let's think about that and discuss it when you get back to Buffalo tomorrow."

"I was thinking of coming back to Bethlehem."

"Okay. Not a problem."

"I've . . . been thinking about living there, at least part of the time."

There was utter silence at the other end for a moment, then: "This decision wouldn't have anything to do with last night's bombshell, would it?"

Bethlehem being such a small town, Tom had little doubt that his proposal to Holly had become common knowledge before the morning church services had let out. Though it had seemed a good idea to speak up in front of her employees last night, he regretted it now. Holly's friends and neighbors weren't likely to be in favor of her doing anything at all with him.

"Maybe it came as a surprise," he said grudgingly. In twenty-four years he'd never explained himself to anyone, and he didn't want to start now. At the same time, he felt Ross had a right to some explanation.

"A surprise? Mrs. McBride's scene at the dance was a surprise. Aliens carrying her off in their spaceship would have been a surprise. But you wanting to get married—and to Holly, no less—that's much more than a surprise."

"And what's wrong with me wanting to marry Holly?" Tom asked crossly. He wasn't ideal husband material. He knew that. But he could learn. He'd always been very good at the things he chose to learn.

"There's nothing wrong with it. It's just . . . Well, hell, you and Holly. It took me by surprise, that's all. I guess I never figured you for anything so permanent."

"You could have figured wrong," Tom said dryly. "After all, you bought this factory only a week before it blew up."

"True. I'm obviously not infallible. Look, you want to marry Holly, great. I wish you all the luck in the world." Ross's voice took on a strangled quality, as if he was trying hard not to give in to laughter. "Trust me, you're going to need it."

Ten minutes later, as he dialed the number for the inn, Tom admitted that his boss was probably right. Holly's greeting was as friendly as could be . . . until he spoke. Then there was a decided chill on the line. "Sorry about leaving so early, but I had to get to Alabama and I didn't think you would appreciate my waking you up just to tell you goodbye."

"You thought wrong. Telling you goodbye would

have been the most pleasant part of this entire weekend."

He imagined it would have been one of the more original kiss-offs he'd ever gotten, too. He gingerly asked, "Have you considered my offer?"

"Oh, yes. I've considered whether to strangle you, or bar you from ever again setting foot on my property. I've considered hiring someone to remove you from my misery. I've even considered going somewhere for a nice, long vacation until this is all forgotten and I can walk through my own home without being badgered by nosy people. In fact, I've considered nothing but your asinine proposal!"

The sharp edge to her last words made him wince. "Okay, maybe I shouldn't have said anything in front of your employees, but—"

"Maybe?" she shrieked. "*Maybe?* You've subjected me to twenty-four hours of fawning, effusive congratulations on something that's never going to happen, and you think *maybe* you shouldn't have said anything? Where in the hell did you even get such an idea, anyway?"

"I want to get married. I've done everything else. I've accomplished everything I set out to accomplish. Now it's time to have a life. To find a wife."

"Wonderful. Great. But there must be hundreds of women in Buffalo whose only goal in life is to marry a rich man. Why not pick one of them?"

"Because I picked you."

"Why?"

"Because you *don't* want to marry a rich man."

"News flash, Tom. I don't want to marry *any* man. For God's sake, you don't even know me!"

He knew enough. He knew she would never bore him, be unfaithful to him, or make unreasonable demands on him. He knew he enjoyed being with her. Liked talking to her. Wanted her too damn much.

He bent one arm over his eyes. His shirt smelled of smoke, and he felt grimy from head to toe. He needed a shower, aspirin, and sleep.

Almost as much as he needed her to say yes.

"You're right," he agreed. "There's a lot I don't know about you."

She remained cautiously silent.

"So we'll take some time to get acquainted. I'll spend some time in Bethlehem. You can visit me in Buffalo. We'll go out on dates. Talk. Do the sort of things people in a new relationship do." Although frankly, he didn't know what people in relationships did. Usually he didn't bother to learn much about a woman, because she wouldn't be around long enough to matter.

"Really?" Suddenly Holly no longer sounded angry or frustrated, but rather intrigued. "All the things people in a relationship do?"

"Except have sex."

"That's a joke, right?"

"No."

"You expect me to have a relationship with you, to date, to pretend to be normal people going through a normal . . . courtship, for lack of a better word, and yet sex won't be a part of it?"

"Right."

She scoffed. "That's ridiculous. That's the most idiotic thing I've ever heard. People who are dating have sex, Tom. It's the most important part of a relationship!"

"No." He breathed deeply. "Every relationship you've had, every one I've had, has been based on sex. That's all you and I give—well, that plus expensive gifts. I want more."

"How much more do you think there is?"

"I don't know. I've never been in a position to find out."

"Then let me tell you. There is no *more* with me. No hearts and flowers, no commitment, no marriage, no love, no nothing. Sex is all I give any man. It's all I'm offering you."

"I don't want it," he lied. "Not yet, at least."

She was silent for so long he might have thought she'd hung up if not for the agitated tapping of a fingernail against a hard surface. After a deep exhalation, she said, "This is ridiculous."

"You said that already."

"You want to go out with me, spend time with me, get to know me, but you don't want to have sex with me?"

"I didn't say I didn't want sex. I do. But just once I'd like to know a little more about a woman than just her name before I find myself waking up beside her. Just once—" He broke off, swallowed. He wasn't a sentimental man, but he remembered when sex was harder to come by, when it was more than just a physical act between two interchangeable adults. More important. More satisfying. "Just once I'd like to think it meant something."

While he spoke, the fingernail tapping slowed, then stopped. After another brief silence, she said, "All right. We'll get acquainted. We'll date. But I won't give up the idea of seducing you."

"And I won't give up saying no," he agreed, then added, "At least, not until the time is right."

Her laugh was shaky, her tone sarcastic. "So how do we start this? When? Where?"

"I'll be back in Bethlehem tomorrow. Maybe we could have dinner."

"Oh, gee, you sound so enthusiastic."

He grimaced. "Will you have dinner with me tomorrow night, Holly?"

"I suppose so."

"Talk about enthusiastic . . ."

"Oh, yes, Tom," she said in a sultry voice. "I'd love to have dinner with you tomorrow night. I can't think of a single thing in the world I'd rather do more. Thank you so much for asking me. I'm just so flattered."

"Knock it off," he said with a chuckle. "I've got a meeting with Ross as soon as I get into town. Should I call you to set a time?"

"Sure. Whenever you get a chance. But don't think because I've agreed to this ridiculous suggestion I'm going to change my mind about marrying you. We'll tell everyone it was a mistake. You'd had too much wine and it went to your head."

"Is that my cue to say it wasn't the wine that went to my head but you?"

"No, that's your cue to agree there'll be no further talk of marriage."

Since there was no way in hell he was going to agree to that, he ignored it and said quietly, "See you tomorrow, Holly."

BETHLEHEM MEMORIAL HOSPITAL WASN'T one of Holly's favorite places, but that wasn't enough to keep her away Monday afternoon. She'd called J. D. Grayson's office earlier and was told he would be free at four o'clock, and the open door signified as much. The sounds coming from inside, though, suggested different.

She stopped in the doorway, folding her arms across her chest, and watched the scene. Gracie, J.D.'s six-year-old adopted daughter, was sitting on his lap at the desk and reading aloud from a kids' book, while his four other kids filled him in on the day's events. It was thirteen year old Caleb who noticed Holly first.

"Dad, you got company . . . or your next patient."

"Next patient, huh?" Holly mussed his hair as she entered the office. "I'll make you somebody's patient, young man. Hey, Graysons and Brown-Graysons."

"Miss Holly, I can read. Wanna hear 'bout Harry?" Gracie asked.

"I don't know. Who is this Harry? Is he single? Old enough for me to date?"

Gracie giggled as her year-older brother, Noah, rolled his eyes. "Harry's a little boy, like me."

"Well, are you old enough for me to date?"

He considered it thoughtfully, but it was Jacob who replied. "Pro'bly. But he has to be in bed by eight-thirty."

"Well, darlin', I have to be in bed not long after. We'll see what we can arrange."

J.D. lifted Gracie to the floor, then pulled some money from his pocket. "Trey, Caleb, can you take the kids to the gift shop and get them a candy bar, then wait for your mother in the lobby?"

"Sure," Trey replied, swinging Gracie up for a piggyback ride. He was a good-looking kid, bearing a strong resemblance to his father. Caleb was good-looking, too. Both were destined to be heartbreakers.

Once they left, J.D. closed the door, then touched Holly's shoulder as he returned to his desk. It was a simple touch, one good friend greeting another. And J.D. was a good friend. For a very short while, they'd been more . . . or was it less? They'd shared a few good laughs, a few great nights, then put an end to a relationship that wasn't meant to be. Since then, he'd become one of her best friends.

He leaned back in his chair, studied her for a moment, then asked, "Well, which are you today? Company or a new patient?"

"Is that your not-so-subtle way of saying I need therapy?"

"I don't know. Depends on whether the rumors are true."

Holly groaned and hid her face in both hands. "I am not getting married."

"But Tom proposed."

It pained her—actually pained her—to admit it. "Yes, but . . ." But what? He didn't mean it? Was that what she was afraid of? Or was she afraid that he did mean it? That he honestly did want to marry her?

Just thinking about it made her stomach hurt, and she was filled with relief when J.D. changed the subject to her other current problem.

"How is your mother?"

Holly shrugged. "Subdued. Embarrassed. Trying to cut back on the booze. It'll last for a few days, and then life will get to be too much for her again. Someone will look at her the wrong way or speak to her in the wrong tone of voice, or the sun won't shine as brightly as she wants, or she'll find a scuff on her shoe."

"Alcoholics aren't very sympathetic people, are they?"

His rueful look made her feel guilty and insensitive. "At least you had a real reason to drink, J.D. You dealt with kids who'd suffered horrific trauma. You had something to escape. You know what she was escaping? Her dreary existence in a town she detested."

"Holly, it doesn't matter what an alcoholic is trying

to escape. What matters is that she, or he, feels the need to escape. Your mother's problems might not seem like much to you, but they're more than she can handle—or more than she believes she can handle—on her own."

"Well, she's definitely more than I can handle on my own." Deliberately Holly turned to something more pleasant. "How's Kelsey?"

"Fine. Anxious for the big day to arrive. She says she feels like a beached whale."

"And do you tell her she's never looked lovelier?"

"Of course."

Holly gave a shake of her head. "Six kids. If I'd thought for a second when I met you that you'd have five kids and one more on the way, I never would have gotten near you."

"Aw, but look what you would have missed out on. So . . ." His expression said, End of reprieve. "What do you think about Tom's proposal?"

"I think the man's crazy. No, wait, let me rephrase that. I *thought* the man was crazy. After the talk we had last night, I know it."

J.D. silently waited for her to continue. It was part of what made him a good psychiatrist—part of what made him such a good friend. He genuinely listened, and genuinely cared, and he usually offered good advice.

"He said he wanted to marry me because I'm not after his money. Isn't that the stupidest reason to get married you ever heard?"

"No, not at all. It's just another way of saying

he wants to be wanted for himself and not his millions. Isn't that all any of us wants?"

Because it made sense the way J.D. put it, Holly ignored it. "I told him he didn't know me well enough to want to marry me, and he said we could get acquainted. You know, date."

"And the problem with that is . . . ?"

"No sex." When his expression remained unenlightened, she scowled. "Tom's insisting on no sex. He's a perfectly healthy man who's asking to spend time with me, the queen of one-night stands, and he doesn't want to have sex—which I suppose proves he's not normal at all, doesn't it?"

J.D. laughed. Wasn't it a big no-no for a shrink to laugh at his patient? she wondered crossly. "Gee, Holly, let's think about it. The man wants to get to know you better before he makes love with you. And you think that makes him abnormal?"

"In my experience, yes. Most men only want the sex. They don't want to get to know me at all."

"Do you really believe that?"

She had no reason to believe anything else. How many men had told her they would call back but never had? How many dates had taken her to a restaurant dinner, a concert, a weekend in the city, and in exchange, got lucky, as Margery had described it. "Even you had trouble remembering my name after the deed was done," she reminded him. "You called me Molly."

His grin faded into utter seriousness. "You were the first for me, you know, after Carol Ann died, losing Trey, and getting sober. It was a hell of a welcome back to life, and I don't remember if I ever thanked you for it."

Her cheeks flushed. "That's me. Holly, giver of great sex."

"That's why this celibate-dating thing frightens you, isn't it? Because Tom wants more than just your body. He wants the intimacy to mean something."

"And I don't want intimacy at all."

"I don't believe that, Holly. You're a caring woman. You're the best friend any of us could have. You help anyone who needs it. You're even good to the kids, despite your insistence that you don't like the little monsters. I don't believe you have none of these warm feelings for the men you date."

"Well, doc, everyone has to be wrong once in a while, and today's your day. Friends, women, kids, and strays are a whole different breed from the men I go to bed with."

"What are you afraid of? Getting hurt? Getting your heart broken? Hurts heal, you know, and broken hearts get mended."

It was Holly's turn to laugh. "Ah, J.D., you've gone soft. That's one of the problems with people who are disgustingly, happily in love. You lose touch with the real world."

"Honey, I live in a three-bedroom house with my pregnant wife, five kids, two dogs, six cats, and my father. Don't talk to me about the real world." After a brief silence, he asked, "When are you seeing him again?"

"This evening. He's in a meeting with Ross. We're having dinner when it's over."

"A real date," J.D. remarked in a teasing voice. "Dinner, conversation, a kiss on the cheek, and a goodbye at the door when the evening's over."

Holly thought of her weekend in Buffalo, when Tom had almost kissed her at her hotel-room door before saying good night. A real kiss couldn't have been any sweeter . . . though the ones Saturday night had been pretty damn special, too.

And kisses were all she was ever going to get if Tom had his way. He was determined to not have sex with her until . . . How had he put it? The time was right. And, considering he'd begun the entire discussion with a marriage proposal, it was a pretty good bet that the time wouldn't be right until she had his wedding ring on her finger. Since that was never going to happen . . .

Slowly she smiled. She had accepted his dating idea with a condition of her own—that she could still try to seduce him. He might be determined as hell . . . but she knew little tricks that would turn him inside out, upside down, and leave him begging for more.

If Tom Flynn wanted another challenge now that he'd met all his previous ones, she would be happy to give him one.

IT WAS A FEW MINUTES BEFORE SIX when Tom walked out of the main headquarters of McKinney Industries. The office complex, designed to blend in with the local architecture, looked like a small, prosperous college campus. The stone and brick buildings looked as if they'd been there for fifty years or more. Not one was taller than three stories, and the setting had been worked with and around to preserve as much of the surrounding forest as possible.

The security lights were on, illuminating the sidewalks that crisscrossed from building to building to parking lot. Except for the guards, he was the last employee to leave for the day. When they had been located in Buffalo, people had thought nothing of working ninety-hour weeks, including Ross. They now called it quits after forty hours, they now had lives. Productivity was up, so were employee satisfaction and profits.

Out of the large group who had lived, eaten, and breathed work, only Tom continued to do so. And he was tired of it, he thought as he drove the company car to the inn. He'd called Holly that afternoon and made arrangements to pick her up at seven. That would give him time to shower and shave—and find some new reserves of control.

He hadn't seen her since Saturday night, when she'd fled after his proposal, and last night's phone conversation had stripped away any remaining illusions he might have had that this courtship was going to be simple in any way. They were both strong-willed people accustomed to getting what they wanted, and now what each of them wanted was directly opposed to what the other was after.

Well, not completely. She wanted sex, and damned if he didn't, too. He'd fallen asleep last night thinking about her, and he'd awakened not long after, his skin slick with sweat, his breathing ragged, and so damn hard that it hurt. If she had any idea he'd been having erotic dreams about her, the contest would be over. She would win, but in the long run her victory could cost them both something special. Something they'd never had before. Something he wanted far more than just sex.

At the inn, he checked into his suite, showered, shaved, and dressed, when a knock sounded. He opened the door and, with the force of a punch in the gut, caught his breath.

Holly stood there looking sexy as hell, wearing a sultry smile and one of those snug-fitting dresses to which she did such justice. This one was purple, and it clung everywhere it touched. He could hardly swallow as his gaze moved down over the silky fabric covering rounded breasts, narrow waist, and shapely hips, to the best legs he'd ever seen, and finally to a pair of three-inch heels, all straps, insubstantial but sexy as hell.

This wasn't a woman dressed for a quiet dinner out. This was a declaration of war.

When he did nothing but stare, her smile widened. "I thought I'd save you the trouble of coming around back to pick me up," she said, coming closer to him, easing past to enter the sitting room. Her voice was husky, and the lazy, languid way she moved promised sweet heaven.

And it was all calculated. This was Holly playing the vamp, the incredibly sexual being who'd brought plenty of men to their knees. Knowing that helped.

His chest was still tight, his hand would probably tremble if he ever let go of the doorknob, and he half expected steam to start rising from his pores, but it helped.

"It would—" He stopped to clear his throat and steady his voice. "It wouldn't have been any trouble at all. Shall we go?"

Standing in the middle of the room, she opened her arms to encompass it—or to give him an even better look at how the dress molded to her body. "One phone call, and I can have the best food in town served right here."

"Oh, gee, and for dessert, we could just go into the next room and feast on each other," he said, grateful he could manage dryness when all he was thinking was how appealing that sounded.

"Well, now that you've suggested it . . ."

He let go of the doorknob, flexed his fingers, and took hold of her arm. "Okay, you've proven you're beautiful and sexy and I want you. Now let's get some dinner and see if we can figure out how this dating thing works."

She didn't reply to his dating comment until they were seated in a booth at McCauley's, Bethlehem's only steak house. "I can tell you exactly how this dating thing works. You ask, I accept. We go out, you spend money, we go back to my place, and I thank you for it."

"So are we trading services, or am I buying yours? Because if that's the case, you're selling yourself cheap." He ignored the tightening around her mouth and the glitter that came into her hazel eyes. "I figure the cost of this dinner ought to get me about an hour of your time, and nothing more."

She was still giving him that hard, annoyed look when the waitress came up. "Good evening, folks. My name's Kate and I'll be—Oh, hi, Holly, Mr. Flynn." When he looked blankly at her, she said, "I work at the inn. My parents own this place and I help out when they're shorthanded. Hey, I understand congratulations are in order."

"No," Holly said curtly. "They're not."

"Not yet," Tom added. "We're in negotiations."

"My dad says you're a tough negotiator," Kate commented. "He owned part of the land you bought for Mr. McKinney's offices."

"I am tough. And I never lose."

Kate took their orders, brought back drinks and a loaf of fresh bread, then left them alone. With very precise movements, Holly cut the end from the loaf, buttered it, then set it down without taking a bite. "For the record, I'm very stubborn."

"Uh-huh."

"I never lose, either. And I always get what I want. I've been called tough, too. If you were offering something I had the slightest desire for, maybe I'd worry, but I've never, ever in my life wanted to get married—not to you or any other man."

"Why is that?"

She shifted on the seat, and the silky purple fabric shifted, too, drawing his gaze downward. Aware of exactly what had caught his attention, she turned on the fake sexy smile and the fake sexy voice. "I have no respect for the institution. Good marriages are hard to find. Bad ones abound. If I want to be miserable, I can be miserable alone, without forcing others to endure it with me."

"So your parents' marriage was miserable. And you're so much like your mother—"

"I am not!"

"Then you're so much like your father . . . ?"

"No," she admitted grudgingly.

"Then why do you assume that because they were unhappily married, you will be, too?"

"I'm not making that assumption. I just don't want—" She muttered a curse. "Why do *you* assume I'm eager to be married? Because I'm a woman? Because little girls grow up expecting to be nothing but wives and mothers? Or do you think you're so incredible I won't be able to tell you no?"

"I'm not assuming anything. I knew from the moment I decided to marry you that I—"

Her sweet smile didn't waver one bit as she kicked him under the table. The shoe he'd admired as insubstantial back at the inn sent a substantial shock of pain through his shin. Grinding his teeth behind a smile as phony as hers, he bent to rub the ache while rephrasing his statement. "I knew from the moment I decided I *wanted* to marry you that it wasn't going to be easy. You *are* stubborn. You don't seek out emotional entanglements. You seem quite happy living the way you do."

"I am. So why would I mess with what makes me happy?"

"Because I can make you happier." The answer popped out before he'd given it any thought. It surprised him as much as her, maybe even more. He wasn't looking to take on the responsibility for someone else's happiness. Unless she wanted money, prestige, or power, he didn't have a clue to how to go about making Holly happy—well, excluding sex.

But then, even the best sex in the world couldn't make a person happy. If it could, both he and Holly would have been the cheeriest people on the damned planet.

The awkward silence that settled between them was broken when Kate brought their meals. After she had gone, he breathed deeply. "Listen, Holly, if you and I get—"

She gave him a look as sharp as the steak knife she pointed in his direction. "Don't say it. I don't want to hear the M word or any version thereof one more time tonight. As I understand it, a date is supposed to be fun. So far, I haven't had any fun. If you expect me to ever agree to another of these little rituals, you'd better start entertaining me *now.*"

"All right. So what do we do besides eat?"

"You can start by telling me why your cell phone hasn't rung even once. This must be some kind of record."

"I left it at the inn. I didn't want to be disturbed."

She stared at him, wide-eyed, open-mouthed.

"It's not like it's a lifeline. I do leave it at home on occasion."

"Name one," she challenged.

"Saturday. When we went to the dance." He smiled smugly.

"Name another," she shot back.

He tried to but couldn't.

She studied him for a moment, then grinned. "I suspected it from the moment you made your indecent proposal. Now I know for sure—you're an impostor. The real Tom Flynn wouldn't think any more highly of marriage than I do, and he certainly would never leave his phone home while he went out. He has a closer relationship with that phone than with the women in his life."

"Woman," he corrected. "There's never been more than one at a time. And I'm doing my damnedest to change that—the relationship part. Not the one-woman part."

"So you're monogamous in your promiscuity. And I suppose you expect the same of me."

He thought of walking away from her at the end of the evening with nothing more than a kiss at her door, and then thought of her with another man who wouldn't stop at her door, or with a kiss. "I do," he said harshly. Damned if he was going to suffer the torment of abstention alone.

"You remind me of a man who divorces his wife, then tries to put stipulations on what she can do and who she can see. He doesn't want her for himself, but he doesn't want anyone else to have her, either."

He studied her over the rim of his glass as he took a drink. Her full lower lip was extended in a pout. He wanted to reach across the table and smooth his thumb over it, to feel the incredible softness that he'd already tasted enough times to remember, to slide around and sit beside her and taste her again. Only the fact that they were in a public place and the dull throb in his shin kept him in place.

But that didn't stop him from smiling his smuggest, most arrogant smile and confidently assuring her, "The difference is, I can't divorce you until I m—" Remembering her ban on the M word, he shrugged to finish the sentence. "And I want you, Holly." Just saying it out loud made him hard and hot. "Oh, man, do I want you. And I don't want anyone else to have you. But trust me, darlin', it'll be worth the wait."

Chapter Ten

WITH EMPTY DESSERT DISHES between them, Holly sat back and indulged in a silent sigh. She wasn't about to admit it to Tom, but she'd enjoyed the evening. Once she'd put an end to the marriage talk, she'd had a nice time, and had learned a few things. He had a sense of humor. He was amazingly appealing for a man who seemed so arrogant. And there was a certain unfamiliar comfort in knowing that he expected nothing more from her than she'd already given.

Though she didn't like the way Tom had phrased it, her flings had boiled down to one of two things—trading services, or selling her own. And she *had* sold herself cheap. Wasn't she worth more than any restaurant dinner, a million concerts, or a year's worth of first-class weekends in the city? She would have liked to think so.

But she wasn't sure.

Because that admission made her feel uncertain and fragile, she pushed it away and focused on him. "Tell me about your family."

He laid down the fork he'd been toying with and shook his head. "There's nothing to tell. My mother died just before my sixteenth birthday, and I never met my father. Her family was disappointed in her for getting pregnant before she finished high school, so we hardly ever saw them, and when we did, things tended to get unpleasant. As for my father, he never wanted to be a father, so he disappeared when she told him the news."

"That was a tough way to grow up."

"It wasn't so bad."

"I meant for her." She couldn't imagine being seventeen or so, pregnant, and abandoned by her family as well as her baby's father. The thought of having complete responsibility for another life was enough to make her shudder.

"Yeah, I guess it was tough on her. But she always said she'd never regretted it. She was a good mother. I—" He looked away and murmured, "I missed her when she was gone."

Holly felt a flush of . . . Guilt? Envy? Resentment? Though she doubted Tom would ever admit it, he'd loved his mother, while the best way she could describe her relationship with her own mother was "forced tolerance." She couldn't honestly say she'd missed Margery even once in the fifteen years since she'd moved away, couldn't honestly claim that she would miss her when she was dead. It wasn't fair that he'd lost the mother he'd loved—probably the only person he'd ever loved—while she couldn't keep enough distance between herself and her mother.

Especially since Margery was still at the inn.

"I'm surprised that once you and Ross began raking in the millions, you didn't have family popping out of the woodwork," she remarked.

"I'm not known for my sentimentality or my generosity," he said with a sardonic tone she didn't quite understand. "I don't value family for its own sake. If my father or my mother's family wanted special treatment from me, then they should have treated her better."

And if Margery wanted something from her . . .

"But people make mistakes," some devil made her say. "They do things when they're young that they regret as they grow older. If they apologize, if they're sincerely sorry and want to atone for those mistakes, shouldn't they have that chance?"

"How do you atone for throwing a pregnant seventeen-year-old out on the streets? For having nothing to do with her for the next sixteen years? How do you atone for humiliating your daughter in front of her friends not once but twice?"

Holly's cheeks burned hot. "I wasn't talking about—"

"Yes, you were. We both have the misfortune to have some worthless people in our lives—or, in my case, not in my life. If your mother wants forgiveness and you want to give it to her, fine. That's a decision that only you can make, because you have to live with it. But it's not a decision I'll ever make. My mother's family was never sorry for what they did to her. My father, to the best of my knowledge, never regretted it either. If they ever do, it will be too late." His smile was thin and unforgiving. "It's been too late for forty years."

She watched that smile, watched it disappear as his features settled in a stony set. *Coldhearted snake.* That was what Maggie had called him until she'd stopped blaming him for Ross's shortcomings. The snake part might be true, especially in his business dealings, but coldhearted? She suspected Tom had more layers of emotion inside him than he realized. How would it feel to be the person who tapped in to all that emotion? Who thawed him out, loosened him up, and brought out not only the passion but the tenderness, the joy, the sorrow, the regret, the gentleness, the love?

She wasn't looking to do any tapping in. She would be perfectly satisfied with the passion, thank you. But for some lucky woman, Tom Flynn the man—the flawed, strong, powerful, fallible, entirely human man—would be a sight to behold.

He glanced around, then said, "Looks like they're getting ready to close."

She looked, too. Kate was pushing a sweeper under distant tables, and her mother was washing down tabletops while her sister refilled the condiments. "My town," she said with a smile. "The only thing open after nine o'clock are the bars, but the quality of their clientele goes down significantly. Shall we go?"

He paid the bill, then helped her with her coat. The silence between them was almost companionable until he turned into the long drive that led to the inn. In a few moments, he intended to tell her good night and leave her alone. She intended to change his mind.

"Front door or around back?" he asked.

"The front's fine." It wasn't as if her employees didn't know she was out with Tom. Coming in with him wouldn't cause any more gossip than—probably not as much as—coming in through her own apartment.

He parked in the nearly empty lot, and they made their way across gravel and frozen ground to the inn's entrance. The lobby was brightly lit and welcoming, everything her guests expected it to be. Though there was no fire in the hearth, the open space was comfortably warm and smelled of mulberry and fresh flowers. It was her single biggest extravagance—fresh flowers delivered weekly from Melissa Thomas's nursery. Holly had neither a green thumb nor the desire to learn to cultivate her own flowers, but she loved the arrangements all the same.

She greeted Peggy, who suddenly found some reason to disappear behind the desk into the office Holly shared with Emilie. Alone with Tom, she slipped her coat off, folded it over her hands, and gave him a practiced smile. "Can I interest you in a nightcap? I imagine we can have the library to ourselves again."

"What do you have that's nonalcoholic?"

"Soft drinks, coffee, milk, juice, mulled cider, tea. You forget, we're a full-service restaurant, too."

"How about cider?"

"Not a problem. Why don't you build a fire in the library, turn on the music, turn down the lights, and—"

Grinning, he took hold of her elbow and turned her down the hall. "Better yet, why don't I go with you to the kitchen, and we can drink it there."

Holly didn't protest. The kitchen was that much closer to her apartment—literally just steps from her bedroom. With Bree now settled in her own room and Margery upstairs in a guest room, she didn't think it would be hard at all to coax him into her apartment. *One of my employees is sleeping next door*, she could innocently say, *so why don't we go to my apartment so we won't disturb her?*

A dim light burned in the kitchen. She turned on only the lights she needed, leaving much of the room in shadow, then handed her coat and bag to Tom and gestured toward the corner table. "Have a seat."

Mulled cider was one of the inn's specialties, available anytime night or day with a minimum of fuss. Gallon jars of cider lined the shelves in the pantry, with the additional ingredients—brown sugar and spices—premeasured and stored in small plastic bags, one bag per half gallon. Even

Holly, whose kitchen abilities didn't extend far beyond sandwich making, couldn't mess up.

Once she had everything simmering in a pan on the stove, she turned to find Tom leaning against the opposite counter. He'd set down their coats, removed his jacket, and loosened his tie. With his dark hair in its perpetually mussed state and his rugged features looking even more rugged in the shadows, he looked . . . incredible. And tired, she added as he hid a yawn. "What great catastrophe took you out of here before sunrise yesterday?"

"There was an explosion and fire at one of our factories. It happened around four, they'd tracked me down by five, and I was in the Gulfstream on my way there by six."

"Was it bad?"

"One man dead, several others injured. The plant was destroyed."

She stirred the cider, half-surprised that he'd ranked the human toll above the business loss. It was a common conception that people didn't mean much to Tom. Even she had always assumed that people were more or less interchangeable with him. If he got tired of one blonde, he simply traded her for another. If an employee annoyed him, he fired him and hired another. It was said that he didn't bother to learn people's names because they were disposable. Soon enough others would take their places.

Apparently, that was a common misconception. "So what do you do now?"

"We're in the process of deciding. We'd just bought the plant. If we take the insurance settlement and walk away, we take a substantial loss. If we add to the insurance settlement and rebuild, we take an even bigger loss in the short term. But if we don't rebuild, it will devastate the town. The plant was the biggest employer in the county, with more than seventy percent of the jobs. Virtually every business in town will go under without the factory employees' dollars."

Opening a cabinet, she bypassed delicate china cups for sturdy porcelain mugs. "Which action are you voting for?"

When he didn't answer, she glanced over her shoulder. He looked chagrined, a bit embarrassed. Because he wanted to take the money and run? It made good business sense, but there was no denying that it was coldhearted. Or did he want to rebuild and help save some little blue-collar burg from extinction? Not the best action for the bottom line, but the decent thing to do, if the company could afford it. And McKinney Industries certainly could.

She ladled the hot cider into the mugs, offered one to him, then turned and leaned against the counter. While waiting for his answer, she blew carefully on her cider, creating ripples in the amber liquid, sending fragrant wisps of steam into the air.

"Whatever we do, a loss these days isn't necessarily a bad thing," he said at last. "With our profits climbing steadily, we could use a tax break. And if we don't rebuild, all we have is the insurance money. If we do rebuild, sure, it'll cost us more up-front, but in return, we get the potential for greater future earnings. The factory was self-sufficient and made a product we needed. That's why we bought it. We still need the product, and there's no reason the plant can't be self-sufficient again in a few years."

"So you're voting to save the town."

He looked stiff and uncomfortable. "I'm voting to take the action that seems wisest in the long run."

"Which just happens to include saving the town." She grinned. "You *must* be an impostor. I heard the real Tom Flynn would sell his soul for a profit if—"

"If he had one," he said dryly. "I'm not concerned about the town. I'm just looking at where we'll stand in five or ten years if we rebuild, and if we don't."

"It's okay, Tom. I'm not going to tell anyone that way down deep inside, you have a tiny streak of sentimentality and generosity." Then she teasingly added, "Not that anyone would believe me if I did tell."

They finished their cider pretty much in silence. By the time Tom's cup was empty, he was dead on his feet. She thought about bringing him wide awake and seducing him anyway, then decided to take pity on him. She still wanted to sleep with him—and she didn't expect that to change until after she'd succeeded—but she wanted him wide awake, with all his wits, his inventiveness, and his creativity at peak performance. He'd promised her it would be worth the wait, and she intended to hold him to it.

She put their cups in the sink, then got his coat. It smelled tantalizingly of him, and it took every ounce of her resolve to resist burying her face in it and breathing deeply enough to fill every pore in her body. "I had a nice time," she said, offering him the coat.

He blinked, but the drowsiness didn't fade from his dark eyes. "That's it? No kisses? No sultry invitations? No promises of soul-deep pleasure?"

"If you had a soul," she said with a faint smile. "No. No seduction. I want you, but I want you awake, alert, and energetic. Otherwise . . ." She lowered her voice and damn near purred, "You just might not survive."

He took hold of his coat and caught her hands, too, pulling her near. Without touching her anywhere else, he gave her a sweet, chaste, innocent kiss. "Good night, Holly," he murmured, then he slipped past her and was gone.

Her eyes fluttered shut, and she remained where she was for a long time. She swore she could still feel the incredible softness of the cashmere on her fingertips, still smell the exotic-spice scent of his aftershave, still feel the gentleness of his mouth against hers. No man had ever made her feel so fragile, so special. No man had ever made her tremble with such a nothing kiss, or brought tears to her eyes by doing nothing more than walking away.

Finally, she opened her eyes, shut off the lights, and started to her apartment. She stopped for a moment, though, at the dining table, where she gazed out the window at the stars. Was it too late, she wondered, to change her wish?

But what would she change it to? *Don't wish for me at all?*

Or, *Wish for us to have it all?*

She didn't have a clue.

WEDNESDAY WAS THE FIRST OF BREE'S two days off. She celebrated by sleeping late, then was on her way out the front door when an imperious voice commanded her to stop. Slowly she turned to face Margery McBride. "Where are you going?" the woman demanded.

"T-to town. This is my day off."

"Where in town?"

Bree shrugged. "The bank, the drugstore, the grocery store."

"I'll go with you."

"But—" Spending her few hours away from the inn with Margery McBride sounded more like hell than a pleasant change. She forced an excuse. "It's awfully cold outside, Mrs. McBride, and I'm walking."

"Good. I can use the exercise."

"But—"

"Wait one moment. I simply need to change shoes and get my coat." Margery turned to start up the stairs. "Don't think about leaving without me. I don't feel kindly toward people who disobey me."

Because she didn't have the nerve to disobey, Bree waited, shifting her weight from foot to foot, listening to the grandfather clock tick off the seconds. When finally Margery returned, she'd changed clothes as well as shoes, pulled a knitted cap over her head, and put on her full-length fur. With the cap and the heavy-duty, top-dollar Nikes, the fur looked silly. Not that Bree would have minded looking silly if it meant keeping as warm as Margery appeared to be.

"Why are you walking to town?" she asked as they started down the drive. "You obviously don't need the exercise. You're thin enough as it is."

"I don't have any other way to get there," Bree replied.

"Where's your car?"

"I don't have one." From the corner of her eye, Bree caught the incredulous look on Margery's face. How nice it must be to take for granted all the little luxuries that made life easy, like a car, a fur, enough money to pay the rent and the bills and still have groceries, too. Margery had never wanted for anything in her life, but look where it had gotten her. Her husband was dead, her daughter wanted nothing to do with her, and she was a drunk.

Maybe it wasn't so nice having life easy.

"Do you have a boyfriend?" Margery asked.

"No, ma'am."

"Why not? You're a pretty enough girl. In fact . . ." She studied Bree intently for a moment. "You look rather familiar. Have we met?"

"N-no, ma'am."

"Are you sure? Because I rarely forget a face, and yours seems . . ." With a sudden loss of interest, she waved a hand to dismiss the topic. "When I was your age, I had young men lined up for the chance to take me out. I lived in the city and went to the ballet, the symphony, the opera, and I attended the most fabulous parties and more opening nights than I can remember. Oh, I had the most wonderful times in the city."

Why did she talk about New York City as if it were the only city of any consequence in the entire state? Bree wondered. And what was so special about the ballet, the symphony, and the opera? She couldn't imagine many worse ways to spend an evening. Her activities at home had been much simpler and cheaper—high school football games, free concerts in the park, a hot afternoon in a cool movie theater—but at least she'd never been bored to tears. She wouldn't have survived long in the life the older woman spoke of so longingly.

"I met Holly's father at the opera, you know," Margery said, then laughed. "Of course you don't know. How could you? It was *La Bohème*. He was so handsome, and I was quite a beauty then. We were the perfect couple. Everyone always said so."

"My father wouldn't have been caught dead at the opera. He liked movies and carnivals and zoos."

"Oh," Margery said with a patronizing look. As in, Oh, how common. Or, Oh, that explains a lot. Then she went on. "So . . . Why are you working for my daughter as a maid?"

"I needed a job."

"Don't you have any ambition? Don't you want to better yourself?"

"My dad always said there's nothing wrong with honest work."

"Don't you want to go to school? Find a better job? I don't know what my daughter pays, but I'm sure it's not enough to balance the indignity of cleaning up after strangers." Margery laughed scornfully. "I'm sure there's not enough money in the world to make *me* take such a job."

Pausing on the curb, Bree gave her a narrow look before announcing, "You're a snob, Mrs. McBride."

Margery wasn't the least bit offended and kept walking. "Well, of course I am. Being a snob is the only thing I do well."

That, and drink. And boss people around. And make her daughter miserable.

"I was an only child, and nothing made my parents happier than to make me happy. Nothing was too good, or too expensive, for me. I got what I wanted when I wanted it, and no one—" she pointed a gloved finger in Bree's direction "—no one ever dared tell me no." Then she grudgingly added, "Until my husband forced me to move to this god-awful place."

Bree gave the "god-awful place" a close look. The houses they were passing were neat and pretty. Downtown Bethlehem lay ahead, a half-dozen blocks of businesses in old buildings, with a grassy square and friendly people everywhere. The town was everything she'd expected—lovely, quaint, artsy, old-fashioned. The instant she'd stepped off the bus, she had felt a connection to her past. Lately she'd begun to think her future might lie there, too, if she didn't screw it up in the present.

"I like Bethlehem," she said stubbornly. "It's a lot nicer than where I grew up. Everyone's friendly, and it's safe to walk the streets, and it seems like a good place to raise kids."

"God, that's what my husband used to say. He never bothered to find out that I wasn't looking for a place to raise kids because I wasn't planning any kids to raise. Holly just sort of . . . happened. After she was born, there was no way I could get him out of that awful old farmhouse or this detestable little town. I was stuck."

A snob and self-centered, too, Bree thought as they crossed another street. There she stopped and gestured toward the bank. "This is where I'm going. If you need a ride back to the inn—"

Margery smiled. "Run along and take care of your business. I don't mind waiting."

"But—"

"Go on. I'll just stand out here and recite all the things I hate about this— Oh, hell, I'll come in and hurry you along." Taking Bree's arm, she pushed her into the bank lobby, then waited at the door while Bree cashed her check. If she got the chance to stay in Bethlehem long, she would open a checking account, but for the time being, she needed to keep all her money handy. She never knew when she might have to leave.

When they stepped out into the cold again, Margery gave a huge sigh of relief. "God, did you see the way those people looked at me? I could never stand that—everybody in town knowing everybody else, along with all their secrets. Where are you from?"

"Rochester."

"Well, no wonder Bethlehem looks good to you. My husband spent a great deal of time in Rochester. Once he even suggested we live there." Margery shuddered. "I told him I should think not! If I can't live in the city, I might as well not live at all!" Without pausing for breath, she exclaimed, "Oh, look, here's Harry's. Let's go in and have something warm to drink."

"I'd rather not—I have other places to—"

Ignoring her protests, Margery took her arm and steered her toward the door. "You chose where we stopped first. Now it's my turn, and I want to stop here. Don't worry. It'll be my treat."

It was easier to go in with her and be embarrassed

than to cause the scene it would have taken to free her arm from Margery's grip. Hoping it was both Maeve's and Harry's day off, she drew a deep breath as Margery propelled her through the door. The first voice she heard, though, was Maeve's.

"You're a stubborn old man, Harry. You'd rather beat your head against a brick wall than admit you're wrong."

"Maybe I would," the old man retorted. "If I'm ever wrong, I'll let you know."

Ducking her head, Bree headed toward the nearest empty booth. Once seated, she kept her knit cap pulled down over her hair and turned slightly to face the town square across the street. It didn't do her any good, though.

Maeve slapped two menus on the table, then said, "Why, if it isn't our friend, Bree. How are you, hon? How do you like that job at the inn?"

Her cheeks burning, she straightened on the seat, pulled off her cap, and combed her hair. "I'm fine, Maeve. And the job's fine, too."

"I hear Holly's made room for you to stay there."

"Yes, ma'am."

The waitress shifted her gaze, and the warmth and friendliness faded from her smile. "Margery. You're looking better."

"Than what?" Margery asked.

"Than the last time I saw you. Let's see, that would have been Saturday night at the dance."

Two sentences that just about knocked Margery

off her seat. Her face turned as pink as Bree's, and for a moment her mouth worked without making a sound. Maeve filled their coffee cups, murmured something about another customer, and walked away.

"That woman never did like me," Margery muttered when she recovered her voice.

With good reason, Bree thought, but she clenched her teeth to keep from saying it aloud.

After a moment, Margery waved one elegant hand as if brushing the subject away, then studied Bree thoughtfully. "You really do look familiar. Are you sure we haven't met?"

Bree nodded.

"Maybe I met your mother. Does she have ties to the city? Do you look like her?" When Bree shook her head, Margery shrugged. "Oh, well, it'll come to me. It always does."

Bree slid out of the booth. "When Maeve comes back, I'd like a cinnamon roll and a cup of hot chocolate. I'll be back."

"But where are you—"

In the nights she'd slept in the café, she had discovered that through the door marked Rest Rooms, all the way to the end of the hall and around a corner was a pay phone. She dug a few coins from her jeans pocket, dropped them in the slot, then hesitated a long moment before dialing the number.

On the sixth ring, the phone was answered by a sweet, soft, familiar voice. She wrapped her fingers tightly around the receiver, blinked back a tear, and said, "Mom? Mom, it's me, Sabrina. How are you?"

PUSHING AWAY FROM THE DESK, TOM rubbed his eyes, then swiveled his chair around to face the windows. The winter sky was dull, the color of well-used pewter, and the temperature, according to the weather report, was easing toward the single digits. Another typical winter day. A warm beach somewhere was starting to sound good. And if he could persuade a certain innkeeper to share that beach with him . . .

Behind him, the door opened, then closed. "Mr. Flynn, there's someone here to see you," his secretary said with a disapproving note in her voice. "She doesn't have an appointment, and frankly, she doesn't look like someone who'd have legitimate business with you. Shall I send her away?"

As he turned to face her, he wondered what someone with legitimate business looked like. "What is this person's name?"

"Sophy." The secretary wrinkled her nose as if the name alone supported the judgment she'd already made. "Sophy Jones."

"Send her in."

"But, Mr. Flynn—"

He gave her a look that silenced her protest, prompted her to nod and leave the room. A moment later, Sophy strolled in. Her look *was* different for the building. The long coat flapped around her ankles, and she wore clunky tennis shoes that looked far too big for her.

"In the neighborhood?" he asked dryly.

"Yeah. Thought I'd come by to see you."

He folded his arms over his chest. "How did you get past the guards?"

"I told them I had important business to discuss with Mr. Flynn."

He shook his head. "It wouldn't work."

"I made myself invisible and walked right past them."

This time he raised his eyebrows.

With a sigh and a shrug, she pulled off her knitted cap and came a few feet closer. "I sneaked in. I thought about waiting in the street for you to run me over again, but . . ."

Her choice of words made Tom flinch inside, but Sophy grinned.

Clutching her cap in one hand, she took the long way around his desk. The paintings on the wall received a thorough look, as did the oriental rugs on the floor. She seemed particularly taken with the collection of jade netsuke he'd bought on trips to Japan.

Finally she stopped on the other side of the credenza and sat on the windowsill. "How is Holly?"

Holly was beautiful, soft, warm. She was intelligent enough to carry on any conversation. When they danced, she fitted in his arms as if she'd always been there. After only a few kisses, her taste was a familiar one that he'd begun to crave. She was a better daughter than her mother deserved, and a better woman than he deserved, but he was going to marry her anyway, even if it took the rest of his life to persuade her to say yes.

"Holly is fine," he said.

"Have you asked her to marry you yet?"

"Not that it's any of your business, but yes."

"And she said . . . ?"

"Something along the lines of 'Not only no, but hell no.' "

Sophy gave him a wide-eyed look. "Good heavens, what did you say to her? Exactly what kind of proposal did you make?"

He rubbed one hand over the back of his neck, debated confiding in her, then decided there was nothing to lose. A woman's take on the subject might be helpful, and she was the only woman with whom he could remotely imagine himself discussing anything so personal. "I told her that we were a good match. We each find the other interesting. We're both in business so we understand the demands on our time. Neither of us wants a family, and she's not interested in my money. Our getting married is a perfectly reasonable, logical decision. What more could she want?"

Sophy stared at him, her expression utterly appalled. "Oh, gee, I don't know. How about, 'I love you, I need you, you make my life complete'? Marriage is a matter of the heart, not a business merger. *Do* you love her?"

He waited a moment before stonily answering, "I . . . like her."

Her features screwed into a wince. "You haven't

had much experience expressing sentiment, have you? What if you never saw her again? Would you miss her?"

He considered life without Holly. Endless evenings with women like Deborah and Cyndi. Meaningless sex. Terminable boredom. The answer was clear, but it wasn't easy to give. "Yes," he said grudgingly. "I would."

"See? That wasn't so hard. Do you feel better when you're with her? Do you enjoy being with her more than other women? When you're not together, do you think about her? Wonder what she's doing, if she's thinking of you? If she pays attention to another man, are you jealous?"

He settled on a shrug for an answer.

"Then tell her so. Don't talk about reason and logic. Tell her what you think, what you want, what you *feel*." She stifled a chuckle. "Good grief, you deserved to be turned down with a proposal like that."

Tell her what he felt . . . Not a bad idea, if he knew exactly what that was. If he had any experience at all in feeling anything, or in identifying feelings. If he was convinced he wouldn't be placing himself in a position of weakness. Any businessman worth a damn knew you couldn't negotiate effectively from a position of weakness.

"Holly's not a very sentimental person," he remarked.

"Maybe not, but she turned down your level-headed business-merger proposal. If you really want to marry her, try something a little more personal. A little more human. Does she like flowers?"

"I don't know."

"Chocolates? Jewelry? Perfume?"

He shrugged again.

"Well, find out. Give her gifts that are unbearably romantic. Let her know that she means more to you than simply closing your latest deal. Let her know you . . . like her."

Long after Sophy left, her words kept echoing in his mind. Finally that night, he picked up the phone in his home office, dialed the number, and curbed the impulse to hang up before it rang.

She answered in the voice that had fueled his fantasies and fevers. He had to swallow hard, had to force his fingers to loosen their white-knuckled grip on the receiver. "Holly, it's Tom. I, uh . . . just wanted to say, uh . . . I've missed you. . . ."

Chapter Eleven

HOLLY'S FRIDAY LUNCH ROUTINE with her female friends was in full swing by twelve o'clock. She sat between Emilie and Maggie and listened to the latest gossip, as well as watched her friends graciously tiptoe around the preceding weekend's fiascos. No one mentioned either her mother or the marriage proposal, for which she was grateful, though she wouldn't hazard a guess on how long they would avoid the subject of marriage.

Not long, it turned out, though the lead-in came from a different tack. "Kelsey, I saw Bud's car parked in front of the Winchester house twice this week," Maggie remarked.

"And I saw him at the hospital yesterday, hanging around the Information desk during Miss Agatha's shift," Melissa added.

"He's moving kind of fast, isn't he?" asked Shelley.

Holly snorted. "At their age, they have to move fast."

"Yeah, they don't have the time for a leisurely courtship like some people," Emilie replied with a sly grin.

"I'm not being courted," Holly said sternly, daring any of her friends to argue with her. Even her fiercest scowl didn't deter them.

"Of course you are," Maggie disagreed. "Tom wants to get married, and he's spending time with you to try to change your mind. Sounds like a courtship to me."

"Tom doesn't know what he wants. As soon as I get through that thick skull of his, he'll see that." Holly indulged in her most seductive of smiles. "And then *I'll* get what *I* want."

"Tom Flynn has known what he's wanted since he was sixteen," Maggie argued. "He's the most decisive, reasonable, logical man I know—after Ross, of course. And what he wants, Holly dear, is *you*."

Holly wanted to argue, wanted to say, Oh, yeah, then why had he made what must surely be the most unromantic proposal on record? Why had he spoken of things like money and reason instead of commitment, emotion, and forever?

Why hadn't he said even once that he loved her?

But she didn't say any of that, even to her best friends in the world, because . . . truthfully, she was embarrassed. It was a sure bet not one of their husbands had made such a cold, unemotional proposal. They'd talked about love, happiness, growing old together, about sharing each other's lives, about wanting no one or nothing more than they wanted their wives. Each of her friends had gotten the hearts-and-flowers routine, while she'd gotten a business proposition.

Of course, there was a very simple explanation for it. Tom didn't love her. His happiness didn't depend on spending the rest of his life with her. She couldn't make his life complete, and there were plenty of things that were more important to him than she was.

She didn't want hearts and flowers. She was way beyond all that. But something personal . . . That wasn't too much to ask, was it? Some little something that indicated she was special, not interchangeable with any other woman he could find who wasn't after his money?

"Speak of the devil," Shelley murmured, her soft tone drawing Holly from her thoughts.

She followed their gazes across the dining room to the lobby, where Tom stood amid a pile of luggage that would do *her* justice. She'd known he was coming for the weekend—he'd booked the suite during their phone conversation the night before—but he usually traveled light. One small bag was all he'd ever needed, along with his laptop computer, of course, and his briefcase. So what was up with all the rest?

"Excuse me." Holly stood, letting her napkin

fall to the floor, and went to the lobby, stopping a few feet behind him. Once Janice finished her usual welcome-to-McBride-Inn spiel, Holly cleared her throat, and Tom turned to look at her.

She didn't want hearts and flowers, but she was a sucker for butterflies and shivers and long, lazy looks from incredibly dark eyes. Her mouth went dry, her palms grew damp, and her temperature rose a few very warm degrees. She opened her mouth, and her suspicious question about all the luggage disappeared, to be replaced by a sappy, silly, "Hi. You're here."

"You sound surprised. Did you forget I was coming?"

Janice snorted indelicately, and Holly shot a warning look that her employee pretended not to see. "No, I didn't forget. I just didn't expect you until sometime this evening . . . and I certainly didn't expect all this luggage."

"I told you I was staying awhile, didn't I?"

"You said through the weekend."

"Hm. I guess I didn't specify which weekend."

Her suspicions doubled. "I guess not. Why don't you do that now?"

"Actually, I don't know. Your assistant,"—he nodded toward Janice—"and I agreed it would be best to book the suite for a month, then go from there."

A *month*? Holly tried to shriek, but her voice wouldn't work. She swallowed hard, cleared her throat, and took a few quick breaths to stave off the panic that tightened her chest. Aware of Janice watching from behind the desk and all her friends from the dining room, she clenched her jaw and forced a smile and a few words through her teeth. "Let's go someplace private and talk about this."

"There's nothing to talk about. I've already paid for the first thirty days."

"I don't like renting my rooms by the month."

He grinned, something he rarely did, and it didn't please her that it was in response to her annoyance. "You're a smart businesswoman, Holly. You like renting your rooms any way you can. Now, where's the bellman to help with the luggage?"

Instead of calling the handyman, who doubled as a bellman when he was available, Holly shouted Bree's name with enough force to make the air vibrate. It was followed by the unmistakable sound of a crash in the library. To Tom, she said, "I hope she manages to set it all on fire between here and your suite—and don't laugh. She could do it." Then she stalked away—through the kitchen, into her own apartment, out the back door, and toward the woods. She knew he was following her, but as long as he was willing to be ignored, she was perfectly happy to do the ignoring.

That lasted . . . oh, maybe three minutes. Then Tom caught up with her, grabbed her arm, and pulled her to a stop. "What are you so upset about? We agreed that I would spend some time in Bethlehem."

"Some time," she agreed, none too gently jerking free. "Not a month. Not living in my house."

"Where would you suggest I stay?"

"You have a perfectly good home in Buffalo. How about there?"

He studied her a long time as if she were something foreign to his experience. She felt foreign to herself. Why should she care that he planned to spend the next month at the inn? She should be glad. Seeing him was infinitely better than not seeing him. Being able to talk to him in person was much more satisfying than relying on a telephone. And as for seducing him . . . well, it might be difficult in person, but it was downright impossible long distance.

But a month seemed so long. So serious. So unexpected. Yes, he'd said he would spend time in town, but, after all, this was the man who'd turned down his boss's request that he move to Bethlehem with the rest of the company because he preferred the city. The man who'd persisted for months in describing her town in a sardonic voice as a little burg, who had tolerated his time there and always looked forward to returning to the city.

Until he'd gotten the crazy idea to marry her. And suddenly there he was, willing to spend an entire month there, maybe even longer. For her. Because changing her mind about marriage was damn near impossible long distance.

He truly was serious about this marriage thing. Which meant she truly had to get serious about this seduction thing.

"Do you want me to go home?" he finally asked.

She turned her back to him, filled her lungs with the pungent, woodsy scent, then exhaled loudly. "No."

"I've got to tell you, your managerial style leaves a little to be desired. I've stayed at hotels all over the world, and this is the first time the owner or manager wished for my luggage to catch fire, then ran away."

She faced him again, stepped closer, and wrapped her arms around his neck. "Is it also the first time you've been greeted like this?" Rising onto her toes, she brought her mouth into contact with his, but before she could go any further, *he* did, sliding his tongue between her lips, slipping inside her mouth, greedily, insistently stroking, exploring, tasting.

She'd been kissed countless times by countless men, but not like this. Sensations spread through her with every thud of her heart—heat and need and an ache that threatened to become unbearable. She was grateful for his hands at her waist, because without them, she thought she just might collapse at his feet, weak, dazed, needy. It was just a kiss, but oh, what a kiss. The start of a slow burn that could consume them both.

Too soon Tom ended it and caught her hands, holding them firmly between his. She hoped she didn't look as shaken as she felt—wished he didn't look so damn smug. He knew that kiss had turned her on more than any kiss should have, and he was amused by it.

She would teach him to be amused. Leaving

her hands in his, she moved seductively against him, using her sexiest, sultriest voice to suggest, "Let's go back to the inn."

"And finish this in private?" Grinning, he unplastered her body from his and pushed her away again. "Not yet. Not until the time is right."

Backing away, she folded her arms across her chest. "What's to stop me from saying the time is right, then admitting in the morning that I lied?"

"Trust me. When it's right, we'll both know." He watched her for a moment, then gestured in the direction they'd come. "Still want to go back?"

She shook her head. "You go ahead if you want. I've been inside all week. As long as I'm out here, I might as well take a walk."

"Then I might as well come with you."

She looked him over, from his well-worn leather jacket to khaki trousers to deck shoes that had probably never seen any deck. "Have you ever taken a walk?"

"Of course."

"In the woods?"

"Never."

"We could get lost," she teased.

"You've never been lost a day in your life. Go on. I'll follow."

She found the narrow trail that led to the pond and set off, considering how wrong his last words were. She'd been lost plenty of times. In fact, she was feeling lost right at that moment. Years ago she'd set a path for herself, one consisting of shallow friendships and shallower affairs, without commitment, love, or trust. In the past few years she'd found herself making real friends, but the affairs had remained meaningless. Now Tom wanted more. She'd told him there wasn't any *more,* but there he was, trying to prove her wrong. And there she was . . . hoping to be proven wrong.

She was crazy. Sex had stood her in good stead for her entire adult life. She shouldn't tamper with what worked, on the slim chance of finding something better. She should be satisfied with what she'd had. She always had been.

"Do you like flowers?"

Holly needed a moment to collect her thoughts before tackling the slope that would reveal her lake. "Yes, I like flowers," she said as if it weren't an odd question. "That's why I spend so much of the inn's profits at Melissa's Garden."

"Do you like chocolate?"

"Of course. I'm breathing, aren't I?" She started up the slope, her loafers slipping on the bare dirt. With his hand on her bottom, he gave her a boost to the top, where she stood motionless for a moment to let the peace start to seep in.

"What about jewelry?" He joined her at the top and apparently found the view quite interesting, because he certainly wasn't looking at her.

"Well, let's see . . . I'm wearing one emerald pendant, two emerald earrings, one diamond and emerald ring, and one watch. And that's just for an average day at work. Yes, I think it's safe to say I like jewelry. Why do you ask?"

"I believe it's called getting to know you, and it

was one of the requirements you put on marrying me."

She gazed from him down the hill to the water's edge. "Don't give me cause to push you in the water," she warned. "The fact that we don't know each other very well was one of the many reasons I gave for *refusing* to marry you. And we agreed not to discuss that any more, remember?"

"We didn't agree. You suggested it, and I ignored you." He slipped his arm around her waist. "And you can push me in if it'll make you feel better, but I'm taking you with me."

In need of a subject change, Holly indicated the pond with one hand. "Welcome to Holly's Lake."

"You named it after yourself?"

She elbowed him in the ribs. "My father named it for his favorite daughter."

"Who also happened to be his only daughter."

"I was also my mother's only daughter, but I wasn't her favorite, by any means. This place holds a lot of memories. I caught my first fish here, drank my first beer, and even lost my virginity right over there." She pointed to a clearing on the far shore. "I was fifteen. He was sixteen and clumsy, and the sex was a disappointment."

Tom watched her gaze at the clearing and wondered if she had a clue how vulnerable she looked. He'd never seen quite that expression on her, and it made him feel . . . inadequate, because he didn't know how to make it go away.

"I was probably twenty before I found out that

sex could be good for the girl, too. I'd already finished with the high school and college boys and had started on the grad-school boys. They knew a lot more tricks than the younger guys did."

"If it wasn't good, why did you keep doing it?"

She smiled faintly as she moved away from him. "Because the sex wasn't the point for me. What I wanted came before. Sex was just the trade-off for it."

The kissing, the holding, the affection. Her mother had been a miserable, abusive drunk; her father had been gone a lot, and dealing with his own unhappiness when he was home. Maybe they had loved her and simply hadn't shown it, or maybe they'd had no emotional energy to spare for her. Either way, she'd gone looking for affection elsewhere, and she'd found it with every boy willing to trade a few kisses and embraces for sex.

You want to go out with me, spend time with me, get to know me, she'd said, *but you don't want to have sex with me. Well, you're the first male in twenty-two years to say that.* At the time, he'd thought she was referring only to the sex part. Now he knew she meant all of it—the going out, spending time, and getting to know her.

"What about you?" she asked as she made her way to a rock near the water. There she sat down, then drew her knees to her chest and wrapped her arms around them. The defensive posture made her look even more vulnerable.

He leaned against a boulder near her. "I was

seventeen. We went to school together, and her family attended the same church my mother had." He didn't mention that he'd been in church every Sunday, too, for his first sixteen years. "She was the youngest of six daughters, and her parents, having failed to produce a son for the priesthood or to get a single nun out of the older five, were determined that she would dedicate her life to the church. She was equally determined to be the first girl in our school to have sex with every guy in the school. She succeeded, too."

"What became of her?"

"I don't know. I haven't thought of her in years. A lot of the kids I grew up with aren't around any longer. Some are dead, some are in prison. All are pretty much forgotten."

"Except you. You made a name and a few fortunes for yourself."

"I did okay."

"Did your mother have great hopes for your becoming a priest?"

"If she did, she never mentioned it. It was all she could do to get me in church once a week. I was never much interested in following other people's rules, soul searching, or doing penance."

"What were you interested in back then?"

He gazed across the water, watching ripples spread from where some creature had broken the surface, and considered all the things he'd wanted—escape, freedom, power, wealth, success. They could all be summed up in one word. "Survival."

"Me too," she agreed softly. She gave him a weak smile. "Who would ever have thought we'd have something in common?"

It was ironic. Holly, with her privileged upbringing in a storybook town and her prestigious family name, and Tom, raised poor in a hellish neighborhood, with his nothing name. For her, survival had meant feeling wanted, even if only for the length of time it took an eager young man to finish the sex act. For him, it had meant getting everything in great measure.

And they'd both succeeded—too well, in fact. She couldn't imagine a man who would want her for anything besides sex, and he couldn't find a woman who wanted him for anything besides the success.

"What's your favorite color?" he asked.

"You tell me."

He glanced at her clothes—black trousers and red sweater under a tan jacket—then remembered the dresses she'd worn each time he'd seen her in recent weeks. "Green." It flattered her in all its shades, played up the creamy tint of her skin, and highlighted the red in her auburn hair.

"What's your favorite color?" she asked.

"Green."

She grinned. "I should have guessed. The color of money."

"The color you look best in," he corrected. The green dress she'd worn to his birthday dinner. The flashy, sexy dress that Saturday night in Buffalo. The deep, dark green she'd chosen for the dance.

"Smooth answer," she teased. "What's your favorite holiday?"

"You and your holidays. Just because you never outgrew them doesn't mean other people didn't."

"What does that mean? You can't think of any to name? Let me help you. There's Christmas and Easter and the Fourth of July. That's when the town fathers blow a small fortune on fireworks in the sky. Come on, your favorite holiday," she prodded.

It was easier to think of the ones that weren't his favorites. He'd outgrown Halloween pretty quickly. Valentine's Day was just an excuse for people to expect expensive gifts. Even with a good Irish name like Flynn, St. Patrick's Day wasn't noteworthy. Christmas and Thanksgiving were family holidays that left him feeling nothing so much as alone. "Fourth of July," he said, choosing the answer by default.

"Why?"

"Because I like fireworks, and I don't mind the risk of getting burned."

She smiled seductively at his answer, but went on with her questions. "What's your favorite word?"

"Oh, come on. No one has favorite words."

She got to her feet and came to stand in front of him, hands in her pockets. "Sure they do. Think about it. What one word do you like to say? To hear? What word makes you feel good?"

Looping his arm around her waist, Tom pulled

her close, ducked his head, and murmured his answer before kissing her. "Yes."

For a moment she held herself stiff, then abruptly she melted against him, bringing her body into full contact with his. The rock behind him was hard, her body soft. The air was cold, the kiss hot. Hungry. Demanding. Greedy. Better than the last.

When he pulled away, she blinked and whispered, "Wow."

"Thank you."

"No," she said, dazedly shaking her head. "That's my favorite word. Wow." She moved away as if she didn't want to, then gave a final shake of her head to clear it. It didn't make her sound any more alert, any sharper, or any less well-kissed. "It's snowing. We'd better head back."

It was a light snow, tiny flakes that melted before they hit the ground, but Tom didn't argue with her. He followed her up the embankment, then back down again. When the trail widened, he moved to walk beside her, then slid his arm around her and tugged her closer. After a moment's resistance, she came willingly, even going so far as to put her arm around him.

But only until the inn came into sight. Then she pulled away, putting distance between them. Was she worried that someone would see them and think she was softening to him and his proposal?

He wanted to think she was, but he wouldn't bet on it yet. Sure, she'd been perfectly willing to kiss him out there, but her kissing him wasn't the problem. She'd been willing to do that practically from the day they'd met. It was all part of her goal—seduction. Which conflicted with his goal of abstinence until marriage.

Then he looked down at her—her hair glistening with melted snowflakes, her cheeks pink from the cold, and her mouth kissed free of lipstick and looking damned inviting—and amended the statement of his goal. Abstinence was fine up to a point.

The point where she said yes.

MARGERY SAT ALONE IN THE LOBBY, staring at the family portrait on the wall, and wondered why the hell Holly had chosen to display that particular photograph. It wasn't as if she hadn't had other choices. The farmhouse had been filled with portraits of dead McBrides when she and Lewis had moved in—dead, judgmental McBrides, who'd stared down at her with condemnation. For a time she had believed that they'd known how much she hated their house, their town, even, at times, their descendant.

On one of Lewis's countless trips away—his stupid, more-important-than-her trips—she'd ripped every family portrait from the walls and tossed them into boxes and corners in the attic. He hadn't even noticed for a month, and then only because she'd pointed it out to him in a fit of pique. He hadn't cared.

That had been the hardest part to bear. At some

point he'd stopped loving her, and then he'd stopped hating her. He had shown her nothing but indifference. He'd made his trips, had his affairs, ruined her life, and hadn't even cared.

Her fingers curled around the curved arms of the chair where she sat, pressing so hard that she was sure the wood's carved pattern would be visible on her fingertips. All her life she'd been blessed with passion, but too often it appeared in the form of anger, rage, helplessness, and hopelessness. She'd never felt anything in half measures.

Late this Friday evening, she felt hopeless. After last week's humiliation at the dance, she'd vowed to sober up, never again to do anything that might embarrass her daughter. She'd made it through the first few days, when she was sick as a dog with her hangover, when she was struggling with the burden of her shame, without even thinking about a drink. She'd made it through the next few days, too, but booze had been on her mind. Everything she did reminded her of drinking. Everything she ate would taste better, she was convinced, with a glass of wine, a snifter of brandy, or a good Irish beer. Awake, she craved it. Asleep, she dreamed of it.

Late this Friday evening, she'd given in to it.

She had waited until everyone was asleep and the desk clerk had gone home for the night before creeping downstairs to the kitchen. Not wanting to be greedy, she'd poured herself one watered-down drink. One, and that was all. It would satisfy her craving and still leave her as sober as a preacher.

One drink. She could handle that.

But one drink hadn't even taken the edge off her hunger. The second had done that. The third had begun to dissolve it. By the time she'd finished the fourth, she'd begun to feel normal again. The uneasiness was gone. The shakiness was disappearing, too. She was starting to feel like her old self again.

The trick was moderation. No more getting falling-down drunk. No more drinking to the point where she lost control of her tongue. No more appearing in public obviously intoxicated. She could have a few drinks—a mimosa with breakfast, wine with lunch and dinner, a cocktail or two in the evening. If that wasn't enough, then she would drink in her suite. Alone. Away from disapproving eyes. No one would find reason to complain, and Holly would have no cause to give her those looks. God, she hated those damning-her-to-hell McBride looks!

"What are you doing?"

Startled, Margery jumped, then watched her daughter emerge from the shadows of the back hallway. "You frightened me," she said, raising one hand to her chest in mock alarm. "For a moment I feared it was Millicent McBride come back to haunt me."

Holly stood utterly still, debating, Margery knew, whether to stay and talk or to flee her presence. She held her breath while waiting, then gave a tiny, inaudible sigh when her daughter moved closer. "Millicent hasn't shown herself in the last fifteen years."

"Of course not. I was gone. She never showed herself to anyone but me. Your father thought I was hallucinating. You thought I told charming tales . . . until you got older." It seemed as if it had happened in an instant. One moment her little girl had been bouncing on the bed, pleading, "Tell me about the ghost, Mama," and the next, she'd given her that haughty McBride look and asked coldly, "Drunk again, Margery?"

Holly's gaze shifted from Margery to the glass on the table beside her. Suspicion darkened her eyes, and her mouth tightened in a way that reminded Margery so much of Lewis. It created a tightness in her chest that threatened to suffocate her, that made her long for just one more taste of scotch to ease it. Instead, she smiled faintly. "It's just plain orange juice. Would you like some?" Her hand was less than steady when she offered the glass, but her gaze didn't waver as she watched Holly lift the glass, sniff, then take a sip. She'd had her scotch in the kitchen, then washed the glass well before filling it with juice. She was glad for the precautions as, with a flush, Holly returned the glass.

"Why are you sitting here looking at that picture?"

"I've been wondering why you chose to hang it. It's not exactly a portrait of a happy family."

"No, it isn't. But then, we weren't a happy family, were we?"

"And that was all my fault."

"I didn't say that."

"You didn't have to. It's what you've always thought. You never blamed your father for one thing, but me—" Catching herself, Margery dragged in a steadying breath. She'd promised herself before she'd come here that she was not going to do this. No arguments, no accusations, no laying blame. She'd done enough of that in her life.

Seeking a softer, less defensive tone, she asked, "Having trouble sleeping?"

"A bit."

"I—I like your young man."

Wariness changed to annoyance. "What made you think of him? The mention of the word sleep in connection with me? Do you just automatically assume that there's always *someone* in my bed?"

"N-no, no, not at all. It's just . . . I just assumed that he's the reason you're having trouble sleeping. Aren't men usually the reason women lose sleep?"

Holly still scowled at her, but the anger was slowly seeping from her pretty eyes and incredible mouth. Whatever problems Margery and Lewis had shared in their lives, and there had been plenty, they'd certainly created a beautiful daughter. Even without makeup in the middle of the night, she was lovely enough to make a mother's heart ache.

Even though she believed her mother didn't have a heart.

Grudgingly, Holly sat down in the opposite chair, tucking her bare feet underneath her. "Did you have a lot of sleepless nights with Daddy?"

"More than I could count." Once she'd found out about his affairs, she'd fretted every single night he'd slept someplace else. She'd wondered if he told his lovers the same sweet lies he'd once told her, if they were prettier than she, if they knew something she didn't and that was why he preferred their company to hers. When he came home, she'd always confronted him, and at first he'd sworn there was no one else. Then one day he'd stopped denying it. He'd simply given her that look, then ignored her. For the rest of their marriage.

"Why?"

Blinking, Margery looked at Holly.

"Why did you lose sleep over Daddy?"

There had been times when Margery had relished the idea of telling Holly every sordid detail. She'd threatened Lewis with it in arguments, had threatened to tell his precious little girl exactly what kind of man he was, and he'd threatened her right back with promises of divorce. He'd died before either could make good, and since then . . . A person was entitled to at least a few illusions about their parents. Since Holly had none about her mother, she should be allowed to hold on to the ones about her father.

"Living in Bethlehem, his travel schedule." Smiling weakly, she waved her hand. "Just things. You'll find out when you and your young man settle down."

"We're not getting married," Holly said through clenched teeth.

"I heard you'd said that."

"Then why didn't you believe it?"

"Because, baby girl, Tom Flynn didn't get to be one of the most powerful men in the state by taking no for an answer." Margery gave her a sidelong look. "What do you have against him?"

"Nothing."

"Then it must be the marriage part that's putting you off. Why?"

"Well, gee, let's consider that. It couldn't be because you and Daddy were so happy together. Couldn't have anything to do with the way you two fought all the time, now could it? Or the way you both got so angry and went off to lick your wounds and forgot all about me?"

She looked as if she expected an argument. Margery didn't give her one.

"You're right, we did. We were terrible parents, and we punished you for our own and each other's sins. But you're not like us, Holly. You're a lovely, intelligent, capable, generous woman. Any marriage you make will be in a different universe from ours."

Once the surprise disappeared from her face, Holly said, "That's not the only reason. I have no desire to be married. I don't need a man in my life."

"No, of course not. But they certainly come in handy from time to time."

"You mean sex. I can get that without the constriction of marriage."

"Actually," Margery said with a delicate smile, "I meant when things go wrong. When the car won't start or your tire goes flat or you turn on the heat in the middle of a blizzard and get nothing but cold air. But, dear, as long as you mentioned it, that, too. Though if you make a good choice, it won't be just sex. It'll be lovemaking, and there's a difference. Trust me."

"I'm perfectly capable of calling a mechanic or a repairman to handle those kinds of problems, and whether you call it sex or lovemaking, it's still the same act. There can't be much of a difference."

"Spoken like a woman who's never been properly loved," Margery said with a sorrowful sigh. And was that her fault, too? Had she and Lewis neglected their daughter's emotional needs so completely she'd buried them away? Because they hadn't loved her the way they should have, did she believe she was unlovable? Or had she convinced herself that she was immune to love—didn't want it, didn't need it, was never going to have it?

God help them, she and Lewis had a lot to answer for.

Rather than respond, Holly left her chair and stalked barefoot across gleaming wood floors to the doors. "Is it still snowing?"

"I don't know. I haven't looked." Margery followed her, but kept her distance. When Holly leaned against the jamb on one side of the double doors, she leaned against the other. "Oh, it is. Isn't it lovely?"

"I've never heard you say anything the least bit complimentary about this house or this town."

Margery smiled. "Snow covers a myriad of sins. Even you would find beauty in New York blanketed by snow."

"Maybe." Gazing out again, Holly casually said, "You must be missing it. When are you going back?"

Truthfully, Margery did miss it, but not the way she had before. The older she got, the more acutely she felt the emptiness in her life, regardless of where she was. The things she'd missed so terribly about the city weren't the things that, in the long run, truly mattered. If they were—if life in the city were so perfect—why did she drink to cope there, just as she had in Bethlehem? If her life was so good there, why was she so damned lonely?

"Don't worry, dear. I'll get out of your hair soon." Before Holly could feel obligated to respond graciously, she changed the subject. "I like that girl Bree. You know, she seems so familiar to me. Does her family have some connection to Bethlehem? Are they people I might have met?"

Holly gazed at her for a moment, then the wariness slowly faded. "I doubt it. As far as I know, she has no ties to the town. She just left home without much money and wound up here. But you're right. There is something familiar about her."

"One of these days I'll figure it out." Margery faked a yawn, then glanced at the grandfather clock that had tormented her every waking hour when she'd lived in the farmhouse. Now she found its steady ticking and relentless chiming of passing hours oddly comforting. "It's almost two o'clock. We'd better get to bed." She started up the stairs, then turned back. "I enjoyed talking with you tonight, Holly. Thank you."

Turning away from her daughter's puzzled, distrustful look, she held her head high and climbed the stairs to the second floor. There she let herself into her room, closed and locked the door, sat down on the bed . . . and began to cry.

Chapter Twelve

THE SNOW STOPPED DURING THE night, leaving a few inches on the ground that quickly turned to slush in the streets. Bundled against the cold, Agatha Winchester stood on the porch of the house she shared with her sister and watched the activity in the yard. Nathan Bishop was shoveling her driveway, and Brendan, his young nephew, was at work on the sidewalk. Considering that Brendan's shovel was child-sized, and he had to cope with both the tool and Ernest, his beloved stuffed bear, he was making good progress, Agatha thought, and she didn't hesitate to tell him so. With a heart-tugging grin, he thanked her, persuaded Ernest to give her a wave, then returned to work.

"Miss Agatha, come build a snowman with us," Josie, Brendan's eight-year-old sister, called. She and Alanna, the oldest of the Dalton children, had gathered a rather dirty snow-body and were starting to work on the head.

Rather than point out that there really wasn't enough snow for a proper snowman, or question the appropriateness of a woman her age building snowmen at all, Agatha went down the steps to join them. Josie met her halfway and enveloped her in a hug. "Guess what, Miss Agatha? Lannie's birthday is coming soon, and she's gonna' be twelve years old, and guess what she wants?"

"Josie!" Alanna warned, but that didn't deter her sister one bit.

"Caleb Brown!" Josie declared. "All she wants for her birthday is Caleb Brown with a great big bow on his head!"

Alanna made a grab for Josie, caught the hood of her jacket, then smashed a handful of snow on her blond curls. "Shut up, you little brat, or I'll bury you inside this snowman."

"Uncle Nathan, Lannie told me to shut up, and Aunt Emilie says we're not s'posed to say that!"

Nathan looked up from the driveway. "Girls."

It was all he said, all that was needed to make Josie roll her eyes, then brush the snow from her hair. Alanna rolled her eyes, too, then muttered, "She's such a pest."

"She's a little sister, dear. That's what she's supposed to be." Agatha gave the girl a smile. Alanna Dalton was quite possibly the prettiest girl in all of Bethlehem, not that Agatha was prejudiced, of course. Everyone knew she had a crush on Caleb

Brown, the eldest of J.D. and Kelsey's adopted children, and everyone knew her feelings were returned—everyone, it seemed, but Alanna and Caleb. They were so cute together, so innocent and sweet. Theirs well might be one of those rare childhood loves that lasted forever.

Or, she acknowledged silently, it could be a meaningless infatuation that would soon pass. But the romantic in her hoped for the former.

Most folks would laugh at the notion that a romantic lived within her. She was past seventy, an old maid. Her time for romance had come and gone. Plenty of her friends would tell her to put such foolishness out of her head.

But she was old, not dead. And if she wanted to pass her days dreaming of a certain man's attention, that was her business and no one else's. After more than fifty years without Sam, she was entitled to whatever foolishness in which she chose to indulge.

"Ready, Miss Agatha?"

Jarred from her thoughts, Agatha realized they were ready to lift the ball onto the snowman's base. She bent, slid her gloved hands underneath and listened to Alanna count.

"One, two, thr—"

"Hey, Lannie, there's Caleb," Josie teased. "Quick, go comb your hair an' check your clothes an' pretend you're not 'magining him with a great big dumb birthday bow on his head." She made loud smooching sounds, then said breathily, "Oh, Caleb! I'm so glad to see you. I've missed you so much."

"Uncle Nathan!" Alanna pleaded at the same time as he spoke her sister's name in a warning tone.

Agatha turned her attention to the vehicle pulling to the curb. The instant she saw Bud behind the wheel, she fought the girlish urge to check her own appearance. She was too old for that sort of nonsense . . . but not for the shivers that danced down her spine. She would never be too old for the giddy pleasure the mere sight of the man brought her.

The children approached first, respectfully greeting her and Nathan before joining the Dalton children. Bud acknowledged Nathan with a nod and a jocular greeting about some shoveling needed at their place, if his back held up. Then he slowly finally—brought his attention to her. "Miss Agatha," he said politely. "This cold weather has brought a bloom to your cheeks."

Feeling shy, charmed, and tongue-tied all at once, she demurely lowered her gaze. "Why, yes, I—I suppose it has. What brings you into town this fine morning?"

"I promised my grandchildren lunch in town—and my son and daughter-in-law a few hours of peace and quiet. We're having a bit of a disagreement, though. The kids want burgers and hot-dogs at Harry's, while I was envisioning something a little more refined. I understand the restaurant at the McBride Inn is very good."

"Yes, it is."

"Trey and Caleb were eager to propose a

solution, of course. They feel they're quite capable of looking out for the younger children for an hour or two. Seeing that Caleb took care of them for nearly two full months after their father's death, I'm inclined to believe them."

"I'm sure it's an excellent solution." She'd never seen a more capable child than Caleb—or Trey.

"There's just one problem." Bud removed one glove and combed his hand through his white hair. "After my wife died, I never did get the hang of eating alone in restaurants. It's difficult to enjoy good food when you're wishing for someone to talk to. So I was thinking . . . If you don't have plans . . . and you wouldn't mind . . ." Getting a bit of a bloom in his own cheeks, he took a deep breath, then rushed the words: "Would you do me the honor of having lunch with me, Agatha?"

Slowly she smiled. She felt as if the sun had come out on a dreary day, or an unexpected hot spell had driven winter's chill away. "It would be my pleasure, Bud," she said. And she truly meant it.

WHAT DO YOU NORMALLY DO WITH your free time?"

Holly regarded Tom through the steam rising from the china cup she held carefully with both hands. "What free time?"

"You get weekends off."

"Well, I'm spending this one answering questions from you. My last weekend off, I went to Buffalo, where you were much less inquisitive."

"That was before you turned down my proposal. Before you insisted we get to know each other first."

"I did not—" Seeing his grin, she swallowed her protest and settled on a sigh instead. "You know, most couples get to know each other by simply *knowing* each other. You find out that I like to shop by spending time following me in and out of stores. I find out that you like action movies by getting dragged to every one that comes out."

"I don't like action movies."

"It was just an example."

"But a bad one. Don't you know anything you could use as a good example?"

"All right." She studied him for a moment longer, decided she liked the view better without the steam, and lowered her cup to the table. "I find out that you had a difficult upbringing by your reluctance to talk about it."

True to her statement, he said nothing.

"The point is, people don't usually get to know each other by playing Twenty Questions."

"Couples."

She blinked. "What?"

"This time you said people. Earlier you said couples."

"No, I didn—" Scowling, she said, "Well, I didn't mean anything by it."

"Come on, Holly, you admitted we were a couple. 'Couples' are totally different from 'people.' Couples are romantically involved. People are just . . . people."

She sat back, folded her napkin neatly, and laid it on the table. "Apparently, I'm spending my free time this weekend listening to nonsense."

"Everyone in town thinks we're a couple." He gestured around the dining room. "Did you see their faces when we walked in together?"

"They wouldn't think a thing, if you would give up this ridiculous idea of our getting married."

He stared at her, his rugged features unreadable. "I want to marry you. I like being with you. When we're not together, I think about you. I wonder what you're doing, who you're with, if you ever think about me. I want you, Holly. What's so ridiculous about that?"

The delivery was stilted, the words certainly words she'd never expected to hear from him. But then she'd never expected a marriage proposal from him, had she? Even so, there was a part of her that would find it incredibly easy to believe his little speech. A part of her that *wanted* to believe it, that was tempted to throw caution, good sense, and intelligence to the wind, to let him tell her his lies, to let herself believe. Thankfully, her rational side was stronger.

"What *isn't* ridiculous about it?" she asked coolly. "It's all part of a game to you, Tom. Go into business. Check. Conquer the local business world. Check. Conquer the global business world. Check. Amass more money and power than you could possibly ever need. Check. What sort of challenge is left? Gee, find a wife. You don't have a clue what being married is about. You don't have a sentimental bone in your body, you don't give a damn about anything but yourself, your wealth, and your power, and you for damn sure don't have a heart, but what the hell. Get married anyway. Great. Wonderful. But leave me out of it."

His expression didn't change even fractionally, but somehow his eyes seemed darker, colder. The set of his jaw was harder. He sat there, motionless, looking at her. Just looking. For a moment she thought he might get up and walk away, or unleash the coldly devastating anger he was famous for and leave her in shreds on the dining-room floor.

She *didn't* think he might very slowly, very coolly, smile and softly say, in a tone sharp enough to cut, "And here I thought you didn't know me at all."

His sarcasm pricked. It made her face flush, and her gaze lower to the table. "I'm sorry. I shouldn't have said any of that."

"Why not? It's true. I don't have a clue what being married is like. Where I grew up, the only married people were women who had been abandoned by their husbands. A lot of the women there, like my mother, had never been married. I've never lived with a woman, never shared any part of my life with one. I have certain expectations of marriage, I admit, but I have no idea whether they're at all realistic."

"What expectations?"

He studied her for a moment, as if debating

whether to trust her. Then he shook his head and changed the subject. "What do you do on a Saturday afternoon after lunch?"

His conclusion that she couldn't be trusted stung. She felt as if she'd been offered something important, then lost it because of her bad behavior. Five minutes ago, she hadn't even known she wanted to know. Now she wanted it badly. "I give no peace to people who refuse to answer my questions," she teased gently. "Since I'm the one you have these expectations of, don't you think you should tell me what they are? Maybe they'll make it seem . . ." She was about to say "less ridiculous." Instead, she substituted, "More reasonable."

Before he could answer, or refuse to, two departing lunch guests interrupted. "Holly, Mr. Flynn," Miss Agatha said cheerily. "I do hope we're not intruding."

Holly forced an extra dose of friendliness into her smile. "Not at all, Miss Agatha, Bud. Did you enjoy your meal?"

"Oh, it was wonderful, as always. You might have heard the compliments flowing if you hadn't been lost in your own little world with your beau. You two make a lovely couple."

Under the table, Tom nudged her foot with his, and he lifted one brow in an I-told-you-so way. She kicked him and smiled sunnily. "That's one of the advantages of being beautiful," she said in a carelessly vain voice. "No matter which man you catch me with, we're always a lovely couple."

"Have you set a date yet?" Bud asked.

"We're not get—"

Tom grasped her hand in what appeared to be an affectionate gesture. Instead, it cut off the blood flow to her fingertips. "Holly wants to do it right away, but I think we should take the time to plan a proper wedding. After all, we're only going to do this once. There's also the problem of where to live. Her apartment's much too small for the two of us, so I thought we should build a house. Not far from here, of course. Perhaps beside her lake."

Indignance fled, and Holly stared at him. She was vaguely aware of Agatha's and Bud's voices and of their leaving, but she couldn't pull her attention from Tom long enough to say goodbye. The instant they'd turned the corner into the lobby, she demanded, "Who told you that?"

"What?"

"That I always wanted to build a house out there."

He shrugged as if it didn't matter. "No one told me, but it's a good location. It's close enough to the inn that you'd be able to keep an eye on things, and yet maintain your privacy at home. The site is basically cleared, it has easy access, and—Why are you looking at me like that?"

It wasn't a big deal, she told herself. So what if, out of the blue, he had picked the one place she would have chosen? It didn't mean a thing. He didn't have any insight into her. They weren't in sync with each other in any way.

In spite of the breath she drew, she sounded a bit

shaky when she asked, "Is that an occupational hazard for you? I'm kissing you, and you're noticing ways to benefit from my property?"

He relaxed his hold on her hand, eased her fingers flat, and lifted her palm to his mouth for a lazy, innocent, intimate kiss. "For the record, *I* was kissing *you*. And I wasn't noticing anything except how good it felt."

She thought about freeing her hand from his, but if she did, he couldn't repeat that hot, damp kiss and would have to stop rubbing the pad of his thumb across her wrist. "You—" She cleared her throat. "You shouldn't have told Miss Agatha and Bud that I want to get married right away."

"I didn't. I said you wanted to 'do it' right away, and you do."

"But they thought—"

"Who cares what they thought?" He didn't kiss her hand again but clasped it firmly between both of his. It was amazing how his warm touch could raise goose bumps beneath her sweater and send a delicious shiver down her spine. "You never did tell me what you do on Saturday afternoons."

And he had never told her his expectations of marriage. But she let that slide for the moment. "How about watching a movie in my apartment?"

"All right."

"Damn. If I'd known you were going to be so agreeable, I would have suggested an afternoon of mad, wild passion."

"Not until the time is right, darlin'." Standing,

he kept her hand in his and pulled her to her feet. She resisted being tugged around the table long enough to ask one reluctant question.

"What if the time is never right, Tom?"

He gave her a long, intense look that hinted at regret deeper than she'd suspected he could feel, and he quietly replied, "Then that would be my great loss."

The words knocked her levelheaded, never-a-sucker-for-a-pretty-line feet right out from under her. He would consider losing her a great loss? Not a relief, not inconsequential, but a *loss*? No man in her life had ever thought such a thing, much less said it aloud. "Wow."

He smiled faintly. "Your favorite word?"

"No. I'm impressed. I never figured I'd be a great anything to you besides a headache."

"As I told you, you sell yourself cheap. You've got a lot more to offer a man than just pleasure and pain. Someday you'll realize that." He started toward the lobby, pulling her along behind. "Come on. Let's catch a movie."

THE AFTERNOON REMAINED VIVID IN Tom's mind. On Tuesday he could still feel the totally unexpected stab of pain at Holly's words after lunch: *You don't have a sentimental bone in your body, you don't give a damn about anything but yourself, your wealth, and your power, and you for damn sure don't have a heart. . . .* The fainter ache at her surprise that he would regret losing her. The incredible sense of satisfaction when the afternoon was over.

They'd done nothing—just watched movies, eaten chocolate, and talked very little. She'd pulled the shades, turned off the lights, and sprawled on the couch with him. At some point in the second movie, he'd fallen asleep, only to awaken to a blank screen in a dark room with her head tucked under his chin. There'd been no phone calls, no pages, no faxes, no interruptions whatsoever. He couldn't recall the last afternoon he'd wasted with such laziness.

Or accomplished so much. He'd watched movies and eaten junk food. He'd held Holly. Dozed off beside her. Kissed her awake. Endured her talented caresses in those moments before she awoke enough to understand that he really meant no. He'd spent the hours the way every man he knew might have spent them. Doing normal things as if he were in a normal relationship.

But how normal could it ever be when she believed he didn't give a damn about anyone but himself? And after spending much of his life not caring about anyone else, how could he convince her that now he did? She had said couples learned by being and doing things together, by observing and experiencing. But pair her insecurities with his inadequacies, and it would take a lifetime for him to make her understand.

"So we've decided to rebuild the Alabama factory

at the North Pole, next to Toyland, so shopping for the baby will be easier."

As Ross's words filtered through his thoughts, Tom slowly blinked, then looked around. He was sitting in the conference room one floor below his office, where he had apparently zoned out halfway through a meeting. Water glasses and coffee cups were scattered along the length of the table, chairs pushed back haphazardly, and everyone else was gone except his boss, who sat across the table from him. "Huh?"

Ross laughed. "Thank you. That's the most profound statement you've made this afternoon. Wish you could have made it to the meeting. Things went pretty well. I'd ask where you were, but I've got a pretty good idea. How's Holly?"

"Stubborn."

"Most good businesspeople are. I hear you two are building a house."

That focused Tom's attention more fully. "We're not . . . I just said that . . ."

"The communication network in this town is amazing. However, a house isn't a bad idea. Her apartment's fairly small. If you choose an architect now, they should be ready to break ground by spring."

Tom scowled at him. "You think she's going to marry me? Because I have zero desire to live here if she turns me down."

"She's already turned you down. You mean if she does it in a way that you have to accept." Ross curbed his grin. "I don't know what she'll do. My first impulse is to believe she'll say no and mean it. But people can surprise you. You, for example. I never imagined that you would ever want to get married, and certainly not to her."

"Why wouldn't I want to get married? Everyone does it. Am I so different?"

Looking uncomfortable, Ross shifted in his chair. "It's just . . ."

"The coldhearted-snake thing. The unfeeling bastard. The shark."

"No," Ross said sharply. "It's not that. You can't be as tough as you are in business and not get called names. Hell, you can't be a lawyer without getting called a name or two. It's about your job, not you."

Except that every woman he'd ever had an affair with had called him bastard at one time or another, and the woman he wanted to marry believed he didn't give a damn about anyone, least of all her. That made it about him.

"Where does it stand now?" Ross asked.

"She's still saying no. So am I."

Ross looked surprised. "You mean, you're not—you haven't—sweet hell, everyone sleeps with Hol—" Abruptly he broke off and swallowed. "I'm sorry. I shouldn't have said that."

"Have you?" The question came out colder than Tom meant it to be, not because he was suspicious or angry but because he made it a point to not pry into people's lives. Ross's personal business was his business. But for reasons he couldn't begin to understand—reasons that felt amazingly the way he thought jealousy and possessiveness would feel—he needed to know.

"No. I'll never give Maggie reason to leave me again. The breakup of our marriage, and putting it back together again, was the toughest thing either of us had ever been through. Trust me. We'll never go through it again."

Tom did trust him. Otherwise, they wouldn't have been having this conversation. Still, he hadn't discussed his sex life with another man since he was fifteen, and he hadn't had one then. Just comparisons with his buddies of how far they'd gotten and how much farther they had to go. "Look, I know Holly's history, and she's well aware of mine. Given that, it would have been normal for us to fall into bed the day we met, but we didn't. We haven't. We're . . . waiting."

"For what?" Ross asked. "Until you're married?"

"Until she realizes it's not about sex."

As he stood up, Ross gave a shake of his head. "I'm . . . impressed. After all those years of my knowing exactly what to expect from you, now you're surprising me every day. You're going back to Buffalo tonight?"

"In the morning. I've got a meeting tomorrow afternoon with the lawyers from the shipping company. I'll be back Friday night unless something comes up."

"Have a good trip. Be careful."

Tom stayed where he was long after Ross left.

When he did finally leave the conference room, it wasn't to return to work. He walked upstairs, got his briefcase and overcoat, and told the secretary he was leaving.

"But it's only three o'clock," she protested.

He fixed a disapproving look on her. "I can leave early. Ross won't mind."

"Oh, that's not what I meant, Mr. Flynn! It's just that I've never seen you leave early."

"Things change. I'll be at the inn until morning, and then in Buffalo until late Friday."

"Have a good trip. And congratulations on your upcoming marriage. Ms. McBride is a lovely young woman."

"Yes, she is." He was beginning to understand how tired Holly was of telling everyone that they weren't getting married. Of course, there was an easy solution, as he told her twenty minutes later.

"And what would that be?" she asked dryly.

"Say yes."

"Ah, your favorite word."

" 'Yes' is full of possibilities. 'No' takes them all away. How could I not like it more?"

They were walking through the woods on their way to Holly's Lake. He'd suggested it as soon as he'd arrived at the inn and she'd agreed, all the while grumbling about having to change the gorgeous blue dress that was to die for for trousers and hiking boots. He wondered if she had any idea that it wasn't the dress that was to die for, but *her.* She looked damned good no matter what she wore.

That's the sort of thing you should be telling her, a soft voice that sounded remarkably like Sophy's whispered in his mind. Just what he needed—Sophy dispensing advice to the lovelorn inside his head. That was what he got for confiding in a twenty-something girl.

They'd reached the slope where the trail narrowed. Holly scrambled up first, then bent to retie one boot. When she straightened, she turned to look down at him. "Aren't you coming?"

"I was admiring the view."

"What view? All you can see is dirt and a few trees and . . . Oh. Oh, yes, I look so lovely in these clothes."

It took him less than a moment to reach the top and stand beside her. "It's not the clothes that make you lovely, Holly. You're beautiful no matter what you're wearing."

For a long time she was silent, simply looking at him. Then she slipped her hand into his, murmured a quiet thanks, and said, "Okay, we're here. Now tell me why."

He started toward the clearing on the distant shore, pulling her along. When they reached it, he turned in a slow circle. It really was a good building site. With the water on one side and woods all around, they could be in the middle of nowhere. In reality, he would guess they were only a quarter mile from the houses that marked the edge of town. "What's your favorite architectural style?"

"Oh, so that's why you're holding on to me. So I can't walk away from stupid conversations." She tried to free her hand, but he held it tighter, then caught her other hand, too.

"What's stupid about it, Holly? You want a house here. So do I. If we get started on it now, we'll be ready to break ground as soon as it gets warmer."

"That's what's stupid. You can't have a house on my property. You can't just move in with me."

"I can if you'll marry me."

"No."

"Come on, everyone expects you to say no. Surprise them for once."

"If you'd kept your mouth shut, no one would expect anything because they wouldn't know anything!" She jerked loose, walked away a half-dozen feet, then turned back. "Why in hell would *you* want a house *here*?"

"Answer my question first."

"Greek revival."

The image of a huge white house with massive columns refused to form, and he didn't waste time trying to force it, because he knew she wasn't serious. Instead, he simply waited for her real answer.

After taking an unnecessary look around, she grudgingly said, "Log cabin. *Elegant* log cabin."

Wood, lots of soaring angles, glass, open to the woods, the water, and the sunlight. Peaceful, relaxing, *home*. That was better.

"Now answer my question. Why do you want a house here?"

He'd given her all the logical reasons on Saturday, and they hadn't impressed her. This time he opted for simple truth. "Because you would be here. Because I'd like to live with you here where you caught your first fish and drank your first beer."

"And slept with the first of many, many men," she said coldly.

"Yeah," he agreed. "I'd like to live with you here where you slept with your first man . . . knowing that I would be your last."

She stared at him a long time before turning away, but not before he saw what looked like the gleam of a tear in her eye. "This is crazy," she muttered, covering her face with both hands, muffling her words. "I don't want to get married. Even if I did, men don't marry women like me."

"Why not?"

"Because I'm easy," she said with a harsh laugh. "I give them what they want without demanding a commitment first, and then they go away. If you would forget this whole marriage idea and just sleep with me, then you'd— Hell, you would forget this whole marriage idea."

Tom shoved his hands in his pockets to resist the temptation to give her a shake or two. "You think a couple of good orgasms is all it would take?" He smiled thinly. "I don't know if you're underestimating me or overestimating yourself. Considering what I've learned about you, I suspect it's the latter."

Her smile was equally thin and much more dangerous. "You think I can't make you change your mind about marrying me? Because—take my word for it—you'd be wrong. And just for the record, darlin', it wouldn't be merely 'a couple of good orgasms.' I'd make you forget your name."

"Maybe. But I wouldn't forget yours."

She looked stunned, panicked, and just a little bit . . . He wasn't sure what. Was it wistfulness that turned her hazel eyes shimmery? Or wishful thinking on his part?

Once again she turned to walk away. Once again she came back. "If I decide to build a house, it will be *my* decision. My site. My plans. My house. The only say you'll have in the matter is if I choose to invite you over sometime. Now, I've got things to do. I'm going back to the inn. If you want to waste your time out here, go right ahead. I'm sure you can find your way back."

His first impulse was to let her go. It would be dark soon, and he wasn't so sure he could find his way back, but he could certainly find his way somewhere. But being with an angry Holly, he was quickly learning, was better than being alone, so he started after her, quickly catching up.

This goal was proving much harder than he'd expected. He should have realized it before. All his other goals had dealt with obtaining things—money, status, property. Obtaining a person wasn't nearly as easy, and obtaining this person . . .

It would help if he were a different person. Someone like Nathan Bishop, described a lot as an all-around nice guy. Or Alex Thomas, the least snakelike of all the lawyers he knew. Like Ross, who'd been normal before he'd struck it rich and had never forgotten it. Or maybe someone like Holly's good friend J.D. As a psychiatrist, maybe he had some insight into Holly that Tom was lacking. Surely he knew ways to undo the damage her parents and years of meaningless affairs had done.

But Tom wasn't anyone else, and didn't want to be. He just wished he understood people better. Wished he were better with words, with feelings. Wished he were persuasive enough to change the way Holly saw herself, resourceful enough to change the way she saw him.

He wished he'd known how impossible this goal would turn out to be. He still might have chosen to pursue it, but at least he would have been prepared for the very real possibility of failure. And if he failed this time, there was no doubt the next time he would succeed.

Because if he couldn't marry Holly, then it wouldn't matter who he did marry.

THE SOUND OF THE GRANDFATHER clock marking midnight was so faint that Bree, in her room at the back of the house, might have thought she'd imagined it if she hadn't lain there in bed, watching the hands on her alarm clock. She'd gone to bed two hours ago, dozed a bit, and now was wide awake again.

Things had been a little awkward around the inn that evening. Tom Flynn had moved up his scheduled trip to Buffalo by about fourteen hours, and after he had gone, Holly had gotten all moody and irritable. Margery was drinking openly again—just one drink with dinner—and the sight had pushed Holly from being angry with Tom to being angry with the world. After nearly breaking a delicate plate and spilling half a bottle of expensive wine in the dining room, Bree had retreated to her room before doing any serious damage. She didn't want to lose her job just because the boss had argued with her boyfriend.

Now everything was quiet. Their only guests were somber businessmen, all there for meetings at McKinney Industries. The kitchen staff had gone home several hours ago, and she'd heard Holly pass her door earlier, too.

Deciding she wasn't likely to fall asleep anytime soon, Bree got up, pulled on her robe, and headed for the kitchen. The pastry chef seemed to like her when he wasn't busy being petulant over one thing or another, and that evening he'd set aside one of his special desserts for her. She would have just a taste of chocolate with raspberry sauce and whipped cream, then find a book or magazine to read until she could sleep again.

A few lights burned in the kitchen, showing long gleaming counters, racks of scrubbed pots . . . and Holly. She too was dressed for bed, and her auburn hair, always so perfect during the day, looked as if it hadn't seen a comb in months. An empty dessert plate with traces of raspberry sauce sat on the table, along with a dozen sheets of paper. Clutching a pencil in one hand, she was bent over yet another sheet.

Bree was hesitating in the doorway, considering returning to her room, when Holly spoke without looking up. "Come on in. Get whatever you wanted."

With a deep breath, Bree found the dessert in the refrigerator, got a fork, and sat down across from Holly. "Hav-having trouble sleeping?" she ventured.

"No. I enjoy being up in the middle of the night when my work day starts around six."

Properly chastened, Bree took a few bites before curiosity got the best of her. "What are you drawing?"

Holly added one last line, dropped the pencil, and slid the paper toward her. It was a fairly good drawing of a lake with trees all around and a house in the foreground. It was built from logs, but there was nothing at all primitive about it. The lines were simple, elegant, with sharp angles and soaring peaks. Other sketches showed different views of the same house. Bree liked the back view best, where the deck extended ten feet over the water. "Is this the house you and Mr. Flynn are building?"

Sliding both hands through her hair, Holly said through gritted teeth, "We are *not* building a house. We're not building anything. And we're *not* getting married!"

So the argument, and Tom's leaving earlier than he'd planned, had been more serious than Bree realized. "You called off the engagement?"

"We were never engaged! He asked me to marry him. I told him no. He didn't listen."

Bree figured her boss was pretty close to taking off her head, but she swallowed hard and pushed on anyway. "Why don't you want to marry him? He seems—he seems to really care for you."

Holly's response was a snort, followed by a curt question. "How old are you?"

"T-twenty-two."

"Twenty-two. Ever been married?"

Bree shook her head.

"Then spare me the advice. Grow up. Live a little. Have a few relationships before you presume to advise me on my affairs."

Knowing she should keep her mouth shut—should take her dessert and flee to her bedroom—Bree hesitantly pointed out, "From what I hear, you do fine with your affairs. It's just the relationships that are impossible."

For a moment they were surrounded by utter silence. The refrigerator, the furnace, the wind dancing wildly through bare branches outside—all went silent. Even her own heart seemed to stop beating for a moment.

Then Holly slowly, regally, stood up and glared coldly down her nose. "Perhaps I didn't make myself clear enough. Shut up. Mind your own business. Don't speak to me."

This time she made it almost to the door before Bree screwed up her courage again. She spoke quickly, hurling the words across the space, and prepared to take cover. "If you really, truly don't want to marry him, why are you so upset about arguing with him? Why do you care so much that he left early?"

Holly stood frozen. An eternity passed before she slowly turned. With her hair standing on end and the anger radiating from her eyes, she looked like the wicked witch in some twisted children's storybook. "Who are you?" she demanded. "Why have you come here to torment me at the same time Tom has chosen to do so?"

"I'm not tormenting you."

"Oh yes you are. Trust me."

"I'm just curious about people and why they do things. When I was going to college, I thought I might be a psychologist someday. People interest me." It wasn't entirely a lie. She had taken one semester of college courses before deciding she couldn't handle work and study at the same time, and she'd aced the one psych course she'd taken. She would have taken more if she'd had the chance.

"Why did you quit school?"

"Money. The college wanted it. I didn't have it." She shrugged. "It was okay. I mostly wanted to go because it had been important to my dad. But he didn't prepare for it before he died." She shrugged again. "He thought he had time. He didn't intend to die so young."

"They never do." Holly came back, sat down again. She glanced at the sketches, then gathered them in a neat stack. "I was about to graduate from college when my father died. It was like I was a little kid again, awakened in the middle of the night by a nightmare. Only this time he wasn't there to hold me. I thought he would always be there. Even though I was grown and out of the house, I truly couldn't imagine that one day he might be gone."

The nightmarish feeling was one Bree remembered well. The day her father had died, she had gone home from school to find her mother sobbing brokenheartedly. Bree had questioned her and gotten no answers. Growing more frightened, she'd dissolved into tears herself before Allison had finally choked out, "Your father's dead."

Across the table, Holly dragged her hands through her hair again. "I—I'm sorry. I swear, I'm not normally short-tempered. But that man . . ."

For a moment, Bree concentrated on her dessert. After the last bite, she licked the fork clean, then said, "He's awfully handsome."

Holly grinned unexpectedly. "Yes, he is."

"Nice body, too."

"Uh-huh."

"Great mouth. Looks like a great kisser."

"The best." There was more than a little dreamy satisfaction in Holly's sigh.

It made Bree smile. "Of course, he's closer to my mother's age than mine."

"Gee, thanks for reminding me that you're a mere child." Holly gathered her papers and stood up once more. "Good night, Bree."

"Night." She sat alone at the table for a while,

drawing patterns with the fork in the sauce that remained in her dish. When finally a yawn screwed up her face, she put her dishes in the sink and headed back to bed. This time she went right off to sleep.

Chapter Thirteen

NOT SINCE HER FATHER'S DEATH had Holly gotten close enough to any man to miss him when he was gone, but by Friday evening she couldn't deny she missed Tom. She'd picked up the phone a half-dozen times to call him, had even gone so far as to call Ross and get his cell phone number, but something had stopped her. Pride? Common sense? One last-ditch effort at self-protection? He would be back. He *had* to come back, and when he did, she would . . .

Greet him coolly as she always had before his birthday? Pretend the last few weeks hadn't happened? Apologize?

She didn't have a clue. But she would find out soon. It was eight o'clock, and according to Maggie, Tom was due back sometime after eight. She had a bottle of wine and two glasses in the library. The lights were turned low, a fire crackled in the fireplace, and her favorite CD was on the stereo. The scene was set for seduction—or romance. She didn't care which one.

Provided he was even speaking to her, she thought as she paced to the west window. He hadn't said one word to her since his last comment at the pond on Tuesday. I'd make you forget your name, she'd bragged to him, and he had quietly responded:

Maybe. But I wouldn't forget yours.

Sometimes it seemed as if she'd been forgotten by everyone who mattered in her life. Her parents. Her boyfriends. She had wonderful friends, but there was no doubt she was less important in their lives than they were in hers. They all had husbands and families, and all of them but Melissa had or were having babies. That didn't change the way they felt about her. It was just that their priorities were different.

It was just that *she* was different.

She'd always been different. When she'd first realized it, back when she was six or seven years old, she'd tried to hide it. She'd pretended her life and family were as normal as everyone else's. Later, when she'd discovered eager adolescent boys and sex, she'd flaunted her differences. She'd played up her sexuality, used it and abused it, figuring that if she was open and up front, if she had no secrets, no one could hurt her.

Maybe it was time now to be normal.

"I would ask if you missed me, but I'm not sure my ego could take the answer."

Startled, she whirled around to find Tom standing in the doorway. His overcoat was folded over one arm, his briefcase gripped in one hand, and his dark hair sported the finger-combed look. He looked handsome and tired and . . . Hell, purely incredible.

She summoned a cool smile but got one that was quavery. "I didn't hear you come in."

"You were lost in thought."

"Probably. How was Buffalo?"

He took a few steps into the room and laid his briefcase and coat on a chair. "Busy. McKinney Industries now owns majority interest in Transglobal Shipping."

"Congratulations."

"We're rebuilding our Alabama factory. Construction starts as soon as the debris is cleared from the site."

"I'm sure your Alabama town is relieved."

"I'm sure they are. And I hired another assistant to help run the Buffalo office when I'm here."

"Is she incredibly beautiful?"

He looked genuinely blank. "I didn't notice."

Holly's smile blossomed as she started across the room. "Good answer. Would you like a glass of wine?"

"Yes, please."

She crossed to the tray on the table and poured wine. As she picked up the glasses, Tom reached from behind and laid a box on the tray. She handed him a glass, then sipped from hers as she studied the box. It was wrapped in heavy navy-blue paper and secured around the middle with translucent silver ribbon and a silver foil sticker. "What is this?"

He moved to the opposite side of the table. There he met her gaze, but he didn't answer. Clearly, he wanted her to open it without a lot of questions.

The box was the right size for jewelry. Ross McKinney had been big on giving jewelry, too. If she described the wrapping and the sticker to Maggie, no doubt she'd be able to tell her which very exclusive Buffalo store it had come from and just how serious such a gift was.

"It's too late for Christmas, and too early for my birthday. Valentine's Day is already past, and we don't have any anniversaries to celebrate. . . . What's the occasion?"

"No occasion."

Finally she traded her glass for the box. One fingernail under the ribbon loosened the foil seal, and the ribbon curled away, leaving the paper to unfold slowly an inch or two. The box inside was dark green, and nestled on its green velvet lining was a stunning, dazzling, eye-popping necklace. Five rows of diamonds stretched from one end of the clasp to the other, each stone perfectly rounded, the even rows offset from the others by half a stone. It was a magnificent piece.

Holly swallowed hard as she lifted it from the velvet and let it dangle across her palm. Even in the dim room, the gems twinkled and sparkled like stars in the darkest sky. They captured all the light in the room and reflected it back brighter, warmer. She cleared her throat. "Oh, Tom, it's beautiful."

Some tension that she hadn't been aware of drained from him. Had he actually worried that she wouldn't like it? What woman wouldn't think it was fabulous?

Setting his drink aside, he reached for the necklace. "Let me put it on—"

She drew back. Part of her wanted to let him do it, if for no other reason than to feel his body warm behind hers, his fingers brushing her skin, his breath gently stirring her hair. The part of her that loved jewelry wanted to let him just to see how such a fabulous piece would look on her. But the part of her in charge of keeping the rest of her together refused. "I—I can't accept this, Tom."

The tension returned, underlaid by disappointment and confusion. "Why not?"

"It's too much."

"Too much what? Too dressy? Too showy?"

"Too extravagant. Too much money."

Clearly, her answer didn't enlighten him. Was he truly not aware of the sorts of gifts their relationship allowed versus the relationship that would justify a gift like this? Probably. The women he'd favored before her had been interested in his money and had welcomed, if not demanded, such amazing gifts.

"But it wasn't that much. And you said you liked

jewelry. Would you prefer emeralds? Rubies? Sapphires?"

She supposed it *wasn't* that much with an income like his, but for the rest of the world, herself included, it was too much. "No, the diamonds are beautiful. They're incredible. But, Tom, we don't have that kind of relationship." Carefully she tugged the necklace from his loose grip and returned it to the box. She closed the box with a snap and pressed it into his hands. "This is the kind of gift you give someone special. Someone you have a serious relationship with."

He pressed the box back into her hands, then clasped his hands around hers so she couldn't let it go. "Then it belongs to you."

It was a roundabout way of saying she was special, but she appreciated it all the same. "Thank you for the sentiment," she said over the lump in her throat. "But I can't accept it."

"I want to marry you. How much more serious can things get?"

She forced a smile even though she felt more like crying. "But I don't want to marry you," she said gently, and for the first time, it felt like less than the honest truth. "I don't want to marry anyone."

"Why not?" he demanded.

"I told you the other day—"

"That you're easy. So what? I've been told I'm difficult. It'll balance out."

Holly forced her hands free, forced the jewelry box back into his hands. "Please don't do this. I don't want to fight with you. I—I—" She smiled ruefully. "I've waited too long for you to come back."

He stood motionless for a very long time, his head tilted to one side, studying her as if she were alien to his experience. After a time, he blinked, gave an impatient shake of his head, and tossed the box on top of his overcoat. "I can't figure you out."

"Join the crowd," she said with a smile that was unsteady.

"I've given other women jewelry, the more extravagant, the better."

"But I'm not other women. I'm certainly not like *your* other women." She sipped her wine, then returned it to the table. "Dance with me."

He took her into his arms without hesitation, and Holly rested her head on his shoulder, feeling the tension drain from her neck and shoulders. For the first time all week she felt peaceful, satisfied. All the world faded away, leaving just the two of them, the music, the comfort. She could stay alone with him like this forever, with no need of or concern for the inn, her guests, her friends, her mother. Just Tom and this closeness. That was all she wanted.

They were well into the fourth song when he quietly spoke. "If I can't give you diamonds, what *can* I give you?"

Eyes closed, she hid her smile in his suit coat. He was one of the wealthiest, most powerful men in the country, and he truly didn't understand why she couldn't accept the necklace, truly didn't have a clue as to what kind of gift would be appropriate. "Flowers," she decided.

"What kind?"

"Roses. In any color. And orchids. I love orchids. Or chocolate would be appropriate."

"What kind do you prefer?"

"Anything from Hershey's Kisses to Godiva to the most incredible champagne truffles from a little shop on Madison Avenue. A book would be nice, or a CD." Anticipating his next question, she went on. "Anything with a happy ending and anything we can dance to." Then, lifting her head, she opened her eyes to find him watching her. "You," she whispered. "That would be most appropriate."

"Me?"

"All those women you've given extravagant jewelry to . . . You made love to them before giving them the gifts, right?"

"We had sex," he agreed guardedly.

Interesting that he would make that distinction. He'd told her he wasn't sentimental, and yet he wanted to make it clear that his relationships with Deborah and the others were purely physical. As opposed to the relationship he had with her, which was purely confusing. And sweet. Frustrating. Pleasing. Frightening. "So have sex with me, and maybe I'll consider keeping the necklace." She grinned wickedly. "At the very least, I'll wear it and nothing else while we're having sex."

For a moment he cradled her hips to his, rubbing the beginning swell of his arousal against her, but she didn't believe for an instant that his answer was going to be yes. Considering that it was his favorite word, he certainly didn't use it often.

"I'll make love to you," he replied evenly, "when the time is right."

"But only you get to decide when that is."

He gazed down at her for a long while before softly disagreeing. "No, darlin', only *you* get to make that decision."

And what went into making that decision? She had to admit they had a serious relationship. She had to admit that she wanted more than just sex, that she wanted *him,* in her life as well as in her bed. She had to admit she cared for him. She had to open herself to the possibilities. To commitment. To marriage. To getting her heart broken.

She wasn't ready for that. No matter how much she wanted an affair with him, she didn't want it enough—didn't want *him* enough—to lay her heart on the line . . . did she?

"You're asking for the impossible, Tom."

"Nothing's impossible. I'm living proof of that."

She couldn't argue with him. And it gave her an odd feeling in her chest to think she would be his first failure.

"Sex doesn't even mean anything to you," she said, returning her head to his chest. He slid one hand up to stroke her hair, his gentle touch encouraging her to close her eyes. Every breath she took smelled of his cologne, a scent that she would forever associate with power, sexuality, arousal . . . and security. "It's a physical act that brings you pleasure, nothing more, nothing less. You do it with women you hardly know and care nothing about, and yet you won't do it with me. It's not fair."

"I won't do it with you because it *does* mean something to you. You use it as a way to keep men at a distance. If you keep busy having meaningless sex with every guy who comes along, then you don't have time to care about any of them. If I sleep with you, you're going to write me off just like all the rest. But I don't intend to be written off, Holly. I intend to marry you."

She made a rueful face. "I used to say that I liked a man who knew what he wanted. Now I'm not so sure."

His low laughter tickled her ear and sent a shiver down her spine. "Sex is easy, darlin'. But having sex with someone you care about . . . That scares you to death, doesn't it?"

Lifting her chin, she stopped dancing and met his gaze. "Not at all," she lied. "I've done it before and I survived."

"When?"

"The first boy I had sex with," she said airily, as if the memories had no power to hurt, "and the next and the next. They kissed me and held me and told me they loved me, and when I gave them what they wanted, they walked away. No big deal. I survived."

He rubbed his hands up and down her arms, sending a slow, lazy heat through her. She wanted to arch against him like a cat, to lean in to him so he could reach other parts of her body, but she held herself still. "And if I have sex with you, that's what you'll expect from me," he said quietly. "That I'll walk out of your life and leave you alone. But it's not going to happen, Holly. One time with you isn't going to be enough. A hundred times won't be. And having sex with you, knowing I'm no different from every other man who's been there before . . . That's not going to happen, either."

He sounded so sure of himself, so absolutely convinced of what he wanted, that Holly envied him. She had tremendous faith in her sexuality, but very little in herself. Maybe that was because she'd spent half her life cultivating the sexuality and all of it hiding herself. She'd been hurt too many times, had been disappointed too many times.

After refilling her wineglass, she sat down in one corner of the overstuffed sofa, kicking off her shoes, drawing her feet beneath her. "Why marriage, Tom?"

"I told you—"

"That you'd accomplished all the goals you'd set for yourself so now it's time to find a wife. But that's not a reason to get married."

"Then what is?" he asked as he settled at the other end of the sofa.

"Frankly, I can't think of any reason besides children. If you're going to have kids, then you should be married. Other than that . . ." She shrugged. "And since we've already established that neither of us wants kids . . ." After a moment, purely out of curiosity, she asked, "Why don't you? Want kids, I mean."

Tom gazed at his wine, watching it respond to the slightest movement he made, and considered her question. For years his answer to such personal questions had been simple and true—no time. He'd been too busy fulfilling his goals to waste one moment on relationships he couldn't sustain or pursuits that did nothing to further his success. He couldn't recall ever making a conscious decision not to marry or not to have children. They were just things that he'd known instinctively weren't going to happen. Of course, he'd changed his mind about getting married. But he wasn't changing his mind about kids. The only kids he could relate to were ones like he used to be, and he neither needed nor wanted that kind of headache.

"Raising children should be left to those whose lives wouldn't be complete without them," he said. "Like Ross and Maggie, the Bishops, and the Graysons. I never wanted a daughter to worry about or a son to carry on my name. I never wanted to be that unselfish. From the time I was sixteen, I had a plan for my life, and it didn't include the sort of sacrifices children require." Listening to his own words, he smiled faintly. "I sound like a self-centered bastard, don't I?"

"Not at all. I think my parents felt the same. They just didn't realize it until I was already here." She smiled, too, as if it didn't bother her in the least, but underneath the cool disregard was a hint of wistfulness. Somewhere inside, he suspected, there was a part of her that still craved her mother's love. Why else would the woman she claimed to dislike so thoroughly still be in residence?

"*I* feel the same," she went on. "I don't have a maternal bone in my body. I enjoy my friends' kids from time to time, but I have zero tolerance for crankiness, tears, messy diapers, sticky hands, sibling rivalry, or temper tantrums—unless they're mine, of course. I feel no desire to pass on some part of myself to some poor, unsuspecting child. I don't need a legacy other than the inn."

They fell silent for a time. Tom finished his wine and set the glass on the table, then studied her. She was dressed in ivory this evening, wool slacks and a sweater that fell below her hips. With her matching pumps and her auburn hair sleekly styled, she'd looked elegant. With the shoes off and her hair mussed where he'd stroked it, she looked vulnerable. Appealing. Innocent.

"What about love?" he asked without thinking about it. "Is that a reason to get married?"

"Love is a fantasy."

"And some fantasies come true."

"Some people fall in love, and it's the real thing. Some people fall in love, and it isn't. Others never fall."

"Or maybe it just takes them a long time because they're too stubborn to recognize what they feel."

Her smile was broad, her voice edged with mockery. "And how does love feel, Mr. Screw-'em-and-leave-'em? For twenty-four years you've devoted every single bit of your passion and energy to building a power base and earning a fortune. You haven't had a serious relationship in your life. You use women to satisfy your sexual urges and pay them well before discarding them. You have one friend—*one*—and that's more a testament to Ross's ability to offer friendship than your ability to inspire it. You've never been in love with anyone, and no one's ever been in love with you. So tell me, Tom, what do you know about love?"

He knew that if he didn't feel *something* for her, he wouldn't listen to her talk like that and keep coming back for more. He wouldn't feel that odd, empty pang in his gut. He wouldn't be so sensitive to her words, or so susceptible to her contempt.

If he didn't feel *something* for her, he would take her to his suite, screw her brains out, then forget she existed. Like all those men before him.

He also knew it was fear that made her say things like that. Fear of emotions she couldn't control. Fear of coming to care more for him than she already did. She wanted him. She missed him. Now he needed her to need him. He wouldn't ask for her love. Those things would be enough.

"I'm coldhearted, Holly, not blind," he said quietly. "The first and last person to give a damn about me was my mother. But I see people. I know things. I understand emotions." Some of them, at least. Desire, hunger, anger, determination. Since meeting her, he'd become well acquainted with frustration, and since his birthday, he'd had a few run-ins with jealousy, greed, impatience, longing, and tenderness.

He didn't change his tone at all. "I know you want to be with me, and at the same time, you're afraid of being with me. You're trying hard to convince us both that all you want from me is sex, because sex doesn't involve emotions. But your emotions are already involved, and that scares you, too. You're afraid of caring too much, of falling in love with me."

For a moment she stared at him, speechless. The laugh she finally choked out sounded phony as hell. "Lack of confidence has never been a problem for you, has it?"

"No."

"You think I'm falling in love?"

"No." He felt a stab of regret as he answered. He wished she *was* falling in love with him. That would be . . . incredible. "I think you're afraid of falling in love with anyone."

"I *choose* not to fall in love," she said sharply. "I don't want any messy emotional entanglements."

It wasn't so long ago that he'd thought the same thing. He'd actually worried whether Holly's emotional needs would be a burden he couldn't meet. He'd never imagined the day would come—and so quickly—when he would *want* that burden, would feel cheated without it.

"You never answered my question," he said, his tone mild, empty of all he was feeling. "Is love a reason to get married? If two people fall in love and want to spend the rest of their lives together . . ."

"Why not just live together?"

He shrugged. "There's no commitment. It's too easy to leave if you get upset."

"You think a marriage license will keep someone around who doesn't want to be there? For an intelligent man, Tom, you can certainly be naive."

He couldn't argue that point, so he didn't try. "Living together is no big deal. At least getting married requires a bit of effort and thought. And it's a hell of a lot more respectable. I'd much rather introduce you as my wife than as the woman I'm currently living with."

She rose onto her knees and slowly, sensuously, moved the length of the sofa until she was straddling his thigh and leaning close to him, with one hand planted on either side of his shoulders. "Why, Tom Flynn, are you saying that you *care* what people think?"

"I care what I think," he said awkwardly. He couldn't breathe without taking in the sweet, exotic fragrance of her perfume, couldn't move without touching her—and, God help him, he *wanted* to touch her. "And I think you deserve better than to shack up with someone you don't trust not to leave you."

And, yes, when it came to her, he did care what people thought. He already knew the looks she would get from everyone who knew him and the assumptions they would make—that she was just like all the others, that her place in his life was temporary, that he didn't care enough about her to marry her.

"Your concern is sweet," she murmured between kisses to his jaw. "Misplaced, but sweet." She lowered herself, bringing her body into aching, throbbing contact with his, and brushed her mouth tantalizingly across his. "You see, I don't care about effort and thought, or respect, or what other people think. I don't care about being shacked up, or what I deserve. What I do care about is getting what I want, and not getting suckered into a marriage that's doomed from the start, and not letting other people influence my decisions. What I *really* care about is you . . . and me . . . naked and doing all kinds of wicked things. It would curl your toes, Tom, and make you forget all about love and marriage and other such nonsense."

The slow, easy way she was touching him was almost enough to curl his entire body into one tight, hard knot. It was more than enough to make him impossibly hard and relentlessly hot. But it couldn't make him forget. Nothing could.

He slid his fingers into her hair as she left a trail of wet kisses down his throat, loosening his tie, unbuttoning his shirt, pushing the fabric aside. When her mouth found his nipple, he groaned, held her there for one moment's torture, then gently forced her away. "Oh, Holly," he said with a chuckle, "whoever said you were easy couldn't have been more wrong. You're the most difficult woman I know."

Her smile was satisfied and erotic and taunting. "And you're the hardest man I know. Why don't we slip upstairs and lock the door and—"

When he shook his head, her amazing mouth settled in a pout that disappeared the instant he kissed her. It was a hard kiss, demanding a response that she was happy to give. He thrust his tongue in her mouth, tasted her, filled her with a familiar rhythm that made his blood hot, that made him throb where her hips cradled him. When, with a sigh, she went all soft and weak against him, he sent her tension level skyrocketing by sliding his hands underneath her sweater. Her skin was warm, soft as the finest silk, and her breasts were bare. He ended the kiss so he could watch her face as he pressed his palms to her breasts, then teased her nipples to aroused peaks. Her eyes were closed, her lips kissed free of color, and her breath came in short, shallow puffs. When he gently pinched one nipple, she gasped, then gave a great groan.

"Has anyone ever told you you have incredibly talented hands?"

"Most women aren't particularly interested in my hands." He moved, easily lifting her until she was reclining at the opposite end of the sofa, until he was leaning over her. First he gave her a kiss, a simple one, just lips, no tongues, then he kissed his way along her jaw. Her ear was sensitive. The kiss there raised goose bumps, and there was a place behind the ear that made her shiver.

He took his sweet time, caressing, exploring, teasing. He felt her skin grow hotter, felt her tension increase, then ebb, then increase again. He watched her eyes flutter shut and her nipples pucker under his touch, and saw the soft, warm skin of her stomach ripple when he tasted it, and he listened with satisfaction to her uneven breathing, her helpless gasps, her wordless pleas for more.

And then he stopped. "You like that?"

"Yes." The word was breathy, damn near soundless, erotic as hell.

"Good. We can finish when you give the word."

Her eyes popped open, and she sent him a look that should have cut him off at the knees. "Wh-what—? Don't stop—You can't—" Understanding set in, and she scrambled up, tugged her clothes into place, then glared at him. "That's not fair! You can't start something like that, then just stop! You—you—"

"All you have to do is say yes, and I promise, I won't stop." Not for a few days, judging from the tension humming through his body.

Grabbing a pillow, she swung it with a frustrated cry and smacked him, but he easily pulled it away, wrapped his arms around her, and drew her close. "I'm glad I'm back, Holly. I've missed you."

She breathed deeply a few times, and the tension slowly seeped from her body, leaving her soft and warm against him. Eventually she rested her head against his shoulder and admitted, "I've missed you, too."

A simple sentiment . . . but they just might be the sweetest words he'd ever heard.

TOM WAS WORKING IN HIS SUITE SATurday afternoon when a knock sounded at the door. He saved the file, then left the computer to find Holly waiting in the hallway. She held a package in one arm and her coat in the other. "Are you ready?"

"Ready?"

"For the party. You already forgot, didn't you?"

He glanced at the package again, wrapped in white paper bearing pink *Happy Birthdays* all over, and remembered their conversation at breakfast. You want to be married and live in Bethlehem, she'd said, let me give you a taste of what that'll be like. The "taste" was a birthday party for her assistant manager's oldest daughter, and practically everyone in town would be there. She wasn't going to find it that easy to scare him away. "Give me two minutes."

"Why don't I come in and help you get ready?"

He pushed the door up to block her. "All I have to do is turn off the computer, and I've been doing it by myself for a long time. You wait here." Closing the door securely, he returned to the desk to shut down. All he needed was Holly in the bedroom with him. Instead of turning the damn computer off, she'd be turning him on, and after last night, he might not find the willpower to resist.

He was in the corridor with his coat in less than two minutes. The party was at the Winchester house, home to most of Bethlehem's celebrations, it seemed. He hardly knew the two old ladies, couldn't even keep their names straight, but he'd had both Thanksgiving and Christmas dinners there last year.

"It's Alanna's birthday," Holly said as he turned onto Hawthorne Street. "She's twelve, and she's Emilie's niece."

"And she lives with Emilie because . . . ?"

"Because her mother's weak, self-centered, and not fit to raise her, Josie, and Brendan," Holly said tartly. After a moment, she continued. "Emilie's sister is a drug addict and an alcoholic who is in and out of rehab and jail on a regular basis. She had to make a choice between her habit and her children, and she chose her habit."

Tom could think of a number of comments he could make. Obviously, the sister had a problem; the kids were lucky to have Emilie; too bad Holly hadn't had a loving aunt to take over when her own parents failed. Instead he said nothing.

Cars lined both sides of the street near the Winchester house. At Holly's direction, he pulled into the McKinneys' driveway, and they walked across to the old Victorian. Halfway there, a tomboy with blond curls met them, flinging her arms around Holly's middle.

"Miss Holly, guess what? I'm learnin' how to ride a horse. Dr. J.D.'s new neighbor's got horses, and she's gonna teach me how to ride just as soon as it gets warm." Pulling away from Holly, she skipped ahead a few steps, then turned to walk backward. "I don't know why we have to wait. I've got a coat and gloves, and the horse has its own coat. It's not like it's gonna get cold or nothin'."

"No, but maybe Dr. J.D.'s neighbor might get cold, and if she's doing the teaching, then she's got to be outside with you. Say hello to Mr. Flynn, Josie."

"H'lo, Mr. Flynn. I'm Josie Lee Dalton. 'Member me?"

"Yes, Josie, I remember you." She was the chattiest kid in town, with Grayson's little girl a close second. Neither Josie nor Gracie had ever met a stranger or, he suspected, had a thought that went unspoken.

"Ever'one says you're gonna marry Miss Holly," she said, unerringly climbing the porch steps without so much as a glance over her shoulder. "Is 'at true?"

"Yes," he said at the same time Holly answered, "No."

Josie giggled. "You gonna kiss her and have babies with her?"

Holly reached out to tug the kid's curls. "You gonna mind your own business, squirt?"

"Prob'ly not. When I grow up, I'm gonna be a cop like Uncle Nathan, 'cause then I get to ask all the questions I want and if anyone tells me to mind my own business, I'll slap the handcuffs on 'em and haul 'em off to jail."

The living room and dining room of the Winchester house were packed. A young boy took their coats to a bedroom while they worked their way across the room. It was slow going, with Holly stopping to chat with virtually everyone.

"Hey, Holly," someone called from the corner. "Have you set a date yet?"

Before she could reply, Tom did. "We're working on it."

Though her smile never flickered, she brought her heel down on his toe while politely saying, "We're not getting married."

"Yes, we are," he disagreed. To the man who'd asked, he winked conspiratorially and said, "She's just a little nervous. It's such a big step, you know."

She glared over her shoulder at him while continuing to the dining room. "Stop that!" she hissed. "Repeat after me—we're not getting married."

Once the crowd thinned, he moved beside her and slid his arm around her shoulders. "But I *want* to get married."

"No, you don't. You don't get married just because you haven't done it before. Pick another goal. Go climb a mountain. Jump out of an airplane. Sail around the world. And let go of me!"

"I don't want to." It was an appropriate answer to any and all of the preceding.

In the dining room, they located most of her friends, as well as the birthday girl. Holly gave Alanna a hug, said hello to the others, and continued into the kitchen. Tom went with her. The

Winchester sisters were there, fussing over the final details on the birthday cake.

Holly hugged and kissed both elderly women. "The cake looks lovely."

"It's carrot cake," one sister answered. "Can you believe Alanna wanted a carrot cake birthday cake? But the smaller cakes on the table are white and chocolate."

"Alanna's always been older than her years," the other added. She smoothed the last bit of frosting, then stepped back to study Holly. "You look lovely, dear. Being engaged agrees with you."

Tom watched Holly struggle for control. Her eyes narrowed, and a muscle in her jaw twitched even as she forced a smile. "I'm not engaged."

"Why, of course you are." Then the old lady gave him a chiding look. "Of course, it's customary for the prospective groom to give his prospective bride an engagement ring."

"He would," Tom said, "if he believed for a second that she'd accept it. Last night I gave her a necklace, and she wouldn't even put it on."

Both women looked at Holly for an explanation. Face flushing, she said defensively, "That necklace must be at least thirty carats! In diamonds!"

"Sounds lovely," one sister sighed. She was the one seeing J.D. Grayson's father—Agatha, he thought—and the more romantic of the two, because the other just harrumphed before adding, "Sounds extravagant."

Holly flashed him a smug grin. He didn't mind, since the dreamy one had sided with him.

With Holly leading the way, they returned to the dining room, where Emilie offered them drinks. As he stood in the background and sipped his, Tom tried to remember the last party he'd attended in the city where the strongest drink offered was fruit punch, or where children had been welcomed, or when he hadn't been bored out of his mind. He couldn't remember. Kids were never excluded from parties here, with the exception of the Sweethearts Dance, alcohol was rarely served, and he couldn't honestly say he'd ever been bored. He'd felt out of place, a stranger among friends, an oddity deposited into their midst, but he'd never been bored, because he'd always been with Holly.

"Holly, you know, the nursery starts getting a ton of really beautiful flowers in April." Melissa Thomas was trying to contain her smile to an innocent smile. Maggie and Kelsey, on either side of her, weren't succeeding as well.

"Yes, Melissa, seeing that the inn is your best customer in town, I'm aware of that," Holly responded. "Though I can't remember a single time in the past you felt compelled to point it out to me."

"Oh, I was just thinking that"—the smile was losing, and the big, teasing grin was winning—"you know, you might need extra flowers this spring. Some centerpieces and boutonnieres and . . . oh, I don't know, maybe a bouquet, or five or six."

When Holly glowered at her, they all started

laughing. J.D., standing behind his wife, leaned forward. "Just for the record, Holly, the hospital staff is betting in your favor."

"But you've lost the police department," Nathan said. "And the sheriff's department. And the fire department."

"People are *betting* on me?" Holly asked indignantly.

"Well, most of us are betting against you," Kelsey replied. "We love you dearly, but . . . Tom's the one known 'round the world for winning negotiations."

"But he's never negotiated with me." The look she gave him was a definite challenge, and he never backed down from a challenge.

He slid his arm around her waist, drew her against him, and used his free hand to tilt up her face. "I've already begun negotiating with you, darlin', and you know what?" He was so close that his mouth was brushing hers, that he could feel the soft, warm puffs of her breath on his skin. He moved even closer and murmured, "This is one deal in which losing is *not* an option."

Chapter Fourteen

"GOD, THIS PLACE IS AS DEAD ON A Saturday afternoon as it was when it was my home." With too much dramatic flair, Margery collapsed into a chair, flung out a hand, and snapped her fingers imperiously. "Bring me a drink, any kind of drink, and be quick about it."

Bree looked up from the silver she was polishing in time to see the waitress, Kate, make a face behind Margery's back. She smiled faintly before lowering her gaze once more to the serving spoon she held. "You know, most people respond better to orders if you say please and thank you and don't snap your fingers at them."

"She's a waitress. It's her job to respond to orders."

"No, it's not. Her job is to serve people, not to jump at their very rude beck and call."

Margery straightened in her chair and glared haughtily. "*You're* calling me rude? *You?* A nobody from Rochester, of all places, whose idea of culture is carnivals and zoos?"

Bree gave no outward response, though inside she trembled just a bit. Margery might be rude, obnoxious, self-centered, and petulant, but she was still the boss's mother, and Bree was still just an employee who could be fired on a whim. She didn't honestly think Holly would fire her for being rude to Margery, but she really shouldn't be testing the theory—not yet.

"Where is my daughter?"

"Out with Mr. Flynn."

"I cannot believe she hasn't yet accepted his proposal. Doesn't she realize how *wealthy* he is? Why, with him for a son-in-law, there would be nowhere I couldn't go. Every door in the country would be open to me."

Bree gave a shake of her head. Her mother might drive her nuts, but at least she wasn't shallow. If Bree were considering marriage, it would never occur to Allison to try to benefit from it. Her only concern would be whether her future son-in-law loved Bree enough.

Kate returned from the kitchen and set a glass in front of Margery. Stepping back, she folded her hands over the serving tray and waited.

Margery took a sip, grew stiff, and turned a frigid look on Kate. "That's nothing but ice water.

So you have a sense of humor. Too bad I don't. Bring me a bottle of scotch, you little—"

"Mrs. McBride." Leaning across the table, Bree laid her hand on the woman's arm. At the same time, she signaled Kate to leave with a nod. Hesitantly, gently, she said, "My father always said that needing a drink was the first sign that you had a problem."

"My husband used to say that, too. He hardly even qualified as a social drinker. A glass of wine from time to time, a few beers . . . Smug, insolent man." She drew a deep breath, then another, then folded her hands together. "I take it you don't drink?"

Bree shook her head.

"And that allows you to be holier-than-thou with those of us who do."

"I have nothing against people who drink . . . occasionally. And I'm not being holier-than-thou. I just don't understand how alcohol can mean more to you than your daughter, your marriage, and your husband."

"How dare you!" Rising quickly to her feet, Margery raised her hand as if to strike Bree. Bree scrambled to her feet, too, but retreat wasn't necessary. All it took to freeze them both in place was a bewildered voice speaking from the doorway.

"Sabrina? Baby, what's going on?"

For an instant her heart stopped beating in her chest. She felt the color drain from her face and a queasiness stir in her stomach, as she slowly turned toward the door. Margery was turning, too, so pale that she looked as if she might faint. When her gaze reached the door, she staggered back a step or two, then sank into the waiting chair. "You," she whispered sickly. "Oh, dear God, it's you."

Bree glanced at Margery, then crossed the dining room in long strides, wrapping her arms around Allison. "Mom! Oh, Mom, I'm so sorry."

"Bree, what's going on here?"

At the sound of Holly's voice, Bree clung tighter to her mother. God, she hadn't meant for things to happen this way. She wasn't even sure she'd meant for them to happen at all. But her mother was here, and so were the McBrides, and clearly Margery knew who Allison was, and . . .

Gulping in a breath, she freed herself from her mother's embrace and saw Holly and Tom, just returned from the party. He was helping her remove her coat, but her attention was all theirs. Bree brushed back her hair, smoothed a wrinkle in her shirt, then laced her fingers tightly together. "I—uh, I'm sorry, Holly. I didn't—I—I—" With another deep breath, she blurted out, "This is my mother, Allison Aiken. Mom, this is Holly McBride."

Holly took the few steps necessary to shake hands. "Mrs. Aiken. I . . ." Her attention shifted to the dining room, where her mother was slumped in the chair, hands over her face. "I, uh, I'm glad to meet you. Bree—"

"Get her out of here!" Margery surged to her feet and furiously approached them, one finger pointing accusingly. "Get that woman out of here!

I will not be under the same roof with her, do you understand? *Get her out!*"

What in the world had she walked into this time? Holly wondered. After the afternoon of relentless teasing at the party, couldn't she have five minutes' peace in her own home before World War III broke out?

She stepped in front of Margery, stopping her a few short feet from Bree and her mother. Margery was livid, Bree frightened, Mrs. Aiken oddly calm. Margery tried to sidestep her, but Holly was quicker.

"Get out of my way!" her mother shrieked. "If you won't remove her from the premises, I will. I will not tolerate that-that woman's presence in my house!"

"Mother!" Holly snapped. Catching Margery's arms, she gave her a shake. "Calm down and shut up! Just a reminder—this is *my* house, and I will not tolerate this kind of drunken behavior here!"

"I'm not drunk, I'm enraged! How dare she come here? How dare she!"

"Let's go into the library where we won't have an audience," Tom said quietly, slipping his arm around Margery's waist and half guiding, half dragging her across the floor.

Holly glanced around and saw several guests looking on curiously from the stairs. She gave them a strained smile, offered a hasty apology, then gestured for Bree and her mother to precede her into the library. The instant she closed the door after her, she asked, "What's going on?"

Mrs. Aiken pulled away from her daughter and went to stand in front of Margery. "Hello, Margery," she said softly. "Imagine meeting like this after all these years."

"All these years I've wished you were dead!" Margery spat out. She would have lunged at Mrs. Aiken, Holly was sure, if Tom hadn't been holding her by the shoulders. "All these years I've hated you!"

"I'm sorry," Bree's mother said. "I've tried to tell you so many times how very sorry I am."

"Mrs. Aiken—"

She turned toward Holly, her expression gentle. "Ms. Aiken. Or Allison. I kept my maiden name."

"Maiden name?" Margery let out a cruel laugh. "Your *only* name, you mean, because he never married you! He wouldn't!"

Heat flushed Holly's face at the same time as a chill danced down her spine. Panic was welling inside her, urging her to run, run as far as she could. She didn't want to know what was going on, didn't want to know how her mother and Bree's knew each other. She damn sure didn't want to know who *he* was. Desperately she wished she and Tom were back at the party, that they'd accepted Maggie's invitation to dinner at their house, that they were anywhere but here, dealing with anything but this.

But she couldn't move, couldn't unfold her fingers to open the door, couldn't make her feet obey her commands to flee. Instead, she stood there as if rooted to the floor as Allison Aiken came toward her. "Holly, I'm so sorry. I never would have come here if I'd realized that Margery was here. I never would have risked stirring up bad memories for her."

Margery made a vulgar response to that, but Allison ignored it.

"I just wanted to see my daughter, to find out what in the world she was doing here. She's always been so curious about you, so envious. . . ." Allison smiled affectionately at Bree, who came to slide her arm around her waist.

"I'm sorry," Bree whispered, looking more distressed than Holly had ever seen her before.

"I—I don't understand." Holly's voice was unsteady, rough. "Who are you? Why are you here?"

"They're nobody!" Margery said scornfully. "A no-good worthless slut and her bastard daughter! Nobody!"

Holly looked past them to her mother, lost her temper for one instant, and shouted, actually *shouted,* "Shut up!"

In the silence that followed, no one was willing to speak—not Allison, not Bree, not even Margery. Tom had his hands full keeping Margery on her side of the room, and wasn't about to speak up, though he'd already guessed what Holly was trying to avoid. She could see it in the way he looked at her, with tenderness and regret and pity, and it made her want to cry, to curl up in his arms and weep and know that he would keep her safe.

She didn't move toward him, though. Slowly she shifted her gaze once more to the Aiken women, and she summoned the courage to speak once more. "Who are you, Bree, to be curious about me? To be envious of me? How did you know I even existed?"

Her gaze darting everywhere except in Holly's direction, Bree dried her hands on her jeans, folded her arms over her chest, and knotted her fists. Finally she stood utterly motionless, looked Holly in the eye, and said, "Because your father was also my father. You're my half-sister."

HOLLY SAT ON THE PORCH STEPS, staring into the dark night sky. Behind her it was business as usual inside the inn. Dessert was being served in the restaurant, beds were being turned down upstairs, dishes were being washed in the kitchen. Life was going merrily on.

Except for her. She was numb inside, and might remain that way forever.

She heard footsteps behind her. Tom. Who else would have the nerve to approach her? She'd sent him away two hours ago. She'd wanted to be alone, wanted to be with him, hadn't wanted to admit just how much she wanted to be with him. She had asked him politely, calmly, to leave her in peace, and, after one look into her eyes, he had politely, calmly agreed.

How had he known that she'd had enough solitude for now?

He sat down on the step above her, his legs on either side of her, and wrapped a down comforter around them both before pulling her back to lean against him. He didn't say anything but simply held her, warmed her, inside and out.

After a time she clasped his hands. "Did Margery settle down?"

"I called J.D. He sedated her. She won't wake up until morning."

"What about Bree and her mother?"

"They talked for a while, then Allison left to go home. Bree went for a walk and hasn't come back yet."

Holly numbly shook her head. "All those years I wished for a sister, and when I stopped wishing . . . I got one. I just didn't know it. I guess that explains why she was so nervous around me."

"I imagine it would be scary, meeting the legitimate daughter who doesn't know you're the illegitimate one."

"I can't believe . . ."

"You knew your parents weren't happy."

"Yes, but I didn't know my father went out and got himself a whole new family he *could* be happy with!" Belatedly she bit her lip. She didn't want to yell at him. He was the only one who'd done nothing wrong, who hadn't hidden something from her. "I'm sorry."

He hugged her tighter. "He wasn't rejecting you, Holly. You remember what your mother was like. She made life miserable for both of you. He had a chance to be happy with Allison, and he took it."

"I have no problem with that. But why didn't

he divorce Margery first? Why didn't he ever tell me I had a sister?"

"People used to take those vows about 'for better, for worse, until death do us part' very seriously. Maybe he didn't want to put you through a divorce. Maybe he was too big a coward." His shrug rippled through her. "And as for telling you . . . How could he do that without tarnishing himself in your eyes?"

She squeezed her eyes shut to chase away the tears. "I always felt sorry for him. He was a good man. And my mother . . . She was determined to punish him for moving her here. As long as she suffered, by God, so would he. Sometimes I indulged in these fantasies about his sending her back to the city, and he and I would live here to gether, just the two of us, and we would be so happy." She scoffed. "Now I know if he'd sent her away, he would have moved Allison and Bree in, and *I* would have been the outsider. He would have loved Bree better because he loved her mother, and when he looked at me, he would have seen Margery, and he would have ha—"

"He would have loved you as much as he always had."

She wondered if he was right and decided she wanted to believe it regardless. After all, her father was dead. Who was going to prove them wrong?

After a time, she gave a shake of her head. "God, a sister! I just can't believe . . . I'm old enough to be her mother. And I almost fired her because she kept breaking stuff because she was so nervous every time I came around. What if I *had* fired her? What if she'd left without telling me? I never would have known. I never would have—"

Tom slid his hands up to her face, tilted her head back, and kissed her upside down. "You didn't fire her, she didn't leave, and now you know. You just have to decide what you're going to do about it."

She hadn't even thought about that. She hadn't thought about anything besides surviving the shock of her father's affair. No, not affair. Lewis's relationship with Allison had lasted at least eight years. He'd shared a house with them in Rochester, had spent two, three, four nights a week there for eight years. He'd pretended to be married to Allison, had been a loving father to Bree.

"I don't know that I'm going to *do* anything. Get to know her, I guess." She twisted so she could lean back against his thigh and gaze up at him. "How did Margery and Allison meet?" She was sketchy on some details. She'd listened to as much of the explanations as she could, and then she had walked out. She would have exploded if she'd heard one more word, felt one more degree of emotion.

"Before your parents were married, Allison was a maid for Margery's family. That's how she met your father. He was dating Margery but started to get interested in Allison. Margery found out, fired Allison, and pressured your father into marrying her. A few years later he ran into Allison again in Rochester, and . . ."

Oh, God, they'd been together more than eight years—more like twenty-something. A lifetime. Holly's lifetime.

"Listen, darlin', forget about your father, your mother, and Allison. Just concentrate on Bree. You and she are the only ones who matter."

She held his gaze for a long time, drawing strength from it, before finally sighing. "Maybe you should find her. Make sure she's all right."

"Maybe we should." He untangled himself from the comforter and stood up, then helped her to her feet, supporting her until her legs were steady.

She waited until then to shake her head. "I don't want to see her yet. I don't want to talk."

"Holly—"

"Please, Tom. Just find her and bring her back. I'll talk to her as soon as I can deal with it."

He looked as if he wanted to argue, but she didn't give him a chance. She squeezed his hands tightly, then stepped around him and went inside. She knew she should go with him, should talk to Bree right away, but she felt too . . . betrayed. Disillusioned. Hurt.

All her life she'd blamed her mother for making her father so unhappy. It had never occurred to her that *he* might be the cause of *her* unhappiness. All those years he'd been unfaithful to her. All those years he'd lived another life, with another wife, another daughter. No wonder Margery's drinking had gotten out of control. She'd needed to forget.

Holly would have given a lot to forget, to wipe

the last few hours from her mind. She wanted to think of her father once again as a good man. Not a liar, a betrayer, a fraud. Not a cheating two-timer who hadn't cared enough for his wives or his daughters, who had cared too much about his own happiness. She wanted to face his memory one more time with affection and love, not disappointment. She'd *trusted* him, believed in him, felt such great sympathy for him, and he had lied to her, to her mother, to the whole damn world. His entire life as she knew it had been one great, meticulous lie.

And she wasn't sure she would ever forgive him for it.

TOM HAD DONE THIS ROUTINE BEfore, on another cold winter night. Then it had been Christmas Eve, and he'd been looking for Maggie, who'd left home after an argument with Ross. He'd seen more of Bethlehem that night than he'd ever wanted to see, and all he'd been able to think about was what had happened the previous Christmas Eve, when she'd left after another argument and had nearly died on an ice-covered highway.

This time he felt relatively certain nothing so traumatic had happened to Bree. She'd been upset but not that upset. It was cold, but the roads were clear, and it was dark, but this was Bethlehem. The streets were safe.

He was halfway through a methodical search, all the way down one street and back up the next, when he finally spotted her, huddling against the cold in the bandstand in the square. He turned into a parking space, then followed the sidewalk to the bandstand.

Bree sat on one step, an older woman on the next. He couldn't place her until she lit up with a big smile and greeted him with great pleasure. "Mr. Flynt! How nice of you to come. See, Samantha, I told you they'd be worried about you."

She was Gloria, who'd checked coats at the Sweethearts Dance, whom Holly had found trespassing on her property, who couldn't keep names straight to save her life. He greeted her with a nod before turning his attention to the girl—to Holly's sister. The designation sounded strange in his mind. "Bree, are you all right?"

She nodded, though her eyes were puffy.

"Poor girl," Gloria said, patting her arm. "I found her here weeping as if her heart were breaking. Why, last time I heard tears like those, it snowed for two solid days. She was afraid she had ruined everything, but I told her she hadn't ruined a thing. There might have been more tactful ways to break the news that she's Holly's sister, but she can't be blamed because her mother spoiled things, now can she?"

"No, of course not."

An awkward silence settled over them. After a moment, Gloria broke it with a sudden clap of her hands as she stood up. "I'd best be going. Remember what I told you, Serena. Be honest, be patient, and have faith. Mr. Flynt, the same advice wouldn't hurt you any." With a nod, she crossed the bandstand, then stopped and turned back. Though she was smiling, her gaze was oddly intense when it connected with his. "Honesty, patience, and faith. Trust me."

Feeling uncomfortable, Tom glanced away. He was a reasonably honest man, and he could be very patient. He wasn't sure where he stood on faith, though. Luckily, he didn't have to decide at that moment, because when he looked back, she was already out of sight.

After a long moment, he sat down one step below Bree. Beyond good-mornings exchanged in the hallway, he probably hadn't spoken to her twice. But soon, if luck was with him, she would be his sister-in-law.

When he'd decided to get married, he'd expected to get a wife, nothing more. He'd given no thought to mothers-in-law, sisters-in-law, or, in the future, nieces or nephews. He well might wind up with more of a family than he'd ever thought possible.

And that was a more pleasant prospect than he'd ever believed possible.

Finally Bree gave a great sigh and murmured, "I'm so sorry."

"For what? Wanting to meet your sister?"

"Breaking the news in such a horrible way." Fumbling in her pocket, she drew out a tissue and blew her nose. "I'd never dreamed Mom would look for me. . . . Daddy used to tell me he'd bring Holly to meet us someday. After he died, Mom told me to just forget about her. But how do you forget your only sister?"

"So you decided to come and meet her on your own."

She nodded. "All these years I wondered . . . I thought maybe we could be friends, even if we couldn't be sisters. But when I finally met her, she was so . . ." At a loss for words, she shrugged, then rested her chin in her cupped hands.

Holly was definitely *so* . . . Tom silently agreed. So beautiful. Sensual, sexual. Bold, aggressive, independent. So no-nonsense. She'd intimidated the hell out of Bree from the start, and an intimidated Bree was not an impressive sight.

Suddenly she looked at him. "Is she going to fire me?"

"I don't think so."

"Is she angry?"

"She's stunned. And, yes, she's angry with her father. She feels betrayed." He wondered how, or if, that would affect things between *them*. Her father was the only man she'd loved and trusted unconditionally, and now, so many years after his death, he'd broken her heart. Would she use it as an excuse to push *him* away?

She might try. But damned if he was going to let her succeed.

"Our father loved her very much," Bree said softly. "He talked about her a lot."

"Did you know back then that he was married to Margery and not your mother?"

She looked stricken. "Oh, no. Until this afternoon, I believed he'd divorced Margery. He and Mom wore matching wedding bands. He spoke of her as his wife. I never dreamed . . ." Moaning softly, she hid her face in her hands. "Oh, God, it sounds like some TV movie, doesn't it? The honest, upright, churchgoing pillar of the community who secretly has two wives, two families, two lives. No wonder Holly's stunned."

Tom stood up and shoved his hands into his pockets. "We've been out in the cold long enough. Let's head back."

But all Bree did was look up. In the dim light, panic glazed her hazel eyes. "What if she doesn't want me there? What if she doesn't want anything around to remind her of—of what he did? What if she throws me out?"

"She's not going to throw you out." That was the only question he could answer for sure. It was entirely possible that Holly *wouldn't* want her around, that she might fire her and put her on the first bus to Rochester. But that bus wouldn't be running until the middle of the week, and until then Bree needed a place to live, and Holly didn't throw family out. Margery's presence at the inn proved that.

"But what if she hates me? What if she blames me for ruining her life? What if she just tolerates having me there the way she just tolerates her mother?"

"If that's the case, you'll have to deal with it. But you won't know until you face her, so . . ." As if it were something he did every day, he extended his hand and, when she took it, pulled her to her feet. They walked to the car in silence. They'd driven several blocks when Bree spoke. "Are you in love with Holly?"

His fingers automatically tightened around the steering wheel and the muscles in his stomach clenched. His first impulse was to answer no, of course not. He'd been called a coldhearted bastard in fifteen languages, and coldhearted bastards didn't know how to love anything but money and power. His second impulse was to tell her to mind her own business. What he felt for Holly was strictly between him and her. Family or not, no twenty-something teary-eyed kid had any right to pry into his personal life.

But all either response would accomplish was to brush her off. It wouldn't stop the question from echoing quietly inside him. *Was* he in love with Holly?

Aware of Bree's unwavering gaze, Tom felt his face grow warm. "Define love," he said gruffly.

She was silent for a moment, then she said, "Everything in your life is different. You find yourself doing things you never would have done before her, having conversations you couldn't have had. She changes the way you look at life, at other people, at yourself. Things that never mattered before become important to you because they're important to her. You don't care what anyone else thinks of you, but you care what she thinks. You rearrange your priorities to make more time for her. Being with her makes you happy. Being away from her leaves you feeling empty. When she's upset or afraid or hurt, there's nothing you wouldn't do to make it all right. *She* makes *you* all right." Her voice softened. "She's the best thing that ever happened to you, and without her . . . you might not survive."

Well, hell, he thought as he turned into the inn's drive. She'd done a fair job of describing how he felt. So that was love, and he wasn't incapable of it at all.

He parked and reached to shut off the engine. Bree stopped him with her hand on his arm. "You didn't answer. Do you love Holly? Is that how you feel?"

He drew a breath and murmured into the darkness, "I feel scared to death."

Her reply sounded amused. "Yeah, that's part of it, too."

"But right now the problem with Holly is yours. Are you ready to face her?"

"No." She laughed nervously. "My whole plan sounded so much better in Rochester. I thought I would come here, get a job, dazzle her with my efficiency, and after we became the best of friends, then I'd tell her who I was. Naturally, she would be thrilled to finally have the sister she'd always wanted and would welcome me as such." She gave a shake of her head. "Fantasies are always so much better than reality."

"She did always want a sister."

"Really?" She sounded hopeful, but it quickly passed. "Wanting a sister and actually having one are two different matters. A fantasy sister doesn't mess up your life, destroy your good memories of your father, or send your mother into a rage."

True. But fantasies couldn't be as good as reality, because if they were, he might not stand a chance.

And he couldn't stand that.

They went into the inn, past the somber night clerk and through the kitchen to the door to Holly's apartment. After trying it and finding it locked, Tom knocked.

A moment later, Holly's voice came quietly through the door. "What?"

"It's me."

"And me," Bree added, sounding as nervous as she looked.

Everything, it seemed, became utterly still. Each breath he and Bree took was magnified in his ears. The throb of his pulse provided a quiet back beat, and Bree's nervous shifting made her clothing rustle audibly.

After the click of the lock turning, Holly slowly opened the door, but no more than a few inches, which she blocked with her body. She was dressed for bed in a T-shirt and robe, and looked pale and stressed, with lines bracketing her mouth, her arms folded across her chest, her hands knotted tightly. She didn't say a word but simply looked at them.

Bree began. "Holly, I'm so sorry—"

Holly interrupted her coolly, unemotionally. "If you feel like finishing your shift, go ahead. If you don't, that's fine, too." Then she moved to close the door.

Bree stopped her. "Can't we talk?" she pleaded. "Just for a minute? There are so many things I want to say to you, so many questions I want to ask."

"Not tonight. I've heard all I want to hear from you tonight. Go to the kitchen, go to your room, go wherever you want, as long as it's away from me. Leave me alone."

Bree stared at her for a moment, obviously tempted to speak anyway, then spun around, went into her room, and closed the door.

"Well . . . that was certainly the mature way to handle it," Tom said mildly.

Holly moved once more to close the door, but he was prepared for it. He grabbed hold, forced her to back away and came in.

"What was that all about?" he demanded.

"I'm tired, and I have a headache. I don't feel like dealing with her tonight."

" 'Dealing' with her? That's your sister, for God's sake. She waited her entire life to meet you, and you don't feel like 'dealing' with her?"

She started to turn away, but he caught her arm and pulled her back. Suddenly angry, she jerked loose. "I don't feel like dealing with you, either," she said coldly. "So why don't you get the hell out?"

Folding his arms over his chest, he leaned against the door. "Your father betrayed you, Holly, not me. I'm sorry you found out the way you did. I'm sorry you're upset and disappointed. But you're not going to take it out on me, and you're sure as hell not taking it out on your sister."

"She's not my sister! She's his bast—"

Tom freed one hand and extended it until his index finger almost touched her nose. "*Don't* call her that," he warned in a deadly quiet voice. "Don't *ever* call her that."

Too late she realized that her insult applied to him as well as to Bree. It was one he'd heard frequently over the years. Every time he'd seen his mother's father, the old man had called him that, with all the scorn and hatred he'd been able to muster. It had hurt his mother, and shamed him, and he'd hated his grandfather for it.

Holly took a step back and rubbed one hand over her face. "I'm sorry," she said stiffly, and he half believed she was. "But this has not been one of the better surprises in my life, and I need some time. . . . All my life I loved my father, and I resented my mother. I blamed her for everything. It was her fault he traveled so much, her fault he was distant even when he was here, her fault that he was only a part-time father to me, and not a very good one at that. I made all the excuses in the world for him, and laid all the blame on her, and . . . I was wrong. He wasn't running away from Margery. He was running *to* Allison. And Bree. He chose them over us. He wanted to be with them. To hear Bree tell it, he was the best father a kid could have asked for." Her voice softened and grew bitter. "But not to me."

"Bree says he loved you."

"Yeah, he really showed it, didn't he? Every minute of his life was a damned lie. Every time he was here, every time he was gone . . . I thought I knew him, but he was a master deceiver. I didn't know that he was the most selfish person in my life. He forced my mother to live here in a place she hated while *he* went off and lived half his life elsewhere with his make-believe wife and his replacement daughter."

Tom reached for her, but she backed away again. Relenting, he lowered his hand to his side. "Holly, whatever his reasons for doing that, it had nothing to do with you."

"It had everything to do with me!" she cried. "I *loved* him! I *trusted* him! He's the only man in the world I've ever been able to say that about, the only man I thought I would *always* be able to say that about! And I was wrong. How could I love him when I didn't even know him? How could I trust him when his entire life was just one huge deception after another?" She angrily swiped away a tear. "God, I'm glad he's dead, because if he wasn't, I'd want to kill him myself! I hate him!"

"Fine. Hate him. Hate Allison. Hate everybody in the whole damned world . . . but not Bree. And not me."

She stared at him, and he read the sorrow in her eyes. The confusion. The hurt. The fear. Hell, he shared them with her. She was going to use this as a reason to back away from him. He knew it as surely as he knew that he couldn't let her, or he'd lose her forever.

Then she blinked, and the emotions disappeared. It was an impressive feat. Even he, at his coldest, hadn't been able to turn it off that quickly, that completely. She looked cool and composed, as if they were discussing some topic of little or no importance. "I don't hate her," she conceded, "but I don't want her here, either. The family I was cursed with at birth has been enough of a headache for me. I'm not looking for any more trouble. Maybe someday I'll change my mind, but not now. Now I want her gone."

He wanted to touch her, to take her in his arms and hold her and kiss her until she'd forgotten all about her parents and the pain they'd caused her, but in all the time he'd known her, she'd never seemed less approachable. He knew that if he put his arms around her, she would stand stiff and unrelenting. She would refuse to lean on him the way she needed to, the way he needed her to. She would keep herself distant, and he would feel rejected, and so he stayed back.

"You always wanted a sister," he reminded her. "Until you turned twelve and your mother humiliated you in front of all your friends and you decided that you'd rather be an only child and the only target for her temper than subject some helpless, innocent kid to her anger."

"I never said that!"

"But it's true, isn't it? You wanted a sister, but one who wouldn't have to suffer with Margery the way you did. Well, that's what you've got."

Tears filled her eyes. He'd never seen her cry and would have sworn a year ago—hell, even two months ago—that she was no more capable of crying than he was of loving. "But she wasn't here when I was growing up and needed her," she whispered. "Now I don't need her. I don't need anyone."

"You're wrong. You need me."

She shook her head numbly. "No. I don't need anyone, and I never will. Needing someone, trusting, believing . . . It takes too much out of a person. People always let you down, and the disappointment . . . I can't bear the disappointment." Shaking her head again, she went into her bedroom and closed the door.

Tom stood there in the hallway, debating what to do. He could try to talk to her and get nowhere. He could try to hold her and probably get nowhere with that. Or he could take some aspirin, go to bed, and hope things would be better in the morning.

Right, he scoffed silently as he let himself out, then took the rear stairs to the second floor. She'd just received the biggest shock of her life, had found out that she'd been betrayed by the one man she'd thought absolutely could not betray her, and she was on the verge of deciding that she would never trust anyone again, never love anyone again.

He was afraid it would be one hell of a long time before things seemed even remotely better.

Chapter Fifteen

SOME DAYS IT JUST DIDN'T PAY TO WAKE up.

Margery rolled onto her side and squinted at the alarm clock, but she couldn't force the blurs into separate numbers. Judging from the light streaming in the windows, it was at least midmorning, and she was hungry, achy, and hung over. But she couldn't remember drinking the day before. That smart-assed waitress of Holly's had brought her ice water instead of scotch and water, and when she'd tried to deal with her, Bree had—

Oh, God. Bree. Allison. Holly.

She was hung over, all right, from an overdose of emotional distress and a shot of something from Holly's doctor friend, who had mentioned something about one alcoholic to another, and rehab. Everything after that was fuzzy.

So now Holly knew the truth about Lewis.

And Margery would have given anything to spare her. Damn Lewis, damn Allison, and, especially, damn Bree for coming to the inn in the first place. She'd lived her entire life without ever meeting Holly. Why couldn't she have lived the rest of it the same way?

A soft sound from behind her penetrated the thick fog that filled her brain. She glanced over her shoulder, then slowly turned onto her other side.

Holly was sitting in the chair there, looking as beautiful as ever. She wore a green wool dress with a simple rounded neck, long sleeves, and a matching belt cinched around her slender waist. Her hair was perfectly styled, her makeup perfectly applied. There was a distant look in her eyes, and a grim set to her mouth, but other than that, she didn't look like the same stunned woman who'd very quietly, very desperately, left the library the afternoon before.

Margery wanted to say something totally innocent, harmless, maybe amusing—something that Holly couldn't possibly take offense at, that couldn't possibly make her think of anything hurtful or disappointing. But when she opened her mouth, the words that slipped out were all wrong: "She reminds me of you."

It took a moment for Holly to return from her thoughts, to hear and understand what she'd said. She shifted her gaze to Margery and icily asked, "Who reminds you of me?"

Nervously Margery moistened her lips. "Bree. I told you she reminded me of someone, remember? But I couldn't figure out who. It was you. Her eyes, the shape of her mouth, the stubbornness of her jaw . . . You both inherited those things from your father."

Holly stared at her unflinchingly for so long that Margery wished she were still asleep, incapable of causing her daughter any further pain or heartache. After a time, though, Holly asked, "Did you know about her?"

Margery shook her head. "I knew . . . I knew he was having an affair. Multiple ones, I thought, with different women. I never dreamed it was just one, and never in my worst nightmares did I think it could be Allison, or that he would have a child with her."

"I'll never forgive him for this."

"No one would ask you to."

"I'm furious with him."

"You're entitled."

"I'm certainly not going to be her sister."

That remark jerked Margery out of her agreeable mood. "Excuse me? Do you think you have a choice in that, little girl? She *is* your sister, like it or not. You can't just wave your magic wand and make her disappear."

"I can make her leave my inn. I can make her disappear from my life."

"And what would that accomplish? You would be punishing her for things her parents did, and punishing yourself, too. She's waited a long time to meet her big sister."

"I'm not interested in being anyone's big sister. It's too late for that."

"It's too late to share a bedroom and confide all your secrets to each other, or to play dolls or dress-up or giggle about first dates. But you can still have a very special relationship, Holly, different from anything you've ever known. You can give her advice, and she can make you lighten up a bit. You can make her feel welcome in her father's home. You can—"

"It's my home now, and she's not welcome." Holly's temper flared. "How can you take her side? She and her mother helped destroy our lives!"

Margery sat up, discovered she was wearing her favorite black silk nightgown, and wondered who had helped her put it on. One or more of Holly's unfortunate employees, she assumed. It would not happen again. The days of being undressed and put to bed by strangers were over. "Holly, I'm sixty-two years old, and I have been miserable most of my life. I'm too old and too tired to worry about whose fault that was. Some of it was Lewis's. Some was Allison's. Most of it, undoubtedly, was mine. But laying blame doesn't change anything. It doesn't make me any happier. It doesn't give me a better relationship with you or anyone else, for that matter.

"I'm not taking anyone's side. I'm just telling you that being angry and holding grudges and laying blame doesn't do anything but leave you a sad, unhappy, and bitter person. I know that from my own experience. I don't have a real friend in the world, and my daughter—my only family—is happiest when I'm five hundred miles away. But at least you're one up on me in the family department. You've got a sister, and she wants very much to be a part of your life. You can blame her for what your father did and send her away, or you can find out what it's like to have family who loves you and wants to be there for you."

Holly stared at her mutinously. "At least you acknowledge that it's my choice. And my choice is to send her away. If you have a problem with that, well, you're perfectly welcome to leave with her." Moving with tightly controlled grace, she stood up and walked to the door. "Since you obviously survived the night and require no further medication, I've got work to do."

"There is one thing I need, Holly." Margery spoke quickly to stop her from walking out, to get the words out before her courage slipped away. "A favor, if you will."

Holly turned back, a wary look firmly in place. "What kind of favor?"

"Last night your friend, the doctor, mentioned a—a treatment facility for people with . . . problems. Will you . . ." Briefly she acknowledged how much easier this conversation would be with a glass of wine or a cold beer to help the words along. Her mouth actually watered at the thought, until she closed her eyes and cleared the image, the taste, the comfort, from her mind. "Will you call him and ask the name of this—this hospital? I . . . would like to go there as soon as possible."

Holly stared at her—simply stared. Not once in her life had Margery made any real effort to stop drinking. She was sure her daughter had believed the day would never come, but it was time. There was so much she was sorry for, so much she needed to make right, but she couldn't do that until she'd dealt with the fact that she was an alcoholic, and a mean one, at that.

After a long time, Holly swallowed hard, then nodded. "I'll call him as soon as he gets home from church."

Margery nodded, too. "Thank you. I'll be packed and ready to go."

Chapter Sixteen

MONDAY WAS ONE OF THOSE WARM, mild days that came too seldom in February, reminding them all that, though winter seemed endless, spring *was* coming. Holly sat at her desk in the office she shared with Emilie, but she wasn't the least bit interested in the invoices stacked in front of her. Her chair was swiveled around to face the windows, and her gaze was lost somewhere out there in the fields and woods.

She needed a vacation. It had been a long winter, and the past few weeks in particular had been difficult. She needed to be someplace warm and tropical, someplace far from Bethlehem and her problems.

One of her problems, at least, was gone. J.D. had made a few phone calls Sunday afternoon, had picked up Margery soon after and escorted her to the rehab hospital himself. He'd called Holly later that night, close to midnight, when he'd gotten back, and told her that Margery's admission had gone off without a hitch. She'd changed her mind a dozen times on the way there, but she hadn't acted on it. He'd sounded guardedly optimistic, and that was the way Holly felt.

But her other problems remained in residence. Bree was making every effort to stay in the background, unnoticed by anyone, while Tom was determined to stay in the foreground. All day Sunday, it had seemed Holly couldn't take two steps without finding him there. Thank God he'd gone to work this morning. Maybe, while he was gone, she could pack her bags and flee. By the time he got home from the office, she could be lying on a Caribbean beach someplace obscure and isolated where even he wouldn't be able to find her.

Could she stay there until he gave up on her? Until he decided she was more trouble than she was worth? Until he moved back to Buffalo, where he belonged, and took up with some long-legged beauty who wouldn't love him enough to be hurt when the inevitable let-down came?

Not that Holly loved him. She was fond of him—maybe even extraordinarily so. But love? No way. Loving someone was the quickest way to a broken heart, and her heart had been broken enough over the last weekend alone to last a lifetime.

Emilie came into the office, taking a seat at her desk as the phone rang. With a curious look at Holly, she answered, then said, "Let me put you on hold, Tom, and I'll get her."

Shaking her head, Holly waited until Emilie pressed the Hold button to say, "I don't want to talk to him."

"Holly—" With a sigh, Emilie returned to the call. "Tom, she won't come to the phone right now. . . . I know . . . I'll give her the message." When she hung up, she said, "I love you dearly, Holly, but I'm not going to lie for you."

"How convenient," Holly said snidely. "Too bad you weren't so concerned with truth and integrity when you first came here and told everyone that Mrs. Pearce's house and your sisters' kids were yours. Everything you did then was a lie. But now you're too honorable to make one simple excuse for someone else."

Her blue gaze cool and tinged with hurt, Emilie rose once again from the chair. "Tom wants you to meet him at Harry's for lunch. He'll be there in half an hour."

After she'd walked out, Holly pressed her hands to her face. She couldn't believe she'd spoken to Emilie like that. She knew the reasons for Emilie's deception when she'd first come to Bethlehem, knew she'd been desperate to save her nieces and nephew from the same foster-care system that had made life so difficult for her and her sister. Holly understood and admired her devotion to the kids.

Hell, she didn't even really care that she'd refused

to lie to Tom. Even if she'd made a simple excuse, he was no fool. He would have suspected that Holly was avoiding him.

What would he think in half an hour, when he waited alone at Harry's? Would he be angry that she'd stood him up, or would he simply accept it?

But she didn't have to wonder what he would think, because three minutes before the appointed time, she walked in the diner door. He was sitting in a booth, with two menus and a cup of coffee in front of him, and he looked . . . worried.

The look eased a bit when he saw her. He didn't stand to greet her, didn't try to kiss her. She was grateful for small favors, since she knew everyone in the place. Once she sat down, though, he did reach across to take her hand. "I wasn't sure you would come."

"I didn't intend to," she admitted. "I just thought . . ." That she should. That she wanted to see him even more than she didn't want to.

He waited until Maeve poured her coffee and took their orders to speak again. "You look tired."

Her only response was a shrug. She hadn't slept well in two days. Her dreams had been numerous, disjointed, and unsettling, with one common theme—everyone in them, everyone she'd ever cared about, had chosen someone or something over her. With her father, it had been Allison and Bree; with her mother, alcoholic oblivion. The dream—Tom had put up with all he could endure before choosing the solitary peace of his old life over the emotional turmoil of life with her.

"How busy will the next few weeks be at the inn?"

"About average."

"Anything your staff couldn't handle?"

A kernel of dread began growing in the pit of her stomach. "Why?"

"I thought this might be a good time for you to go away for a week or so. With me."

She gazed steadily at him. Less than an hour ago she'd been wishing she were on a tropical beach somewhere, with no responsibilities, no guilt, no anger, no bitterness, and, most important, no pressure. No Bree lurking in the shadows with that anxious, wistful, sorrowful look in her eyes. No memories of Margery walking out of the inn with J.D. at her side, her head held high, her smile confident, and sheer terror making her quake. No Tom hanging around, pressuring her—whether he said a word or remained totally silent—to act like a mature, intelligent adult in this whole mess. Less than an hour ago it had sounded like heaven.

But a tropical beach with Tom beside her? With the proper restrictions in place, that could be heaven, too.

"I thought the word *vacation* wasn't in your vocabulary."

He grinned. "I admit, I've never taken one before, but . . . You and me, away from everyone and everything? The idea holds a certain appeal."

Though she didn't feel like smiling, she couldn't

resist a grudging one. "Maybe then you'd quit telling me no."

"And maybe you'd stop saying it, too. Maybe . . ." He reached into his pocket and pulled out something small enough to hide in his hand. For a moment he hesitated, then he laid the item on the table between them. "Maybe you could use the time to get used to wearing this."

It was a small jewelry box, the right size for a ring, in the burgundy velvet used by Bethlehem's only jeweler. As Holly stared at it, the sounds of the diner faded to a distant roar until all she heard was the rapid thud of her heartbeat and the too-slow, too-shallow sounds of her own breathing. She wanted to reach for the box and open it, wanted to shove it out of sight. Most of all she wanted to jump and run. But in the end, she did nothing. She couldn't move. Couldn't breathe. Couldn't speak.

Tom leaned toward her and lowered his voice to little more than a whisper. "Do you want to see it?"

Mutely she shook her head once.

Disappointment darkened his eyes and tightened his jaw. "It's not extravagant. I think you'll like it. It suits you."

She shook her head again.

Grimly, he swept up the box and folded his fingers around it, making it disappear from sight. She felt a moment's relief, but it was short-lived. His grip tightened until his knuckles turned white, and a good deal of the color drained from his face. With jerky movements, he returned the box to his pocket, then forced a couple of short, choked breaths. "I take it your answer to a trip is also no."

Slowly she nodded. It would have been answer enough, but something inside her made her explain. "A vacation from all my problems sounds wonderful . . . but, Tom, you *are* one of my problems."

"So you'd be happy to go, but not with me."

Thankfully, this time she managed to keep her mouth shut.

Maeve brought their meals then, filling the stillness with friendly chatter. Once she was gone, Holly's discomfort doubled. She picked up a fork and poked at her lunch, then laid it down again. "I'm sorry, Tom. There's just so much going on right now. . . ."

He offered no response.

"Look, don't push me, please. Don't make any demands. I just can't handle that now."

"Let me get this straight. Wanting to give you an engagement ring—that's pushing? And wanting to spend time alone with you—that's making demands? What *can* I do, Holly? What am I allowed to want from you?"

Her hands trembled, so she clasped them in her lap. She was afraid her voice might tremble, too, but it was strong, raw. "Nothing. That's all you'll ever get from me, Tom. You have no right to expect more."

Tom sat back numbly. *Nothing.* That was the way

deals went sometimes. You went into negotiations wanting it all. Sometimes you got it. Sometimes you got part of it. And sometimes you got nothing.

But this wasn't business. It was damned personal. And damned painful.

He'd known from the beginning that the odds were against him, but the idea of losing hadn't been so bad when all it would cost him was a few weeks of his time. But somewhere along the way he'd invested a hell of a lot more than just his time. Somewhere along the way, he'd fallen in love with her, and that wasn't so easy to walk away from.

You have no right to expect more. He'd known that from the beginning, too—had known she deserved a better man than he'd ever been, some one who hadn't spent his entire life looking out for himself. But he'd thought . . . he'd thought he might get lucky, might change her mind. He'd thought she had begun to care for him. The way she kissed him, the way she smiled when she saw him, the way she seemed happy that he was there . . .

Unable to sit still one moment longer, he grabbed his overcoat and slid out of the booth. He dropped a twenty on the table, then looked at Holly. There were a dozen things he wanted to say—arguments, mostly, and pleas. But since he wasn't about to beg her in the middle of Harry's noontime crowd, he simply looked at her and said nothing.

And then he walked out.

His car was parked a block away, in front of the jeweler's. He was tempted to walk in the door, toss the velvet box on the counter, and walk out again. Hell, how was it that, after spending a couple of not-so-small fortunes on jewelry for the women in his life, he'd found a woman who not only didn't want his gifts but refused even to consider them? If he couldn't give her diamonds and emeralds, what *could* he give her?

Distance. Privacy. Freedom from his presence. He'd bet she wouldn't turn those down.

"Tom?"

He opened the car door, then slowly turned. She stood on the sidewalk, looking distraught and even wearier than when she'd first sat down across from him. Fifteen minutes ago he might have wrapped his arms around her and simply held her, stroked her, let her lean on him. At the moment, he settled for shoving his hands into his pockets.

"I told you from the start that I wouldn't marry you," she whispered.

She had, but he hadn't believed her. He'd looked on her refusals as something of a game, a challenge to overcome. He'd thought that with time she would see things his way. He'd thought he would win—at first because he never lost, and more recently because she'd become too important, too much a part of his life.

But she wasn't playing a game. She didn't want to marry him. Didn't want to spend the rest of her life with him. Didn't want him, period.

Except for sex.

"It's not your fault. I thought . . ." He could change her mind. Thought she could find something in him worth caring about. Thought she could come to trust him.

"Nothing has to change," she ventured nervously. "We can still be friends. We can still go out and dance and"—she offered an unsteady smile—"and so much more. We'll just agree not to mention marriage again. Okay?"

His first impulse was to let out an angry roar. Nothing would change? Still be friends? Go out and dance and *so much more*? Not only no, but hell no! If he couldn't have her for his own, he didn't want to be friends with her. He sure as hell didn't want to mean no more to her than the men who had come before him. If that was the way things would be, then he didn't want even to see her again.

Except he couldn't imagine living without her. No, that wasn't true. He could imagine it far too easily—the emptiness, the loneliness—because that had been his life before her. He didn't want to go back to that. But what could be emptier or lonelier than being with a woman who cared no more for him than for the last nobody-special she'd taken to her bed?

"Tom?" she murmured, coming close enough to touch him, though she didn't. "We can still be friends, right?"

"Sure." He had only one friend in his life. He should be pleased by the prospect of having a second. But the friendship she was offering was a poor substitute for what he wanted. Hell, it was a poor substitute for *friendship*. But he could settle for it. For a time. "How about dinner this evening?"

She smiled, relieved. "That sounds fine. Where would you like to go?"

"Let's stay in. One phone call, and you can have the best food in town served right in your apartment. Or so you once bragged."

The smile strengthened. "All right. The cook's best, in my apartment. What time?"

"Seven."

She came close enough to rise onto her toes and brush a kiss across his mouth. "Any special requests?"

"Yeah. Wear one of those dresses."

Her smile was coquettish, seductive. "I have an entire closet full of dresses. Which ones do you mean?"

"The kind that makes every man in the room forget who he's with and stare at you instead."

"Oh, darlin'." She brushed her hand across his cheek in a practiced touch. "Have I got a dress for you. My apartment. Seven o'clock. Prepare to be dazzled."

Tom watched her walk away. When she turned the corner, he realized his fingers hurt from being clenched so tightly in his pockets. He forced them to relax. He would be dazzled tonight, all right. Dazzled, delighted, and, when the evening was over, disheartened, despondent, and dismayed.

Because when it was over, it really would be over.

He ran a few errands before returning to the office. There he sat through a conference with Ross, then answered a stack of correspondence, scheduled a trip to Paris for the following month, and reviewed the reports from the fire marshal on the blaze that had destroyed the Alabama factory.

And he never, not for one moment, managed to stop thinking about Holly.

He left the office at six o'clock and was home—no, not home. He was at the inn by ten minutes after. He showered, shaved, and dressed, took care of some last-minute business, and was downstairs at Holly's door at precisely seven o'clock.

Prepare to be dazzled, she had warned, and she hadn't been kidding. She was wearing a little black dress, very short, very snug, very sexy. The deep V neckline exposed pale creamy skin and the swell of her breasts, and the narrow straps left most of her shoulders bare.

She gave him one of those practiced, seductive smiles, and one of those practiced, coquettish looks. Part of him wanted to grasp her shoulders, give her a shake, and tell her to knock off the games. There was no need for them tonight. At least this Holly wanted to have sex with him. The real one didn't want him at all.

"Do you like my dress?" she asked, resting one hand on her hip, bracing the other against the doorjamb.

"It's nice."

"Faint praise, darlin'. But you haven't seen

anything yet." With that teaser, she slowly turned and sashayed down the hall inside her apartment.

Tom swallowed hard. Truth was, there wasn't much to see from the back . . . except lots and lots of Holly. The two thin straps connected at her nape, and narrow strips of fabric swept down her sides before finally meeting in the middle below the small of her back—way below. The skirt molded over her bottom, then flared into a flirty flounce that tormented and enticed with every step she took.

He watched until she turned into her dining room, then he drew his hand across his forehead. His palm came away damp, and his hand was less than steady. By the time he reached the dining room, he'd regained a bit of his composure. "It's a nice dress, but don't you get a little cool when you wear it?"

She smiled. "Funny. Everyone else who's seen me in it said I looked hot."

And who was everyone else? How many men had seen her wearing nothing but that little bit of fantasy? How many men had helped her out of it?

"Thank you for the flowers. They're lovely. I can't believe you got Herbert Thomas to let you have some of his orchids."

He glanced at the deep red roses on the table, then at the more delicate orchids on the sideboard. He'd asked Melissa Thomas for roses and orchids, and she'd told him her only hope of getting orchids on such short notice was to persuade her husband's uncle Herbert to part with some from his greenhouse. She'd already heard that Tom had bought a ring at the jeweler's that morning, and, assuming that he was going to formally propose to Holly that evening, she'd been more than happy to do what she could to make the evening perfect.

He hadn't bothered to correct her mistake. He'd wanted the orchids and hadn't thought his real reason for them would impress her nearly so much.

Anyone who saw the setting for this private dinner would likely make the same mistake as Melissa had. The chandelier above the table was dimmed to a mood-setting glow, and tall white tapers flickered all about the room. A linen cloth overlaid with lace covered the table, and the dishes were part of the inn's oldest, most delicate set. With the soft music playing in the background, it was the perfect setting for romance.

Too bad her only goal was seduction.

He held her chair for her, his fingers brushing her skin, then took his own seat. While she filled their wineglasses, one of the waitresses came from the kitchen with a loaf of crusty bread, hot from the oven, and salads of fresh mozzarella and roma tomatoes.

Holly was the perfect hostess. She talked steadily about absolutely nothing, but she made the conversation so personal, with private smiles and intimate touches, that he didn't care what she said. She was flirtatious at times, very brash and sexual, and at other times quiet and introspective. At those times he wished he could believe that she was thinking about him—about wanting him, trusting him—but he didn't believe it for a minute. He couldn't.

She talked her way through roasted duck with orange sauce, asparagus spears, and wild rice dressing, through a bottle of wine and a dessert of white pears in crepes. Tom talked enough to keep the conversation going, but mostly he just responded to her—verbally, emotionally, physically. He watched the expressions cross her face and tried to remember each one, tried to imprint in his memory the different tones of her voice. He knew even the best memories wouldn't be enough, but they'd be better than nothing.

At last she rose from the table, blew out about half the candles, then extended one hand to him. "Dance with me?"

Her fingers were so slender, her hand so delicate. *She* was delicate, for all that she was also strong and capable. He could crush her, could overpower her, but he could never defeat her or bend her to his will. He could never make her see reason.

There wasn't a great deal of space in her dining room, but the kind of dancing they did didn't require much space. He drew her into his arms, found himself holding nothing but scraps of silky fabric and expanses of velvety skin, and swallowed back a low groan. She was so soft, so warm, and fitted so perfectly against him. He wanted to sweep her up and carry her to her bedroom, and at the same time he wanted to stay like this forever.

But they didn't have forever. All Holly believed in was the present. She wasn't looking for Mr. Right, she liked to tease, but Mr. Right Now, and the only thing he wanted less to be to her than *right now* was *never*.

The music she'd chosen was older than either of them—lush tunes, big bands, Ella Fitzgerald, songs about love won, lost, betrayed. He held her against him, closer than close, and stroked her back, her sides, all the way down to the edge of the skirt. He made her shiver, sigh, and raise her head from his shoulder to kiss his throat, then his jaw, then finally his mouth.

Boldly she thrust her tongue inside, and he let her tease, probe, taste, before he took control from her. His kiss was hotter, greedier, damn near desperate, and it brought her onto her toes, making her press harder against him, cling to him as if, dammit, she *did* need him. At some point they stopped dancing, though the music continued, and focused instead on the sensations of touching each other, rubbing, creating heat and friction. He felt her fingers at his throat, fumbling open his shirt buttons all the way to the waistband of his trousers. There she stopped and slid her hands inside his shirt, her delicate hands caressing, restlessly exploring. He wanted to grab her wrist and guide her fingers to exactly the place where he needed her touch, but to do so he would have to give up his own explorations. She would find her way there soon enough . . . if he lasted. If he didn't strip off his clothes and that nothing little dress first. He'd waited so long . . . wanted so much . . . needed so badly. . . .

Freeing his mouth from hers, he left a line of kisses down her throat, then followed the deep slash of the fabric to the hollow between her breasts. For a moment he groped with the fastening at her neck, then gave up and impatiently brushed the material aside. Her breast was rounded and soft, a seductive contrast to the hard, swollen peak of her nipple. He dragged his tongue slowly across it and made her gasp, sucked it between his teeth and made her groan. Sliding her fingers into his hair, she held him tighter for a moment, then reluctantly pushed him away.

"You're killing me," she whispered, her voice as taut as his muscles. "Please tell me you're going to stay. Please say"—he slid his hand inside the bodice to toy with her other breast, and she caught her breath—"say we d-don't have to wait."

"Make your choice, quick—the dining table or your bed."

Surprise crossed her face, followed immediately by relief. Catching his hands, she pulled them from her body, pressed a kiss to each palm, then clasped them tightly in hers. "We'll try the table later," she said as she started down the hall. "But right now . . ." Glancing over her shoulder, she gave him a sensual-as-hell smile that sent a shock of lust through him and made him throb. "Right now I want you in my bed."

Chapter Seventeen

THE BEDROOM WAS SHADOWY, LIT only by the light that came through the doorway. Holly walked to her bed, perched on the edge of it, and removed first one strappy black heel, then the other. Standing again, she peeled off the sheer black hose that were all she wore beneath the dress, then raised her hands to the clasp on the straps.

Tom stopped her, not with words but with his hands. He pushed hers away, turned her so her back was to him, and brushed the lightest of kisses to her neck, raising goose bumps all down her spine, weakening her so that her head fell forward. For a time he lingered there, kissing her, touching her skin as if it were a new and different experience. When her breathing had become shallow and heavy, he finally turned his attention to the straps, unhooking them, letting them fall, letting his hands follow their path. His hands were cupping her bare breasts, his erection pressing against her bottom, when he nuzzled her ear, then murmured, "Look at us, Holly. You are so damned beautiful."

Though it required effort, she raised her head and caught sight of their reflection in the mirror across the room. Light from the hallway fell across them in a wedge, showing his hands on her breasts, his fingers dark against her pale skin. It was an erotic sight—Tom fully clothed while her dress bunched around her hips, just waiting for the chance to fall. It was damned tormenting, watching him pinch her nipples and feeling the sting turn to pleasure between her thighs.

She watched in the mirror as his hands slid together over her midriff, her navel, her abdomen, then slowly guided her dress down. At the last instant before it fell, she raised her gaze to his face, saw the corners of his mouth turn up in a smile, saw the smile turn wicked as he touched her most intimately. She sank against him, her head on his shoulder, her muscles trembling uncontrollably. She spoke his name in a whisper. A plea.

"What do you want?" he asked in her ear, his voice rough and hoarse. "What do you want me to do?"

From somewhere she found the strength to turn, to twine one arm around his neck, to slide her other hand over fine cotton and finer skin, over soft fabric and hard flesh. The powerful proof of his desire eased her own weakness, took the raw edge from her voice, and replaced it with greedy demand. "I want you inside me. I want you to make love to me. Make me forget my name. Make me forget the game."

He released her to undress, and she helped, or maybe hindered, judging by his curses as she carefully unbuttoned and unzipped his trousers, then painstakingly guided them over his erection. Once he was naked, he laid her back on the bed, followed her down, settled between her thighs . . . and kissed her—a sweet, innocent, gentle kiss. It surprised her, stunned her, brought a tear to her eyes. It made her breath catch and her heart ache, and it filled her with delight. She'd never felt so wanted, so needy, so connected to another person—and all because of one gentle kiss and one incredible man.

He pushed inside her, stretching her, filling her, and he continued to kiss her—hungry little bites, deep possessive claimings, tender tastes. His hands were never still, stroking, caressing, coaxing. As his thrusts quickened and his breathing grew harsher, she felt as if she were going to explode into a million pieces, but this time she didn't run away. She welcomed the release, the shattering, the rush of emotion. She welcomed the sensation of being overwhelmed, of bursting apart, of slowly, gradually, coming back together. It was amazing, something she'd never experienced before, something more than just two people coming together to spontaneously combust. Exactly how much more—love?—didn't even scare her. It was that incredible.

Recovering from his own release, he rested his forehead against hers for a moment, then dragged in a shaky breath. "Do you remember your name?"

"Hmm. Holly. Do you?"

He kissed between her eyes, one cheek, the corner of her mouth. "John Thomas Flynn, at your service."

She stroked his hair back from his damp forehead, slid her palms over his sweat-slick skin. "John Thomas," she repeated. "That's a good Irish Catholic name. And look how I've corrupted you."

"No, darlin'. You've either saved me . . . or destroyed me."

She must have looked startled, because he grinned and thrust once deep inside her. "It's quite possible you've ruined me for other women. I've never had it feel like that in my life. We are . . ."

When he shrugged, she tentatively, gently, laid her palms against his face. "I know," she whispered, her chest growing tight again.

Leaning forward, he kissed her, nibbling her full lower lip before sliding his tongue into her mouth. Sensation built quickly, spreading through her, burning hotter, until she couldn't remain still one moment longer. She moved restlessly underneath him, thrusting her hips against his, clenching the muscles deep within her body where she sheltered him. His response was also quick, and hard and powerful, and promised such pleasure.

Such soul-deep pleasure.

SOMETIME LATER, TOM EASED AWAY from a sleeping Holly, slipped from the bed, and crossed the hall to the dining room, where he blew out the first candle he came to. As a thin stream of smoke uncurled from the wick and drifted to the ceiling, he remembered his birthday dinner at Ross and Maggie's. What's the use of a birthday, she'd asked, if you don't get to wish for your heart's desire? He hadn't made a wish. A few short weeks ago, he hadn't had a heart's desire. The only thing he'd wanted was a wife, and his reasons had had nothing to do with his heart or with desire.

He should have made the wish. Should have asked for divine help. Should have gotten down on his knees and begged. But it was too late now.

He blew out the rest of the candles, turned off the chandelier, then went into the living room to shut off the stereo. For a moment he stood in the darkness, breathing, smelling, feeling. Then, with a sudden chill, he returned to the bedroom, to Holly. She lay on her side, facing the window, and when he slid under the covers behind her, she scooted back, fitting the curves and angles of her body to his, sharing her warmth with him. He slid his arm over her, sought and found her breast, then pressed a kiss to her neck.

"I love you, Holly." He didn't say it in a whisper or a murmur, didn't get swept up in a moment of passion, but offered it as a quiet, firm statement of truth. She might never trust him, might never believe it was true, but he knew. At the moment, that was the best he could ask for.

HOLLY AWAKENED TUESDAY MORNING with the most incredible sense of well-being—and the most erotic memories. Keeping her eyes squeezed shut against the sun, she rolled onto her back and felt various aches that merely made her smile. Her mother had tried to tell her that there was a difference between making love and having sex. With less eloquent words, so had Tom, and she'd even suspected it herself, but nothing had prepared her for the reality of it.

Quite simply, it had been amazing. More intimate, intense, satisfying, and important than ever before. For the first time in her life, she didn't feel a little dirty or a lot used. She didn't feel as if she'd given herself away cheaply. For the first time in her life, the act of sex mattered, because Tom mattered. Because she . . .

Silently she formed the word she rarely said aloud. It flowed, all soft sounds to match soft emotions. *Love.* Somehow, despite her best efforts to the contrary, she'd fallen in love with him. Sort of. More or less.

Oh, hell. She covered her face with both hands. She was such a coward. The idea of loving anyone scared her to death. She had nothing to offer anyone, nothing to make them love her back. What could she possibly offer Tom?

She didn't have to offer him anything, a little voice whispered in her head. He'd already said that he loved her. Last night. Right there in that very bed. He'd made love to her as if she were the most important thing in his life, and he'd told her he loved her. He'd said it. Clearly. Confidently.

Not that men couldn't lie. The boys and young men who'd broken her heart had lied. Some had accepted it as the price of admission. A few kisses, a few caresses, *Of course I love you,* and they scored, then forgot all about her, except to brag to other boys and young men.

But Tom had no reason to lie. For one thing, he'd said it after they were finished, not before. For another, there'd been no reason for him to coax her into bed with pretty words. She had always been ready and willing. She'd just been waiting for him.

But he hadn't waited for her to wake up. Even though she hadn't opened her eyes yet, she knew he was gone, knew if she stretched her arm across where he had lain, the sheets would be cold. He hadn't awakened her for a repeat performance. He hadn't stuck around to face her the morning after.

Hating the insecurities, she opened her eyes. The bed was most definitely empty. His clothes were gone, and her dress had been hung over the back of a chair. Her heels stood upright, side by side, underneath the chair. A passionate lover, and a neat one, too, she thought, but couldn't manage a smile. What she was calling neatness could be a desire on his part to erase any trace that he'd been there.

Leaving her bed, she got ready for the day as if it were any other day. She didn't rush her shower, took her usual time selecting a dress, applied her makeup, fixed her hair, and chose her jewelry with as much care as always. When she was finally ready to leave the apartment, it was after nine o'clock. Just a few hours later than her usual morning.

She checked in with the kitchen staff, then strolled down the hall to the registration desk. "Good morning."

"Good morning," Emilie replied. "You look lovelier than usual today."

"Why, thank you. I feel better than usual. Do you happen to know if Tom's left for the office yet?"

Emilie looked at her for a moment, then behind her. Holly turned to find Bree standing there, looking like a deer caught in headlights. The girl swallowed hard and shifted as if she might take flight. "What's up, Bree?"

"I—I don't know. He, uh, left"—she guiltily cleared her throat—"about five-thirty. I couldn't sleep, so I was sitting out here, watching the fire, and he—he came downstairs, and I don't think he was going to the office here in town because I, uh . . ." With a deep breath, she rushed it out: "I helped him carry all his luggage to the car."

Holly stared at her, not sure her voice would work, whether it would sound even halfway normal. "Was there some emergency? Did he get a call?"

Bree shook her head.

"All of his luggage?"

"Everything."

"Did he say anything?"

"H-he told me to . . . to take care of you. That was all."

As brush-offs went, it was pretty weak, but then, Tom had never been great at ending affairs. He'd sent her red roses and gorgeous orchids, and made love to her as if she'd mattered more than anything. He'd told her he loved her.

And then he'd left her.

One time with you isn't going to be enough. A hundred times won't be, he'd told her.

Liar. He was a liar, and she was a fool. She'd known better than to trust him. Everything in her life had taught her not to believe him. Everything in her heart . . .

"Holly? Are you okay?"

She gave Emilie a sharp look. "Of course I am. Why do you ask?"

"Because you're crying."

She raised one hand to her face and felt the dampness that streaked her cheek. Angrily she wiped her tears. "I'm not crying. I'm just . . ." Unable to think of an explanation, she spun on her heel and returned to her apartment. Where his cologne lingered in the air. Where the dishes from their dinner still sat on the table. Where the flowers he'd given her still looked beautiful in their vases.

She wanted to hurt someone, to smash something to pieces. She picked up the vase of roses, went outside, and took great pleasure in hurling the vase to the sidewalk. Green glass shattered across the path, and twenty-four red roses scattered in a tangle of stems and leaves. She ground the flowers under her heel until they were bruised and broken and ugly, but that wasn't enough. She needed more.

Returning to her dining room, she got the orchid vase and stalked back to the front porch. She raised the vase above her head—

But stronger hands snatched it away. "This vase is an irreplaceable antique," Bree admonished. "If you're going to insist on breaking things, give me a half hour to go to the store for cheap glassware."

Holly glared at her and saw little more than a blur. "Angry," she said coldly, precisely. "I'm not crying. I'm just angry."

For a moment Bree gazed at her, sympathy in her eyes. Then she moved the vase to her left arm and opened her other arm wide. "I know," she said softly. "Sometimes I have to get angry, too. Why don't you come over here and be angry on my shoulder?"

Holly hadn't had a shoulder to cry on for so long. God knows, Margery had never been there for her. Her friends? She couldn't cry in front of them. She had a reputation to maintain, in her own eyes even if in no one else's.

But Bree was family. If a woman couldn't go crying to her sister, where could she go?

She took two steps and Bree took three, wrapping her arm around Holly's shoulders, pulling her close as the tears flowed. Bree patted her back and stroked her hair and murmured things like, "It's okay," and "Let it all out."

When the tears dried, her eyes were puffy, her nose was stuffy, and her heart was still breaking.

"If it's any consolation, he looked pretty upset when he left."

As she moved away from Bree to lean against the railing, Holly tamped down the bit of hope that flared. "Why would he be upset? He got what he wanted, and he left."

"You agreed to marry him?"

"No. He got—" She discarded the first words that came to mind as certainly applicable but too vulgar, and said instead, "He got laid. And now he's gone."

"But . . . he wanted to marry you."

Holly shook her head stubbornly. "That was what he *said*. But it wasn't what he was after."

"But, Holly, that doesn't make any sense. You would have slept with him months ago. He knew that. The whole town knew it. If that was all he wanted, why would he say no for months? Why would he ask you to marry him? Why would he move here and buy you that fabulous necklace and an engagement ring if all he wanted was sex?"

It *didn't* make sense, any of it. Especially the part where he'd said he loved her. Everyone knew Tom Flynn was a coldhearted bastard incapable of loving anyone. Everyone knew she was promiscuous and easy and undeserving of love. None of it made any sense at all, least of all the fact that she'd fallen in love with him.

"I think you should go to Buffalo."

She shook her head again. When she was fifteen and the boy she'd finally had sex with had begun avoiding her, she'd confronted him at school one day. He'd fidgeted and stared at his shoes and hemmed and hawed before finally admitting that she was too easy. When she was seventeen, the most popular boy in school had stopped by unexpectedly one evening. He'd told her how pretty she was and how much he liked her, and he'd talked about asking her to the prom. After doing the deed in the backseat of his car, he'd gone to school the next day and asked the head cheerleader to the prom. Not having learned her lesson the first time, Holly had confronted him, too. He'd been more than happy to tell her—in front of his friends, no less—that all he'd wanted from her was sex, that he would never go out on an actual date with a girl with her reputation.

Humiliated and ashamed, she'd learned the lesson well. Never question a man who'd had sex with her, then dumped her. Not even when he'd promised he would never, ever do that. Not even when he'd said he loved her. *Especially* not when he'd said he loved her.

"You can't just let it end this way," Bree insisted.

Holly smiled bleakly. "This is the way all my attempts at relationships end. That's why I only have affairs. That's why I never give a damn about any man."

"You love Tom."

"I don't even know Tom." She'd never imagined that he was a liar, a schemer, a betrayer. She'd never thought he was the sort of man who could listen to some of her most painful memories, assure her that he was different, and then do exactly the same thing to her. She'd never dreamed he had a cruel streak like that.

They both fell silent, Holly leaning against the railing, Bree hugging the vase of orchids as if it were precious.

Last night it had been.

Tilting back her head, Holly looked at the sunny sky and thought of the things she needed to do—fix her makeup, get to the office, take care of the usual one hundred and one chores. But when she moved, it wasn't to go to work. Instead she took a seat on the swing at one end, then clasped her hands between her knees. "Why don't you put the orchids inside, then grab a couple of blankets out of the hall closet?"

With a nod, Bree disappeared. She came back moments later carrying the same thick comforter Tom had brought out Saturday night. Holly blinked away the tears spurred by the memory as Bree spread it over them both.

As the warmth began to spread through her, Holly asked, "How long have you known about me?"

"Always. There were pictures of you in our house, and Daddy talked about you a lot. He promised that we would meet someday, that he would bring you to Rochester or take me to

Bethlehem." Bree's smile was fleeting. "I was too little to understand why it never happened. All I knew was that when I lost my father, I also lost my sister."

"I never suspected a thing. I was twenty-two when he died, and I never had a clue he was such a damn good liar."

"Don't. He was a good man, Holly."

"Oh, yeah. The best. The world needs more like him."

"He loved you."

Holly glanced at her. "Did he? He chose to spend half his life away from me. He chose to have another family that excluded me. He couldn't bear being around my mother himself, but he had no problem leaving *me* with her. Is that how you define love?"

Bree's mouth turned down at the corners because she couldn't give the answer she wanted. Then she turned sideways to face Holly. "He used to tell me bedtime stories about how life would be if it were perfect. We would all live here in Bethlehem—him and Mom, you and me, and some dogs, cats, and horses. Every day in the summer we would have picnics at Holly's Lake, and every weekend in winter we would go ice skating. We'd go to church together, and when it snowed, we would make a snow-father, a snow-mother, and two snow-sisters, and we would never want for anything. Life would be perfect."

Holly's smile was regretful. Life had never been perfect for Lewis—or, thanks to him, for her and Bree. Maybe Bree stood a chance—she was still so young—but Holly feared her best chance for a wonderful life had left town that morning, and she didn't think he intended to come back.

"You were only seven when he died. It must have been hard." Her voice was thick with unshed tears. For her father? For Bree? Or for herself? She'd lost so much and survived it all, but she wasn't sure she could survive losing Tom.

"I missed him terribly, just like you did. He used to sing this song." Bree hummed a few bars, then started singing in a clear, steady voice. Halfway through the chorus, Holly joined in.

When the last note faded, she smiled faintly. "I'd forgotten that."

"For years I sang it to myself every night at bedtime, and I wondered about you—if you missed him and me as much as I missed you and him." Bree's sigh was soft, sad. "And you didn't even know I existed."

"Now I know."

"Now you know," Bree echoed, then hesitantly asked, "are you going to fire me?"

"You don't fire family."

"Are we—are we family?"

All the years she'd been alone drifted through Holly's mind. All the holidays she'd spent with friends because she had no family. All the emptiness she'd tried to fill with strangers. And all that time she'd had a sister, who was also in need of family. Taking the secret of her existence to his grave with him might be the one sin she could never forgive Lewis for.

"I always wanted a sister," she said as she got to her feet. She started toward the door, then returned to hug Bree. "Welcome to the family. And about—" Embarrassed to mention the tears, she merely gestured. "Thanks for being there."

Bree smiled, and for an instant, Holly saw what Margery had seen—a little bit of herself—in the girl. "Hey, what are sisters for?"

IT WAS AFTER ELEVEN O'CLOCK TUESDAY night when Tom walked into his apartment. After the drive back from Bethlehem, he'd spent a long day in the office. He would have spent the night there if he'd been able to find something to occupy his mind, but after realizing he'd spent nearly two hours staring out the window, thinking of nothing but Holly and his failure, he'd called it a night.

The apartment was cool, quiet, lifeless. Exactly the way he'd wanted it for years. Exactly the way he would learn to want it in the future. He set his bags down inside the door, then wandered through, turning on lights, working hard to avoid unfavorable comparisons to the warmth and welcome of the inn.

A check of the kitchen turned up a six-pack of beer in the refrigerator. He took one to his office, where he broke one of the few unbroken rules in his life. He opened the safe in the credenza, pulled out the envelope marked *Private* and *Keep Out,* and loosened the tape.

He never opened his list of goals between birthdays. But tonight he drew the paper out, unfolded it, and smoothed it flat on his desk pad. The only goals left to fulfill were on opposite sides of the paper. *Get married* on the front, and *Fall in love* on the back.

He'd thought the first would be easy, the second damn near impossible. Everyone managed to get married. But fall in love? For a man who'd forgotten what love was? He might as well have wished to sprout wings and fly.

But he was farther from getting married than he'd ever been, and he'd fallen in love so easily, so smoothly, that he hadn't even realized it was happening until it was a done deal. As if all he'd had to do was open himself to the possibility, and it had happened.

He didn't kid himself that it would happen again.

Fall in love.

Taking a pen from the desk drawer, his hand less than steady, he drew a thick, black line through the words.

Then, he added another goal. Like getting married, it might not be attainable, but he was going to do his damnedest anyway.

Survive.

Chapter Eighteen

THERE WERE WORSE THINGS THAN having everyone tease you about a wedding you hadn't yet agreed to, Holly discovered as the week wore on. There were the sympathetic looks she received wherever she went. The obvious care everyone took not to mention Tom, weddings, diamonds, or Buffalo. The cautious way they acted around her. She wanted to scream at everyone in Harry's that Saturday afternoon that she was all right, that it was no big deal Tom was gone, that she wasn't going to break down sobbing in their midst, that they were driving her *crazy* with their concern.

But she didn't scream anything because the simple truth was that she *wasn't* all right. It was a horribly big deal that he'd left the way he had, and she just might burst into tears and never stop.

For protection, she'd gotten in the habit of taking Bree with her wherever she went. Bree's position as recently discovered illegitimate daughter of a man they'd all thought they'd known well deflected a good deal of attention from Holly's broken heart. When that failed, Bree kept people at a distance and steered all conversations away from dangerous ground. Holly was more grateful to her than she could find words to express.

There was a downside to keeping Bree nearby, of course. She was absolutely convinced that some terrible misunderstanding had occurred. All Holly had to do, she firmly believed, was go to Buffalo and talk to Tom, and everything would be resolved. He would come back. Holly would be happy again. The wedding plans would proceed.

"There weren't any wedding plans," Holly said for the millionth time as she stirred her coffee. "He asked. I said no."

"But you would have eventually said yes if something hadn't gone wrong. You love him, and he loves you, and sooner or later you would have agreed because it's the right thing to do."

"My parents were married and were miserable. Your parents *weren't* married and were very happy."

"But they pretended to be married. I think, in their hearts, they really were." Bree smiled faintly, at least temporarily distracted from Holly's life by her own. "When Daddy died, we couldn't go to the funeral. At the time, I didn't even know what a funeral was, but as I got older, I wondered why Mom and I weren't there when he was buried. Now, of course, I understand. Mom couldn't risk showing up with me."

"Might have made for a more interesting service if she had," Holly said dryly. At twenty-two, she'd been young enough, forgiving enough, to better deal with her father's secret life. It would have been easier to face a grieving Allison, to accept a seven-year-old Bree. She'd come into ownership of the house upon her father's death, and she could have taken them in, and maybe learned what a real family was like. "Are you interested in seeing his grave?"

"I'd like that . . . if you don't mind showing me."

Holly smiled tightly. The cemetery might be the one place in all of Bethlehem where no one would give her sympathetic looks or treat her like an emotional time bomb. On a gray, cold day like today, there weren't likely to be many living, breathing visitors, and the residents had a tendency to mind their own business.

No one else in Bethlehem did.

The cemetery was located on the north side of town. The wrought-iron gates were propped open, and the grounds were neatly maintained. Holly drove to the oldest section, then pulled to the side of the narrow road. The McBride family plot was a large one, with gravestones dating back more than two hundred years to the first McBride. Lewis's grave was near the iron fence, marked with a stone that gave his full name, dates of birth and death, and a simple tribute: *Loving husband and father.*

Holly pointed it out to Bree but didn't follow her through the gate. Instead, she waited beside a tall maple, its bare branches reaching into the leaden sky. Thinking of the words carved on her father's tombstone, she snorted quietly. " 'Loving husband and father.' Yeah, right. Maybe we should add, 'and consummate liar.' "

"Now why would you want to do a thing like that?"

Giving a little cry, Holly jumped, then whirled around to find Gloria leaning against the opposite side of the tree. Holly raised one hand to her throat, then drew a deep breath. "A cemetery is not the best place to sneak up on people, you know."

"Sorry if I startled you. I forget that not everyone finds the same peace here that I do." Gloria came around the tree and stood a few yards in front of Holly. Her cheeks were ruddy from the cold, but she was smiling as if she found it most pleasurable. "Your father was a good man."

"And how would you know that?"

"I know a little about everyone here." She indicated the rows of markers. "I know that, for the most part, they're people who tried to do their best. They made mistakes, like your father, but they tried."

"And which one of us was my father's mistake? Me? Or Bree?"

"Babies are never mistakes!" Gloria declared. "Your father loved you both dearly. He never would have given up either of you."

But he had. In the last seven years of his life, he'd spent as much time in Rochester as he could. He'd neglected Holly to be with Bree.

Already feeling about as blue as she could bear, Holly said, "I'd really rather not discuss my father anymore."

"All right. You were talking about epitaphs. What would you like on your tombstone someday?"

Holly glanced past her at the graves. The engravings on most McBride women's markers were unoriginal: *Beloved wife to . . . Loving mother of . . .* "I suspect mine will say one of two things, depending on when I die. 'She was easy,' if I die young, or 'One classy broad,' if I have enough time to improve with age."

Gloria didn't look amused. "Ask me what mine would say . . . if I were to have one, of course."

Grudgingly, Holly did.

" 'She made wishes come true.' " She gave Holly a sly glance. "You made a wish. And I, with a little help, of course, made it come true."

A shiver raced down Holly's spine. She huddled deeper in her coat and worked up her best scoff. "Everyone makes wishes—on shooting stars, in idle conversation, on birthday candles."

"Not everyone makes a wish on someone else's birthday candles."

Holly was speechless. Then a logical explanation popped into her head. "You've been talking to Emilie."

Gloria shook her head. "Wishes, dreams, prayers . . . That's my job. You wished for Mr. Flynt to wish for you."

"Flynn," Holly corrected impatiently. "His name is *Flynn*."

"Well, of course it is. You wanted him to want you, and now that he does, you're pushing him away."

"I'm not pushing him away! I didn't push him out of bed Tuesday morning. I didn't push him all the way back to Buffalo without so much as a 'So long.' "

"No, but you made it impossible for him to stay. He loved you, Holly. He wanted to marry you. And yet when he asked you what he was allowed to want from you, you told him nothing. *Nothing.* Not your time, your love, your friendship, not even the smallest bit of your affection. Is it any wonder he left?"

Anxiety tightened Holly's chest and started a pounding in her head. "That isn't why he left! He left because—" She'd finally given in and had sex with him? They both knew that wasn't true. "Because—" He was a coldhearted bastard who cared about no one but himself? They both knew that wasn't true, either. "He left because—"

"You took away his hope, Holly. He thought he would eventually win you over. He thought he could earn your trust, that someday he could deserve your love. But you told him he couldn't have *anything*. No hearts and flowers, no commitment, no marriage, no love. Just sex. You offered him nothing you weren't willing to give every other man in your life."

Holly turned away from the woman and her kindly, motherly concern and stared across the grounds. *Just sex*. That was a hell of a description for the most incredible lovemaking she'd ever experienced. She'd given him passion that she hadn't known she possessed, trust that she hadn't known she could give. She'd fallen *in love* with him. And he'd walked away. Like every other man who'd never wanted her after he'd used her.

"He *left* me," she said, her voice unsteadier than she wanted, her eyes damper than they should have been. "He didn't even have the decency to tell me he was going. He just *left*."

A long silence fell and when it was broken, it was by Bree, not Gloria. "So go to Buffalo and tell him it was a lousy thing to do. And as long as you're there, tell him you love him, and you miss him, and you want him back. But before you do that . . ." A puzzled tone came into her voice. "Who were you talking to?"

Holly turned in a slow circle, but she and Bree were the only people around. It was entirely possible that Gloria was just out of sight behind another tree or one of the memorials placed around the grounds. She would have to have moved pretty quickly, but it was a more logical conclusion than the only other option—that she'd simply disappeared. "Myself, apparently," she said with a sigh. "But Gloria *was* here."

"Gloria? Older lady, graying hair, very maternal? Pops up in odd places?"

"Knows more than she should? Then disappears?" Holly met Bree's gaze and knew that her own eyes mirrored the disbelief in her sister's. Goose bumps rose on her arms, and the tiny hairs on the back of her neck stood on end. Then, as if on cue, they both laughed.

"It's a cemetery," Bree said, as if that explained everything.

"Right. And you can't keep any secrets in Bethlehem."

"Well . . . Daddy could."

They exchanged looks again, then laughed again. It felt natural, cleansing, and made Holly feel about ten years younger. She slipped her arm around Bree's waist, and they started toward the car. "I need a favor, Bree. Can you take care of things at the inn for a day or two?"

Bree stared at her. "Me? In charge of the inn? Holly, what if I break it?"

"You can't break a building." Though she could burn it down or blow it up. But Holly couldn't concern herself with that. She had more important things on her mind. "Don't worry about it. You'll be fine."

After studying her for a moment, Bree took a deep breath as if drawing strength, then smiled. "You're right. I'll be fine. Where are you going?"

"Buffalo." Holly mimicked her strengthening breath. "I've got a few things to take care of."

IT HAD BEEN A TYPICAL SATURDAY FOR Tom. Up at five, breakfast at his desk, then the entire day alone in his office. After a solitary dinner across the street, he would go home alone, have a drink alone, go to bed alone. If he was lucky, he would sleep a few hours, then find the strength to get up and go through the whole routine again.

If he was lucky...

He was about to close his briefcase when a blue box caught his eye. Taking it out, he pulled the diamond necklace free and let it puddle, row by row, in his palm. He'd managed to forget it, even though he was in and out of his briefcase every day.

What he only pretended that he'd forgotten was the ring box in his coat pocket. Now he dropped the necklace into the same pocket and left the office.

The restaurant on the twenty-fifth floor was crowded, as usual. He put his name on the list, then found a table in the bar. Within minutes, a woman dressed to entice approached him. "It's busy tonight. Do you mind if I join you?"

When he nodded once toward the tall stool, she eased onto the seat and crossed her legs, displaying a tremendous amount of skin. A few months ago, he would have automatically considered her a likely prospect for a short diversion. She was leggy, blond, beautiful, and sexy—his type of woman.

In the past.

Her name was Lacie, and they chatted about nothing.

If he'd met her before he'd gotten involved with Holly, he thought as he ordered a second round of drinks, he probably would have proposed to her. She met all the requirements on his initial list. And she had one definite advantage over Holly—she would never be able to break his heart.

"Do you like diamonds?" he asked when a lull came in the conversation.

"What woman doesn't?" she replied with a husky laugh.

He reached into his pocket, then drew out the necklace. "Hold out your hand." When she obeyed, he placed the necklace into her palm. "Happy . . . Saturday."

For several moments she stared at the necklace, slowly stretching it out from end to end. Her face went pale, and her lips parted on a soundless gasp. "Oh my God . . . These are . . . Are these . . . ?"

"Real? Yes."

"My God, they're beautiful! I've never seen anything so—" Abruptly, she glanced at him, and a sympathetic look came into her eyes. "What about the woman you bought this for?"

"No story there. I wanted to get married. She wanted to have an affair." He shrugged as if he didn't care, and wondered if it looked as phony as it felt.

She pressed the necklace into his hand. "You can't just give it away like this. Maybe she'll change her mind. Maybe someday you can give it to her for a wedding gift. Maybe—"

The bartender stopped beside their table and put down Tom's drink hard enough to make it splash. He intended to give her an annoyed look, but was too surprised when he saw Sophy glaring at him. "Hey, Mr. Flynn. Long time no see."

"Sophy. How is it you only fill in here sometimes and it's always the times I'm here?"

"You're just lucky, I suppose." She set down Lacie's drink, then rested one hand on her hip. "How is Holly?"

The muscles in his jaw tightened as he fixed his gaze on the pool of liquor on the tabletop. "Holly is . . . not open for discussion."

"You screwed things up with her, didn't you?"

Jerking back his head, he glared at her. "How did you—"

"Of course you did, or you wouldn't be here with another woman. What did you do this time? Turn your marriage proposal into a marriage contract? Ask her to sign a partnership agreement? Try to negotiate a topping clause, wherein you could get rid of her if someone better came along?"

He continued to glare at her as he quietly, coldly answered, "I told her I loved her."

Clearly surprised, Sophy fell silent. Lacie took advantage of it to leave.

He hardly noticed. Though he owed Sophy no explanation, he drew a deep breath and offered it anyway.

Sophie stared accusingly at him. "And so you

did what everyone else has done. You left her. You proved to her that she's right to be afraid. You asked her to marry you, you told her you loved her, and you left her without even saying goodbye. You did what everyone else has done. You took from her, and then you walked away."

Tom opened his mouth to argue, to insist that it hadn't happened that way at all. She'd told him she wouldn't love him, wouldn't marry him, wouldn't give him anything at all. After that, how could he have stayed? How could he have seen her every day, held her, kissed her, made love to her, knowing that the most important relationship in his life meant nothing to her?

But from Holly's viewpoint, it had happened exactly that way. After swearing to her that he would never do what the first boy, and the next and the next, had done, he had. Exactly.

Panic tightened his chest and formed a lump in his throat. He'd never meant for her to look at it that way, had never intended to do anything that might hurt her.

Dropping the necklace on the tabletop, he raised both hands to his face, rubbing the heels of his palms over his eyes. "I never meant for her to think . . . I just couldn't stay there, knowing she was never going to let me be any more important than every other man she'd—"

"Tom."

He looked up, and saw that Sophy was gone and standing in her place . . .

"Holly," he breathed. Reaching out one unsteady

hand, he touched her cheek, her jaw, before sliding his hand to the back of her neck, pulling her close, and covering her face with kisses. "I'm so sorry," he murmured. "I never meant . . . I've missed you . . . I need you. . . ."

She slid her hands into his hair, holding him still for a sweet, gentle kiss. Then she leaned back and took a deep breath. "Listen up, because I'm going to tell you something I've never said to any other man in my entire life. I love you, Tom Flynn. I tried not to, because the possibility of loving and losing you scared me to death, but I couldn't stop it from happening. No matter how much I ignored it, no matter how much I pretended you were just like all the others, you weren't, because I never cared about the others and I . . . I love you."

He raised one hand to her wrist, kissing the palm, and felt the rapid beat of her pulse. "I left Tuesday morning because—"

"I took away your hope. I thought I could keep you in my life without having to take any chances, without risking a broken heart. I didn't consider what that would do to you. I was selfish." She kissed him again, then nervously smiled. "Do you still want to marry me?"

When he opened his mouth, she hastily covered it with her fingers. "No, don't say it. Just . . . Ask any question you want, because I'm about to say your favorite word."

He had a lot of favorite words, starting and ending with Holly. But he knew the word she was talking about. *Yes,* he'd told her, because it was full of possibilities. Like them. He slid his arms around her waist and held her close. "Hmm . . . Do you understand the difference now between having sex and making love?"

She smiled slowly, seductively, but in a whole different way from what he was accustomed to. The old seductiveness—that was Holly putting on an act for any man in the area. This was Holly playing to him, and only him. "Yes."

"Did it mean something to you?"

"Yes."

"Did you hate going to bed without me and waking up without me and spending the entire day without seeing me even once?"

"Yes. Terribly."

He felt her breath on his jaw, smelled her fragrance when he breathed, swore he heard the faint thud of her heart. Or maybe it was his heart pounding. He'd never felt so nervous, so lucky, so incredibly grateful, in his life. He brushed his mouth across hers, just a quick taste; then, able to manage little more than a whisper, he asked, "Do you really love me?"

"Yes. Oh, yes."

"And will you marry me?"

"Ye—"

Before she could finish, he kissed her, thrusting his tongue into her mouth, hungrily, greedily, claiming her. Heat rushed through him, making him hard and desperately in need. Painfully aware that they were in a public place, he forced her back, then tenderly stroked her face. "One more question: Will you come home with me and make love with me and make me forget my name?"

She smiled that intimately seductive smile again, making him ache inside, and whispered, "Oh, yes. Every night for the rest of our lives."

Epilogue

THE CLOCK ON THE OFFICE WALL gave two soft *bongs* at midnight. It was now officially the second Sunday in March. More important, Tom thought as he opened the safe, it was the day after he'd achieved his second-most-crucial goal. He and Holly had been married the day before. She had looked more beautiful than ever, and he had felt . . . blessed. He'd known without a doubt that she was the best thing ever to happen to him. It was nothing less than a miracle that she felt the same about him.

Her pastor had performed the service in the church where her family had worshiped for two hundred years, and Father Shanahan had been there to offer his own blessing, along with most of the residents of Bethlehem. Josie Dalton and Gracie Brown-Grayson had served as flower girls, and Bree had been maid of honor. Margery, doing well enough in rehab to merit a day out, had watched from the second row with tears in her eyes.

At the reception afterward, Agatha Winchester and Bud Grayson had had eyes only for each other, leading to whispers about the possibility of another wedding soon, and Harry and Maeve, he'd gathered from the gossip, were becoming quite a couple, too.

Tom grinned. He was remembering people's names, keeping them straight, learning the details of their lives. He was going to fit in in Bethlehem just fine. The only thing missing from the celebration had been Sophy. He had tried to find her, had driven the streets of the old neighborhood, asked everyone about her. No one had known anything.

Father Shanahan had chuckled. "Oh, Sophy . . . She's an angel, you know."

At the time, Tom had written it off as an old man's fondness for a kind young woman. In odd moments since, he'd wondered. He'd struck her with his car, and yet she'd been uninjured. She'd waltzed into his office past the tightest security in the city. She'd known things she shouldn't know, popped up every time he'd needed her, and given him the pushes necessary to achieve his goal. He'd needed assistance, and she'd provided it.

Divine assistance? Was it possible . . . ?

Smiling at the notion, he opened the envelope for the third time that year, took out a pen, and drew a line through a goal. *Get married.* He'd done it, once and for all time.

Before he could return the paper to the envelope, a shuffle sounded in the hallway. "Tom?" Holly murmured an instant before appearing in the doorway. Her hair was mussed—his fault—and her eyes were glazed with sleepy satisfaction—his fault, too, he thought with a grin. She was wearing the top half of the pajama set her friends had given her as a gag. He wore the bottoms.

She climbed onto his lap, dangling her legs over the arm of the chair, and gave him a kiss. "Working on your wedding night? What did I do wrong?"

"Not a thing. I'm not working."

"Then what's that?"

He glanced at the paper on the desk pad and thought that someday he would share it with her, but not tonight. "It's just some notes. If I carry you back to bed, will you give me a chance to make you say your favorite word again?"

Her grin was lazy and wicked and did wonderful things to his body. "You do what you did earlier, and I'll say any word you want."

As he reached to turn off the lamp, his gaze fell on the paper again. He blinked, closed his eyes, then looked again. *Survive* had been lined out, and a new one had been written underneath. The ink was the same—hell, the handwriting was the same—but he knew for a fact he hadn't added that new goal. Not that he had any problem with it.

And live happily ever after.

Who knew where it had come from? Maybe from the same good luck—the same miracle—that had given him Holly.

He turned off the lamp and carried her out of the office, down the hall to their bedroom, where a few candles burned. He was about to blow one out when she stopped him. "On your birthday, when Maggie put the candles on your cake . . . What did you wish for?"

He recalled that night easily enough, recalled sitting at Maggie's table and thinking about beginning his search for a wife. He hadn't put a wish into words . . . or had he? He'd certainly gotten everything he'd been thinking about and then some.

Leaving the candles burning, he lay down, wrapped his arms around her—around his wife—and pulled her close so she fitted snugly against him. "You, darlin'," he murmured, brushing his mouth against hers. "I wished for you."

About the Author

Known for her intensely emotional stories, Marilyn Pappano is the author of nearly forty books with more than four million copies in print. She has made regular appearances on bestseller lists and has received recognition for her work with numerous awards. Though her husband's Navy career took them across the United States, they now live in Oklahoma, high on a hill that overlooks her hometown. They have one son.

Look for

Marilyn Pappano's new novel

available from Bantam Books

Summer 2001

Too wicked, too sexy, too unreliable . . .
That's how women describe Ben Foster.
Then a dying wish sends him to
Bethlehem where, with the help
of guardian angels, he just may find
two good reasons to finally settle down.